KEISHA THE SKET

KEISHA THE SKET

JADE LB

1 3 5 7 9 10 8 6 4 2

#Merky Books
20 Vauxhall Bridge Road
London SW1V 2SA

#Merky Books is part of the Penguin Random House group of companies
whose addresses can be found at global.penguinrandomhouse.com.

Penguin
Random House
UK

Keisha the Sket copyright © Jade LB 2021

Jade LB has asserted her right to be identified as the author of this
Work in accordance with the Copyright, Designs and Patents Act 1988.

Sexc © Candice Carty-Williams 2021
Sex and Masculinity in the Endz © Caleb Femi 2021
A Million Footsteps © Aniefiok Ekpoudom 2021
The Blacker the Berry, The Penger the Juice © ENNY 2021

First published by #Merky Books in 2021

www.penguin.co.uk

A CIP catalogue record for this book is available from the British Library.

ISBN 9781529118919

Typeset in 13/16 pt Bembo MT Pro
by Integra Software Services Pvt. Ltd, Pondicherry

Printed and bound in Great Britain by Clays Ltd, Elcograf S.p.A.

The authorised representative in the EEA is Penguin Random House Ireland,
Morrison Chambers, 32 Nassau Street, Dublin D02 YH68.

Penguin Random House is committed to a sustainable future for
our business, our readers and our planet. This book is made from Forest
Stewardship Council® certified paper.

MIX
Paper from
responsible sources
FSC
www.fsc.org   FSC® C018179

This book is dedicated to Us Lot.

Those of us finding a home here, carving out our
place via art and culture – *The* Culture. Creating from
our hearts, allowing our spirit to lead, knowing the
God our parents and grandparents fed us would never
see us go hungry.
May We continue to know ourselves.

And to my teenage self, who didn't know what
she was doing.
Producing this project was equally painful and
grace-filled; it's funny how this healing stuff works.
This is evidence of how infinitely blessed you are x

Contents

Author's Note

Sitting down to write this author's note, there's a pressure to make it bare profound, more than I've noticed feeling throughout all aspects of this project. Writing this is confirmation that this book, which has been in the works in some capacity for almost two decades, is about to meet people in a very official way. Even now, in June 2021, I engage with so much of this project with a numbness because I still *cannot believe this.*

I'm mindful that I could very easily go on and turn this note into a mini book of its own if I delved into all of the twists and turns, so I'll stick to the basics. For readers new to this work, I started writing *Keisha the Sket* (*KTS*) at thirteen years old. It was popularly known as 'Keisha da Sket' at the time, and the tale reprinted in these pages (in 'The OG' section of the book) was a product of some enterprising creativity and pretty meagre resources. I'd been gifted a desktop PC for my thirteenth birthday in 2005 with only the default applications available for me to knock myself out with, while dial-up internet remained outside of the household budget for some time.

When we finally got AOL later that year and I caught up to my peers with the then must-haves (an MSN, a Face-pic.com account and a Piczo site), I vividly remember uploading the first of about six chapters I'd so far written of this story on to my Piczo site as a flippant bright idea. Over the next few years, *KTS* ingrained itself in the adolescence of inner-city Brits coming of age in the noughties, alongside many other heirlooms we look back on fondly and acknowledge as the foundations of what we now refer to as 'The Culture'.

This book is made up of three parts.

The preserved OG text I wrote between the ages of thirteen and fifteen exists in these pages for the first time in official print (so, excluding all the school printer paper it graced). It's here as a reminder of where it all started and I'd gently advise you to have the Urban Dictionary on hand whilst reading. I hope new readers inquisitively picking up this book use the OG as a portal to access intimate and intricate parts of black girlhood they may not have had the opportunity to witness otherwise. For readers familiar with Keisha, I hope you will smile, laugh, cringe, and see her anew all these years later, riding each wave of nostalgia the text invokes.

On this project I've collaborated with some giants, who have expertly spoken to what *KTS* means to them and to The Culture in the form of essays. It felt important to archive some of the multitude of conversations and considerations *KTS* inspired, via the writers we will look back at and say, 'They spoke for, to or about me,' in years to come. These essays make up the final section of this book.

Then there's the rewrite. I had so many editorial conversations about the direction of the book. We went back and forth on what should be included, how everyone could be served and what I wanted. This project with #Merky Books has been in the works (unofficially) since 2019, and for a lot of that time my ego wanted to offer something more reflective of adult me. We played around with the OG text, made a mess, but settled finally on this rewrite and I churned it out under the maddest of time constraints.

I've endeavoured to bring Keisha's story to literary life – creating better imagery to invoke some real rushes of nostalgia, applying some literary devices to help it hang together better, and giving more texture to the characters to further bring them to life. I've also tried to keep the story as authentic as possible without violating the OG. As it stands, the rewrite is a reoffering that honours a younger Jade's original creation while keeping *KTS* alive and contemporary.

I have an appreciation for every individual who has bought into me via *KTS* that's very difficult to articulate and express in this brief author's note. If you're familiar with *KTS* and reading this author's note, you have likely engaged with my creativity and/ or the memory of it several times over the last fifteen or so years. Perhaps you read *KTS* as an amused teenager, or shared a tweet about it once or twice, or maybe you flippantly asked old friends: 'Do you remember *KTS*?' In doing so, you helped turn my grassroots creativity into what will be remembered as a cultural touchstone.

Thank you to everyone who collectively and very literally conspired to bring about this book. As I write this author's note, I'm in bed and we've nearly wrapped this project. I'm overwhelmingly reminded of how I stand on the shoulders of my generation and how I carry a deep gratitude for the people who have unknowingly (or knowingly) held up my work and, inevitably, me.

Enjoy x

'Is *Keisha the Sket* About You?'

Reconciling me vis-à-vis Keisha, and deconstructing my own misogynoir

As far back as I can remember, my favourite and yet most destructive pastime was creating worlds and narratives from the depths of my imagination. Photographs of me as a toddler depict a very serious little girl 'reading' intently or playing dress-up; I had many an imaginary friend, and some evenings my mum would morph into this wacky character who lived under the cherry tree in our garden.

Writing *Keisha the Sket* (*KTS*) was born from being a bit of a bookworm – and, apparently, enterprising. In the black fiction section at the library, where the scanty shelves offered books that told American stories detailing the politics of black, inner-city lives slightly different from mine, I discovered tales that detailed intense sex and depictions of intimacy and misfortune in the lives of characters I could finally relate to, and the opportunity to pen my own came on my thirteenth birthday when I was gifted a PC. In the period between it being given to me and my mum working out what resources could be committed to a monthly AOL bill, I intertwined the American stories I read with what I'd seen in the places I'd lived or the things I'd heard at the back of Science and Geography, and from there tapped out a tale of this black girl from inner-city London, and the politics that governed her womanhood and sexuality.

So much of this essay will be concerned with how and why we create and tell fictional stories, because this element is so central to how Keisha's story was created and assumed. What underpins the purpose of this book, the buy-in from every stakeholder along the way and perhaps your very own readership is a story that has been created and told around me, Keisha and the advent of *KTS*. Readers and writers turned *KTS* into works of fan fiction, writing alternative endings to what they felt was an unfinished tale. Others created their own 'sket' story spin-offs,* and as the anonymous author I was the subject of some wild and wonderful stories too. But beyond the fictional aspects, there is an intimate personal story I told myself in the years between finishing *KTS* and 2018, when I finally answered a (literal) call to come back and look at this story I'd started at thirteen.

---

* Large up Deena + Rochelle

Keisha's story wasn't exclusively a construct of my adolescent observations of the world; equally it was manufactured by my own inauguration into womanhood in the early noughties. It was heavily informed by how we as teenagers spoke about and treated sex. Sex was a conquest shrouded in arbitrary patriarchal rules that we plucked from religion and a hctcrogeneous diaspora culture. My own lens was informed by slut-shaming, the policing of young women's sexual preferences (whether their sexuality or their libido), body counts, and which sexual acts were deemed 'acceptable' to engage in. Your agency to decide whether sucking dick was permissible wasn't yours, while your chances of claiming 'Lady [insert love intercst's tag name here]' was predicated on a reputational report on your exploits coming back clear. The older we got, the more our virginity was revered as a status symbol – implying inherent goodness, worth and female elitism. In the context of inner-city London – or 'endz' as I'll refer to it herein – if you were a young woman considered by young men to be 'stoosh', the title and status of girlfriend or 'wifey' could be bestowed with a pride and contentment in the knowledge that you hadn't been 'had'.

Between the ages of thirteen and fifteen, I was actively writing about Keisha, her love life and her sexcapades, uploading each chapter bold-faced on my personal Piczo site that fully identified me and my government name – pictures of me in school uniform and all. In that context, Keisha's relationships with many of the boys and young men in her story reflect my strange observer's wisdom. Keisha was afforded (albeit unknowingly) grace in my commitment to presenting her as a victim of the narratives that we came of age within and were governed by throughout our teenagehood, whether it was that she'd been raped or viciously accused of being a 'sket'. Reading back, one might assume my early teenage self was not directly judging Keisha, but that I sought to tell a tale of someone who would otherwise not be afforded love and acceptance in her relationships with men, because of her sexual appetite and experiences. My story for young women who looked like me reflected an awareness of how the world we knew interacted with us, and my capacity to articulate that earnestly.

It seems that, in writing Keisha's story, I was very aware of the varied manifestations of sexual violence, like rape and coercive control, along with the ways Keisha's sexuality was policed by others and her inability to acknowledge her own victimhood. Also, aside from Ricardo, I continuously portrayed boys and men as believing they were entitled to Keisha – her body, her as a void to project their lust or rage onto – and, in doing that, I was vividly reflecting the reality of the misogyny embedded in the endz' very own patriarchal structure.

When writing *Keisha the Sket* started to feel like a chore and I cut her story short, leaving things on a cliffhanger (on Keisha's eighteenth birthday she is kidnapped by Malachi, and I imply that her boyfriend Ricardo and best friend Karl come to her rescue), I unconsciously shifted to a new way of telling stories. Instead of being a neutral observer and writing them down, I made myself the object of stories that I kept in my head and allowed to inform my whole world – and stifle me – for over a decade.

As I approached my final year of secondary school, I began consciously carving out ideas about the young woman I endeavoured to be, and became aware of the narrative I wanted to be ascribed to me. I got myopic about the story I anticipated people telling about me, as well as the one I told myself about authoring *KTS*. I subscribed to dense, binary narratives about young women, believing that it now had to be my life's work to live in a way that fit a 'good girl' narrative – because the only other alternative was to be a Keisha, who I'd ultimately turned against. So, at some point, I stripped my Piczo site of any content that could be linked back to me, leaving only Keisha's story. Away from the computer screen, I believed I had to be one-dimensional, so I disassociated from expressing myself sexually and instead purposely pursued the things I told myself embodied 'acceptable' feminine desirability.

By seventeen, I had two jobs and was averaging A and B grades at A level (I was predicted all Cs), and although on some level this was something to celebrate, the context behind it wasn't. Aesthetically, I opted for modesty and made very literal, arbitrary rules for myself – no make-up, no nail extensions, and no sex before marriage. I engaged in periods of not using swear words, and underwent strict no-bash-ment-music 'fasts', all in a bid to separate myself from Keisha and attain some unachievable, false ideal of worth and desirability. The result was to rob myself of two important things: one being a chance to be authentic; and the other the truth that creating *KTS* was, foremost, a manifestation of my capacity to use my meagre resources to conjure up stories that engaged and entertained thousands.

This forced separation between story and self continued. I spent years expending energy willing the legacy of *KTS* to its grave; as time went on, having written it became the single most anxiety-inducing pseudo-secret I kept. When I finished school in 2008, I was certain the memory of it would fade as fast as dummies, cubed hair bobbles and our Year 9 SATs scores, but by the time I got to uni in 2010, not a single year passed where a secondary school friend didn't send me a screenshot of *KTS* trending on Twitter, and each time my heart would sink to my belly with the knowledge that my peers had far from forgotten. Social get-togethers with mixed groups of friends were prefaced by a silent prayer that a loose-lipped school friend wouldn't expose the 'thing' that had started as an an outlet which filled the void of boredom and reflected my eagerness over my first computer, but had now grown into this monstrosity that my new sense of self and respectability politics told me would ruin everything.

In 2018, I started therapy, and although *KTS* was the furthest thing from my mind when I embarked on that journey, the practice forces you to confront yourself and process the full spectrum of your feelings. As I processed the shame that had sat with me from childhood, and acknowledged some unjust things that had happened over the years, I also had to deconstruct the stories I told myself about certain events, people and relationships and realised that they were sometimes assumptions, projections and narratives that were deeply negative and, a lot of the time, made up. The radical confrontation and accountability that therapy eased me into, alongside some loud knocks at the door to come back to *KTS* in some capacity, was a catalyst for facing the host of feelings I'd held on to about Keisha, her story and my authorship – feelings that had consumed me for more than a decade. I had to ask myself, 'Why did I so diligently hide this part of my trajectory? What was the turmoil I experienced at the mention of *KTS*, and why?'

I had to confront the fear and apprehension that enveloped the reality that I'd written *KTS*, and acknowledge that the same resistance had affected my sex life, the relationship choices I'd made, and the lack of empathy I extended to black women (including myself) – and that at the heart of it wasn't much more than my internalised misogynoir.

'Misogynoir' – coined by queer black feminist and academic Moya Bailey, and developed more extensively by Trudy of the (discontinued) blog Gradient Lair in the early 2010s – describes a type of misogyny that is specifically anti-black. Trudy and writers thereafter have applied the term to a plethora of examples in mainstream media and entertainment, from the hyper-sexualisation and denigration of black women in various pop-cultural spheres to how well-accomplished black women are depicted in mainstream media. Stereotypical tropes that sit at the intersection of race and gender and are continually levelled at black women also perpet-uate misogynoir. A good example of this is the claim that black women are aggressive; or that black women are, or ought to be, strong; or that black women are 'ghetto'.

Like colourism, misogynoir can be (and often is) internalised – perpetrated and perpetuated by black men and women alike. The current literature that applies the term and illustrates misogynoir is largely American, but turning the lens onto the ways that misogynoir manifests in the context of endz – which provided the backdrop to the writing and setting of *KTS* – I can clearly see how a unique application and consequent internalisation of it followed, which affected the way I interacted with my creation of Keisha and her story.

It was apparent that misogynoir very specifically was the dogma I'd adopted. My lack of acceptance and my disdain for myself – and inevitably other black women – was very much anti-black, and this was highlighted to me when I retrospectively considered a friendship I had with a white girl in school.

Leigh and I became friends in Year 9 when the teacher's seating plan put us next to one another. I really loved Leigh, and although our friendship didn't much venture outside of school, we shared many an intimate secret. Leigh's experiences, beliefs and behaviours went far beyond the binary standard I had begun to curate for myself and the girls and women who looked like me. Leigh was a 'big girl', she experimented with drugs, and she didn't just have sex but dared to have *adventurous* sex. Her life and my view of it involved a level of freedom and permissibility that I and the girls who looked like me weren't afforded. What was noteable was that none of this made Leigh unacceptable or wrong or bad or deficient to me. I didn't even consider that Leigh couldn't be my friend because of the choices she made. I could see Leigh's beauty, I could understand Leigh's reasons, and I could accept that Leigh was a risqué, experimental, and perhaps lost teenager. Looking at myself, though, I couldn't even accept or see beyond the fact that I had written about sex.

I highlight my friendship with Leigh to shed light on my relationship to it. In retrospect, I can see how the narrative around girls that looked like Leigh and girls that looked like me were polarised in my subconscious, and how that informed the space and empathy I gave to Leigh in contrast with the space I wouldn't give to my authorship of *KTS* and the empathy I couldn't allow myself for many years to come.

There are two scenes in the story where Keisha is raped/brutally sexually assaulted (in one scene, by a gang of boys; and in the other, by a jealous lover). Despite the violence of these experiences, particularly after the gang assault, Keisha effectively goes back to some semblance of normalcy where she is engaging with all parts of her life just as she had prior to said assaults. I was asked why I had written Keisha 'back to normal' so quickly – and also why, in revisiting the story sixteen years later, I still wanted to keep it that way. My response was because that's the truth, and that's what happens. Girls that look like me and Keisha bury violations and move on.

By my early teens, I knew girls who'd engaged in sex with men when they were just girls, or who had been bullied into the block and told they weren't leaving until every boy present was satisfied. I also knew girls who'd been assaulted with aggressive words and hostility as a preamble to sex. But in the accounts that were relayed after the fact – on the phone, or

in the stairwell, or in a corner of the playground –
no one ever called it 'rape' or described their experience as an assault.

We didn't comprehend sexual acts in this way, and
we didn't have permission to articulate our discomfort
or the lack of consent as rape either. Rape was rigid,
it was months of tears, and it was never having sex
with that person again. It was time off school, it was
the authorities getting involved and the transgressor
being the subject of ferocious gossip that shamed
them out of the world they'd once existed in. Being
bullied into a line-up was a personal shame-tinged
secret that you told your 'BFFs' one random lunch-
time, and by the time the bell rang and we went into
the next period, it was fire for the supply teacher and
snaffling Pringles behind our blazers. We didn't think
what happened to *us* was rape. It was sex.

There is a distinct culture of silence in working-
class diaspora communities, where we don't complain
too much, and we don't make a fuss, and we often
let burdens rest firmly on the shoulders of women.
This, coupled with the girls we oversexualise – the
ones with the gold hoop earrings, grease-glossed
lips and crusted slicked-down baby hairs; the girls
with the visible attitude and robust bravado that is
often misconstrued as strength but never recognised
as sorrow – ensures we rear generation after generation of girls who leave empathy till last. That's
why Keisha can go back to 'normal' after her

assault – because the world she exists in doesn't recognise what happened to her as a violation, and she knows her expressions of sorrow and shock will be misunderstood. Keisha is dually the product of an outside world which never stops or makes space for her, and an inside one – endz – which lacks the luxury of time and resources to stop, hear and hold space for her.

At the time of writing *KTS*, my age and lack of maturity meant my ability to embrace the complexity and consideration needed for the subject of sexual assault and rape was limited, as was my capacity to afford Keisha the right to process her experiences and heal. At the same time, I had an awareness of the world which I pulled from – the world of silence, of not bringing problems to your front door or shame to the (broken) family name, and of 'getting on with it'. I couldn't write Keisha as the recipient or possessor of empathy, because I myself was inevitably struggling to have any for my teenage self.

The internalisation of my misogynoir and the way I distanced myself from my role in penning Keisha's story also impacted my relationship with sex and pleasure. I couldn't reconcile the fact that someone who was a sexual being and had written *Keisha the Sket*, and someone who successfully fulfilled the ideal of a morally good, acceptable and worthy young woman, could co-exist in one body.

My resistance to embracing sexual expression and being open to varied forms of intimacy reflected my conception of what purity and being a 'good Christian' was; and at about sixteen, I decided that I wasn't going to have sex before marriage. That would mean avoiding and repressing my true sensual nature, and refusing to acknowledge what I wanted or needed to explore physically to experience pleasure. I told myself that remaining a virgin until marriage, and fulfilling this idea of 'righteousness' that us 'on fire for Christ' lot swore by, was more important than developing a healthy capacity for intimacy.

The parameters I set for myself culminated in entering a shit relationship at twenty, losing my virginity at twenty-one and, if I'm to be honest, enduring some pretty shit sex after that. The parts of Keisha's story that felt most alien and yet alluring to me both whilst writing as a teen and reading back as an adult, were where we see manifestations of her confidence and sexual agency, and can perceive her capacity to enjoy a connection to her body and receive gratification from sex. There's a latent belief in her right to experience pleasure which was drastically at odds with what I felt able or allowed to negotiate in the sex I was having in my early and mid-twenties.

My memories of the trajectory of that particular relationship are a lot of enduring, acquiescing and then negotiating how I felt later, either physically or emotionally. One memory I can now laugh at is how my ex-boyfriend would 'play' with me, which would genuinely feel like my clit was being repeatedly scratched like a record on a turntable by an overzealous DJ. My inability to correct him came from a fear of being seen to know 'too much' for someone who had come into the relationship a virgin. Now, as I approach thirty and reflect on my sexual experiences, I think about how deeply I trapped myself in a web of stories that I created in response to Keisha's, and I acknowledge the ways I robbed myself of my own voice and my ability to assert my sexual wants and truly see sex as something I am entitled to equitably enjoy. I can recognise that, through distancing myself from both Keisha and my role as the author of her story, and in fighting to be perceived in a particular way, I cheated myself out of developing a healthy relationship with both myself and sex. In the years that mattered, my focus was not on establishing a relationship with pleasure, but solely on controlling a possible narrative I both feared and considered 'wrong'.

I was mortified about everything *KTS* represented, from the content to the vernacular it was written in, for a long, long time. Revisiting the text now, attempting accountability and acknowledging my internalised misogynoir is central to embracing and feeling some pride in my role in creating a cultural work that a generation enjoyed. Shining a light on where parts of Keisha's story come from is not a bid to absolve myself of the contribution I made to trapping myself, but the context is important. My ideas about how young black women ought to attain desirability and worth weren't established in a vacuum. Reintroducing *Keisha the Sket* and applying my adult creativity and intellect to the story represents a process of relinquishing the internalised misogynoir that has long held me back – in both my writing and the more intimate parts of my life. Being suspicious of people's reverence for your work is no fun, and the constant gymnastics to avoid what is apparently meant to be grows tiring. Shame unchecked becomes irrational fear, which allows one to refuse to accept, like or love who they truly are – and, in my case, what I had created on my journey. At first, I didn't think 'the work', supported by therapy and my tribe, would see me wilfully answer the door to those who knocked on it in regard to *Keisha the Sket*, but here we are. The innumerable pieces of the puzzle that make up the work that has ultimately led me to this point conspire to cultivate a complete, albeit flawed and fragile, masterpiece. It is in fact an honour that I can come back to *this* work and show love to a teenage Jade who felt innately unworthy, unacceptable and unlovable. I hope she can see all she's done.

THE OG ♡

1

'TURN THAT RACKET DOWN!!!!!!!!' Mum screamed. She was only saying that because there was nuff swearing inna this track. She annoys me to DEATH! because when she and dad are having der 'fun' no one elses opinion is wanted or needed! I turned it down and sat back down at my computer chattin on msn.

'Yeh so wot u on?' Ramel allerted me. He was 1 peng boi dat i had been chatin 2 4 tym.

'Arrrr nuttin much ya na ... kina bored ya na ... need sum entatainment ina me likkle borin lyf!' i replied smilin 2 maself dun knoin he wuld replie sumfin funny or jus dutty!

'Arr skn skn, me need a likkle excitment ina my lyf, ina my bedroom, ina my bed!'

'LOOOL, joka, naa gyal aint dat loose'

'Iz jus a likkle fun init, no1 na need fi kno'

'mmm'

'mmmmm ... so das a no den'

'Scroll up da convo ... did i type da word NO??'

'Mmmmm ..... me lyk da way ya tink'

'LoL N e wayz ima b off now i mite chat 2 u 18r ye'

'So ... Can man fone u 18r 2 c if me gna get n e excitment ina me bed 2day'

'Ye, u can fone 18r ... Bless x'

'Ye Bless xxx'

Dat boi iz 2222 peng, i thought 2 my self, 4rm jamrock an jus ova shexi lyk! Black long coolie hair, 1 sexi chocolate color wit sum peng hazel eyes wit green outline, sum sexxxxi soft LL cool J lips and 1 NOICCE body! He woz jus 2 sick annnnnn da boi can SPITTTT! I laid dwn on ma bed an wondered 2 maself 'y da fuck did i go off msn? lyk i hav n e ting beta 2 do' but i didnt bova 2 go bck on coz il jus look lyk a eediat! Ma fone started ringin, it woz a priv8 caller an i fort 'shuld i awnsa it or not?' I decided 2 awnsa it jus incase it woz dat sexi ting. It woz dat stupid fool michael.

'hello' i sed.

'ye, wha gwarn, so wot u na return ma txts?'

'i tel u alredy dnt fone ma fone or txt ma fone agen ya stupid eediat, u iz a eediat dat tink dey can gt peice outa evry gyal in hackney'

'hu u chattin 2 lyk dat?'

'hu iz on ma line??'

'Lisen likkle gyal-'

'NO u lisen ya prick if ya fone ma line agen me goin mek sure u neva c ya likkle limp dick agen ya stupid dickhed!' an i dropped da fone, propa vex. Now i rly needed sum 'excitment'! I lied bck dwn on ma bed an ma fone rang agen, dis tym 'shanice' came up an i awnsered it.

'Ye, wha gwarn gyal, me jus a gt a cal 4rm dat ediat'

'wot did dat wasteman want?'

'Me na kno, but me neva giv im chance 2 tlk im rubbish ina me ears, Ya MAD??!'

'Ahh, ya dred gyal! Gimme nuff joke, so wha u doin 2day den?'

'Duno boi, dat sexc bwoi ramel iz invitin me 2 his yard 4 a lash init but i duno if i gna reach it or not'

'go man!!!! 4rm wot ive seen dat bwoi iz 22 buff!'

'I knooooooo! Oh my dayz! da boi! Wot u on 2day doe?'

'Nuttin rly u kno, u wnna jam an den ill escort u 2 ramelz yrd?'

'Ye, ite den. Arrrr i jus gt 1 gully idea, ramel sed hell fne me, wen he dus ill ask him if he wil bring his bredrin 4 u'

'Wot bredrin??'

'Sean, hes nufffff peng aswel!'

'Wot dus he look lyk?'

'Lite skin, peng green eyes, cain row, nuff tall'

'Yesssssssss man'

'JOKA!'

'Ne wayz cum 2 ma yrd in lyk half an hour?'

'Ye Ye, Kool'

'Bless'

I quickley looked in da mirror jus 2 chek maself, how da hell can i go c dat peng ting lookin lyk dis? So i opened ma wardrobe, it woz a sunny day so i took out sum shorrrrrrrrt white rah rah skirt an a pink vest top. I gt out ma brand nu converses, dey wer white an folded dwn, on da insyd dey had pink swirlz. I completed ma outfit wit a pink nike wrist-band an ma white rosary beads. I looked in da mirror an fort 2 maself 'Oh Rasss' den I ran dwn stairs an told ma mum i wuld b goin 2 shanices yard an will b bck at around 11.

'Ye alrite, c u 2moro'

'byeeee'

And i ran out da house an walked down da road 2 shanices yard. Der woz a group of boiz sittin on a wall jamin, wen i went by dey all started sayin 'arr chung ting' all dat shyt. 1 of dem jumped of da wall an cum up 2 me. He woz bare buff an he musta goes: 'arr so can i gt ya numba' an took out his fone.

i gave it 2 him an den he goes: 'arr ill fone u 2moro or l8r init'

i jus walked an smiled 2 maself.

I gt 2 shanices yrd an knocked da door. Her buff big brova awnsered da door.

'Rarrrr ... u sure ur lookin 4 shanice an nt me!' he sed lookin me up an dwn.

I laughed an jus moved him outa da way an walked in 2 da corridor. He turned round an slaped ma bum. I didnt do nufin bcoz her brova woz ova buff an n e tym i felt dwn or had n e truble wit n e dickhed boiz den i knew i culd turn 2 him 2 shank n e prick inna dem eye!

I ran up da stairs 2 shanices room, she woz in der wit sum bashy music playin full blast, i swung open da door an stood in da door way an started wynin 2 da track. Ricardo, her bro, came up behind me an started grindin an gyratin on me. Da track soon fished an i jus walked in 2 da room, levin him 2 grind on thin air.

'Close da door fool' Shanice sed 2 her brother, he kissed his teef, gave me a wink an closed da door.

'U kool gurl' shanice sed turnin 2 me.

'ye gurl im gud, ur bro iz on me hard doe, did u c him' i sed, laufin.

'i kno, dnt take no notice' shanice replied.

i laughed.

'hey stay her a sec im gna go dwn stairs 2 get sumfin ye'

'okidoke' i sed.

shanice walked out of her room, i herd her footstepz runin dwn da stairs, an den sudenly da bedroom door opened, it woz ricardo. I looked at him an rolled ma eyes.

'Soo wha gwarn sexy, u woz workin manz dick jus den init, show me sum of dat action in MY room' he sed sittin on da bed an started touchin ma thigh.

'mayb 2moro init' i replied lookin in2 his sexc eyes.

'mmmmmm' he sed,our faces gettin closa an closa, 'did i tel u hw damn sexc u b-'

I jus laid ma lips on his sexc lipz, i jus had 2 he woz 2 sexc an he woz seducin me soo slowley i jus culdnt handl it. we sat der lipsin an den wen we stoped he laid on his back an gave me a sexc look, witout tinkin twice i climbed on top of his buff body. wit my bumpa in da air an ma lips on his, kissin him gently slowly pulin ma tung in an out of his mouf. den i remembered shanice dwn stairs. i quickly stopped an sat up.

'wot abat shanice?'

'wot abat her baby, wen me an u r gettin it on she aint gna b der' he sed puttin his hands up my skirt.

'na babe,lets go 2 ur room or sumfin b4 she finds us lyk dis'

'ye ye, im gnna b in ma room, go tell er i gt u 4 a cuple hrs'

I climbed off of him an fixed ma skirt, he got up an stood bhind me feelin up ma batty.

'wait a lil' i sed turnin round an holdin his hands.

I walked away 4rm him an went outada room, runnin dwn da stairs 2 find shanice.

'oi gurl im gna b wit ur bro in his room 4 abit ye'

'he-hey!!!! gurl u a dutty freak u kno, but go get ya mack on newaiz, dat boiz bin on u 4rm dai!'

'safe gyal'

I ran bck up da stairs an entred ricardos bedroom. I had suprisingly neva bin in der b4. It woz blu, he had a double bed wit blu sheets an dark blu curtains dat were drawn 2 giv da room a blu-ish glow. he had sum pine wardrobes an a desk full of condoms, a pc, a tele wit a ps2 bsyd it an a stack of cds an dvds. he woz sittin on his bed. As i entered he gt up an came up 2 me he stood ova me lookin in2 ma eyes. I thought 2 maself, hes so damn sexc y didnt i gt it on wit him earlier? he laid his lips into mine an we stood der lipsin 4 a gud 20 mins. Wen we finaly moved apart he took ma hand an walked me ova 2 his bed. Agen he lay dwn an i climbed on top of him. I took of ma top an he started feelin up ma breasts, caresing them an lickin his sexc lips. Afta a while i moved his hands away an gt off of him indicatin i wanted him on top. i lay on da bed an he gt up, he took ma skirt off an started feelin up ma legs an stomach. He started kissin me around ma belly buton. He moved 2 da upa part of me an started suckin ma breasts an gently/tenderly bitin ma nipples. Afta a gud 5mins he started gently an passion-atly kissin ma lips an touchin ma whole body. he gt up an sat on da end of da bed, probably putin on a body bag, which made me want him evenmore, he looked bck at me, lookin at ma body, admirin itz sexc shape. I gt up an sat on his lap, kissin his lips an his hands moved up ma leg 2 ma pussy as he started playin wit ma pussy lips, it made me wet straight away wit his soft touch an da rythmic finga work he used. I started 2 kiss him even more deeply an bite his botom lip. He slid his 2 fingaz in ma pussy, it felt sooo good dat i let out a lng but quiet 'uhhhhh ...', he slid his fingaz in an out slowly an gently, goin deepa an deepa. He slid anuva finga in, i started moanin his name, 'uhhh ricardo,uhhh'. Ma legs started 2 feel weak an i knu i woz gna cum on his lap. Ma legz started shakin an den i came on him. He woz satisfied bcoz he took his fingas out of me an kissed me deeply. I slid off of his lap dwn his body. I knelt up in front of him an started lickin an gently bitin his chest an nipples, wit ma hand on his dick it hardened wit evry bite an lick! Afta a while i gt a lil bored of dat so i took his warm dick an placed it in ma mouf. I started suckin an blowin on it, it drove him wild an he started moanin ma name. Soon, he got ahold of da back of ma hed an started pushin ma hed towardz his body, fasta an fasta until he came. Wen i finished suckin i gt up an sat nxt 2 him, straight away he gently pushed me bck an climbed on top of me an slid his hard dick in syd of me, in an out, he went fasta an fasta, he woz tearin me out, i woz moanin 'uhhhhhhhh ricar-, ricardO!!' Ma legz den bcame rly weak an shaky an i came on his dick, which was now gettin biga an biga insyd of me. He came in me soon afta me an slowed dwn 2 nufin. Wen he finished he gt off of me an put his boxers on. He looked bck at ma naked body layin on his bed an lay nxt 2 me, strokin ma stomach an kissin me gently. i turned an kissed him passionatly an gt up 2 gt dressed. Wen i woz dressed i turned 2 him an looked in2 his eyes, he bent dwn an kissed me agen, this tym 4 abat 15minz an woz feelin ma body. Wen i finished kissin him i looked at him an he sed 'so, ill c u agen ye?'

'Ye baybe' I replied an turned around an walked out of his room in 2 da passage, I walked bck 2 shanices room wit a smile on ma face. She woz sittin der on da pc, as i walked in she sed 'So lil miz freak r we gna go 2 dis boiz hse or wot?'

I laughed gently an sed 'ye, ye we gna reach dat'

'r u sure u can handle all dat in 1 day' Shanice sed turnin 2 face me wit a worried look on er face.

'I am lil miz freak arent i' I sed starin straight bck at er wit a dutty grin on ma face.

2

Me an shanice left da house at 7 oclock. Ramel had foned me at 6 an asked if i woz stil cummin, i sed ye an he sounded happz! I asked him 2 bring sean along 4 ma frend an he sed ye he can arrange it no problem! So me an shan were at da bus stop waitin 4 a 479 to tek us 2 his yard. He lived in enfield an it woz quite a journey.

'So u gnna cum spend da nite at minez?'
shanice asked.

'Gud idea ya na' I replied, so i took
ma fone outa ma pocket an foned hme, mum
awnsered. 'mum im gna sleep ova at shanices, ok'

'alrite den, c ya 18r on 2moro, take
care'

'bye'

An hour 18r, at da 1st stop we gt off
an walked dwn da road.

'He sed it woz on Crow road'

'Derz crow rd rite der' Shanice sed
pointin 2 a street sign.

We walked dwn da street until we gt 2
numba 14. Wen we gt 2 da door i knocked
it. A few secondz 18r it opened an ramel
woz standin der 2 greet us.

'Cum in' he sed standin bck.

Shanice walked in first an walked dwn
da passage 2 meet her nu 'frend'. I
walked in, as i walked in i felt ramels
hand slap ma bum hard. I turned bck an
gave him 1 of ma dutty grinz an walked
along da passage a lil mor. Ramel closed
da door an walked up 2 me. He stood
bhind me playin wit ma bum while he woz
talkin.

'So sean u hav dwn stairs an imma hav upstairs ye' He sed.

'Ye man' he replied. 'So we gnna tear up dwn here ye sexc' He sed turnin 2 shanice.

'Ye man, most definatly' she sed lickin er lipz at him.

Ramel led me upstairs an i left shanice dwn stairs in da passage wit sean kissin. Wen gt 2 da floor dat his room woz on he opened his bedroom door an looked bck at me wit a sexc look in his eyes. I folowed him in2 da bedroom an closed it bhind me. As soon as da door shut he span round an started lipsin me rly hard an ruff. He woz feelin up al ma body an takin ma top off. He woz alredy topless wit jus jeanz an boxerz on. He gt me dwn on his bed an gt on top of me an put his face in ma chest an started lickin an suckin ma chest. He worked his way dwn an pushed ma legz up an opened dem. Movin ma thong aside he started lickin ma pussy. It felt gud, he woz suckin at da walls an movin his tung bck an forth so gently. Juices started flowin out of me in2 his mouf but he took it all bck. Soon i woz cumin all in his mouf an he stil licked me out. Wen he rose up der woz noo spilage at all, his face wz clean an evryfin. I culd tel he did dis freaky shit on a regz. He woz on top of me, in between ma legz kissin me deeply. He woz rubbin ma legs an i culd feel his handz getin closa an closa 2 ma pussy. Dey reached der in no tym an he started rubbin it an movin his handz dwn 2 ma hole an he pushed his fingaz in. He moved dem round an round pushin his 3 fingaz deepa an deepa. Dwn stairz i culd hear shanice moanin. He took his fingaz out an slid his dick in. He woz ridin me hard an fast, he had no mercy. He woz tearin me OUT! I woz moanin an screamin 'uhhhhhhhh ... uhhhh .... ramelll ..... mmmmm ..... uhhhh ......' den sunddenly i screamed out 'Ricardo!!' He stoped rite der an looked at me an sed, 'lisen u slut, me name na ricardo me name RAMEL, gt it rite na' He sed kisin his teeth wit a sinista an scary look on his face. He gt off of me an went an sat dwn. I gt up an put ma clothes on. I culd c he woz ova vex but i jus didnt make ne eye contact an jus carried on putin ma clothes on. I woz hedin out of da door wen he sudenly sed 'oi, gyal, ya 4gtin ya salary' he laufed. Dat gt me so vex, i werent no prostitute! I looked 2 ma rite, feet glued in itz position. Ma eyes caught a shank. I quickly picked it up an dashed it at him an ran out of da room dwn da stairz. 'SHANICE, SHANICE, PUT YA CLOTHES ON NOWWWW!!!!! WE GTTA GT OUTA HERE!!!!!!!!!!!!!' Shanice ran outada room lookin baffed, 'cum on gurl hurry up! i stabbed da fuka!' Wen i gt 2 da botom of da stairs i grabed er hand an ran out da front door. Ramel woz stumblin bhind me tryin 2 catch me. Wee ran outa da house an dwn da rd all da way 2 da bus stand. Der were several buses so we ran on2 1 an went up stairs 2 da bck an lay on da chairs until da bus started movin. Onli den wuld we even dare 2 sit up. Afta an hour on da bus we arrived at shanices house. Sum boiz started whistlin at us but we ignored dem! Wen we gt 2 shanices yrd we went upstairs, der woz music cumin 4rm ricardos bedroom, sum sexc slow jamz. Shanice woz jus abat 2 step in2 er room den she turned round an sed 'go giv him a suprise' she sed lookin at er broz room door. She smiled at me an i smiled bck an walked 2 ricardos room. I hesitated, shuld i knock? i thought. I knocked an he opened da door. Wen he saw ma face he moved aside an let me in. Wen i walked past him i expected him 2 tuch ma bum or grab me 4rm bhind, but der woz nufin. I sat on his bed an looked at him. He woz standin infront of me lookin at me.

'Wher did u go?' he asked.

'I dnt wnna chat bout it' I replied quickly.

'Did u fuck him?' He asked startin 2 bcum anoyed.

'Ye, but it ment nufin, i even caled out ur name' I sed jumpin up, I didnt kno y i woz goin on lyk dis coz me an him aint even goin out or ne fing, but i knew deeeep dwn i woz in LOVE wit ricardo.

He looked in2 ma eyez an sed 'u kno i luv u'

I jus stared at him 4 wot felt lyk days an den sed 'I luv u 2'

He grabbed me an kissed me. Not a snog, but jus a long passionate kiss. I had neva had 1 b4 an it felt so nice, i knew he woz serious, an 4 da 1st tym in ma LYF i woz serious 2. Wen we finished kissin he sed 'do me a favour b'

'Ye wot?'

'Take a bath'

'r u tryna say i smel or sumfin????'

34

'Naaaa Naaaa, iz jus dat da fort of u an anuva boi-'

'Ite bayb'

I went 2 shanices rom quickly. I walked in, Shanice woz sitin at er pc.

'Wha gwarn step sis' I sed.

Shanice slowly turned er hed 2 me smilin. I walked bck out an went 2 da bathroom. I ran da bath an stepped in an scrubbbbbbbeddd maself lyk i aint scrubed b4. I felt a lil sore afta but i woz satisfyed. I woz clean. I went bck 2 Ricardos room. He woz lyin on his bed wit 1 hand dwn his boxers an da ova 1 wit da remote init.

'Cum bayb' He sed wen he herd me cum in. I sat nxt 2 him an we started watchin tv. We watched tv until lyk 3 in da mornin. Wen he switched off da tele he turned 2 look at me. He jus sat starin at me an i stared bck. I culdnt believe he woz all mine.I remebered 4rm wayy bck, wen I woz lyk 13 an he woz abat 15, he had alwayz had a bit of a crush on me. But now we wer olda an fingz hadnt changed at all. I leaned in an kissed him on his soft lips. He kissed me bck an we jus sat der kissin each ova all mornin.

3

I woke up at 12:00pm, wiv Ricardo sleepin nxt 2 me. I leaned ova 2 look at him, he woz sound asleep, catchin flies which made me smile. I lay bck dwn an jus thought abat all da eventz of yestaday. Imagine dat, I gt lashed twice, gt a hubby an shanked sum1! Rahhh! I gt up half an hour 18r. I went in da shower, it werent my house but it woz ma home away 4rm home. Wen i gt out i dried an putt on 1 of ricardos tshirtz. I went in2 shanices' room. She woz layin in er bed wide awake.

'Hey gurl' I sed closin da door.

'Hey' Shanice replied, abit husky.

I sat on da end of er bed lookin around.

'So ... wotz on da agenda 2dai?' I asked.

'Dunooe boi, cum we go shoppin!'

'Yeeee' I sed.

Shanice jumped outa er bed an went 2 da showa. I waited 4 er 2 cum out n den she provided me wit sumfin 2 wear, blue hipsta jeanz, a short white nike tshirt an i wore ma converses. Wen i went bck 2 ricardos room he woz stil asleep so i wrote him a note sayin 'Wha gwarn babez, naa i aint jus left u hangin lyk dat im

36

goin shopin wit shanice, dnt wrry ill pik
sumfin sexc jus 4 u nuff luv xW!FEY ROCKAx'
I looked at him agen an left da note on
his desk.

Me an shanice hit da shops in wood green
first. Pickin out loadz of stuf. Nike,
adidas, converse, lot29 ... evryfin. At
3:00 ricardo foned me.

'Hello'

'Wha gwarn sexc, u stil out?'

'Ye babe'

'So u cumin bck 2 mine 2nite?'

'Ye'

'Ite gdgd, mek sure u pik up sumfin 4
me 2 enjoy'

I laufed, 'Ye dnt wrry'

'Ite sexc, c u 18r ye'

'Ite den, Bye'

I picked up 1 sexxxxxxxxxcccccccc thong
an bra set. It woz pink an all lacey an
shit. I finished shoppin at abat 6:00 an
decided 2 go 2 my house wit shanice. We
jamed der 4 an hour or so 4 me 2 change
an let mumzy kno i woz gnna b at shanices agen 2nite.

Wen we gt 2 shanices, der wer sum manz
in er yrd, abat 3. Me an shanice jus went
upstairs str8 coz we knew wot ricardo woz
up 2. He woz shottin init. Wen all da

manz had left he came upstairz an opened shanices door.

'Let me chat 2 u 4 a minute' He sed lookin at me.

'Ur soo bate man, u can hav er 4 aslng as u lyk' Shanice jumped in.

I gt up, wit da shoppin bag wit da laudaray in, an walked ova 2him. I closed da door bhind me an jus looked up at him. He kissed me an I folowed him 2 his bedroom. Once we woz in der i put da bag on a chair an he lay on his bed lookin at me.

'Did u hav a gud tym?' He asked.

'Ye' I sed.

'I made sum cash money 2 day sexc, 300 boof, jus 4rm dem guyz an jus 4rm sellin hi grade aswel' He sed takin out bare notez 4rm his pocket.

He handed me a stack of notez an i jus looked at his hand an den him.

'Wot????, Ur ma wifey now an i kno hw 2 treat ma gyal init' He sed lookin at me.

I took da money 4rm him an put it in ma pocket. He put da rest in a draw wiv mor money in.

'So show me woz in da bag init' He sed.

I took out da set, holdin it up against my body an lookin at him.

'Mmmm, so ur nt gna put it on 4 me den?'

'Nope, nt until 2nite' I sed putin it bck in da bag an gttin on top of him an kisin him.

I lay b side him jus starin up at da cielin tlkin abat lyf, us, skool. I woz feelin abit blusky so i slid ma hand dwn his trouserz an started playin wit his dick. We caried on tlkin lyk normal while he felt alova me aswel.

Afta abat an hour i took ma hand out an suggested dat i shuld go keep shanice company, or jus giv er an idea of sumfin 2 do coz she mus b as board as hell by erself! I walked outa ricardos room, not b4 lipsin him 4 a further 10 minz an getin ma bum slaped a cuple timez. I walked acros 2 shanices room, she woz sittin at er desk.

'Oi, y dny u go link a bre or sumfin gurl?'

'Das a guly idea aswel u knooooo, leme link dat boi das bin bellin off ma line 4 da lngst while!! Safe 4 da idea B!'

I walked bck outta shanices room, happy dat we both culd hav sumfin 2 do an dat me an ricardo culd hav da house allllllllll 2 our selves! I went bck in2 his room.

He woz sittin on his bed holdin his dick, topless on da fone. I walked ova 2 him an sat nxt 2 him. He woz on da fone 4 a gud 10 minz an i started 2 gt bored so i started feelin up his chest an bck. I started kissin him softly an lickin his sexc muscular armz sexcilly wit ma eyez on him. I took his hand out 4rm dwn his trousers an slid mine in. I started playin wit it an i culd feel him harden.

'Ye ye look man i gtta go lyk' He started 2 stutta as i took ma hand out 2 take ma top off. B4 his bredrin (jerome) culd even say 'ye bless' he had hung up da fone an woz starin at me, mouf gapin. I jus looked bck at him wit a sexc smile on ma face.

'Dnt jus sit der, cum an gt it' I sed as he jus sat der wit his mouf stil gapin.

Ricardo stood up ova me an i lay bck wit ma legz open, topless. He slid off ma trousers an climbed on2 da bed. I opened ma legz wida an he moved in between dem. B4 i woz even redy he slid his biggg dick in ma wet pussy. I let out a lng moan an he moved his dick in an out fasta an fasta. He cam inside of me afta a gud 15 minz. Afta he came he took his dick out an lay on da bed. I gt up on top of him an sat on his dick, lettin it go in me. I bounced up n dwn. The bed woz creakin an bouncin wit me. Ricardo came a gud 3 tymz b4 i gt off an wnted it 4rm da bck. I slid off of him an gt on all 4'z, ma bum in da air. Ricardo gt bhind me an held da sidez of ma bum firmly an slid his dick in an out of me. It felt soooooooo gud. He woz goin soo fast dat he woz tearin me out!! I moaned loudly, but afta a while i culdnt take it nemor.

'Stop!' I woz screamin, afta a min or so he started 2 slow dwn.

He moved 4rm bhynd me an colapsed nxt 2 me. I colapsed on ma bck nxt 2 him. We both jus lay der, naked, starin at da ceilin.

'Sorry bout dat babe, but ur bare big so i cnt hold out dat long u gt me' I apologised lookin ova at Ricardo.

'Iz ite babe', he replied wiv a smile on his face afta da compliment 2 his manhood.

I turned away wit a smile on ma face finkin 'men aye!'. Suddenly, Ricardo sat up.

'Babe im goin in da showa ... u wnna cum?' He asked wiv a lil smile on his face.

'Ye, ite den'

We both entered da bathroom and i headed str8 2 da mirror whilst ricardo turned on da showa. Wen it heated up i stepped in and so did he. I gt unda da water and ricardo jus stood der, in da steam, his beautiful muscular body gttin fliked wit da hot water. I stopped rubbin at ma body and looked at him. I jus stood der lookin at him wit a lil rude gyal look on ma face dat sed 'wot u lookin at man' wriiten all ova it! He slowly steped ova 2 me into da water and grabbed me. We stood der lipsin 4 a while, the water hittin our bodies and runnin dwn our bcks. Wen we finished lipsin ricardo looked dwn at me wit a lustful look.

'Naa baby not in ere' I quickly sed, knowin xactly wot woz on his horney lil mind. I stepped outta da showa and grabbed a towel. 'Go in da bedroom and dry off an ill put on da ting 4 u' I sed, rememberin ma present 2 him.

He walked outta da bathroom lookin as horney as hell but nt sayin anyfin.

I quickley dried ma body, moisterised it wit coca butta an den put on da thong an bra. I looked in da mirror. I admired ma sexc full body an smiled. I thought bck 2 wen i woz a yute wen i fort i woz so fat an buttaz an used 2 h8 da way i looked. But now, i woz in luv wit ma figure! Blessed wit a big bum an chest, a firm flat stomach an sexc thickish thighs. I walked outta da steamy bathroom wit a dressin gown on. I entered ricardos room. He woz standin up facin his desk. As i entered he looked ova at me wit a puzzled look on his face.

'I came on ma redz' I lied b4 he culd say nefin. I walked past him tryin 2 keep a str8 face.

'Oh, serious' Ricardo replied, disappointment in his tone.

I went ova 2 da bed an lay dwn. He lay dwn nxt 2 me. He closed his eyes. I gt up on 2 ma knees an undid da dressin gown an let it fall around me. It brushed him an he opened his eyes an looked at me. A look of shock creeped on 2 his face an i smiled. He gt up nt takin an eye off me.

'Raah, yuh look sexc gyal' he sed in a soft voice stil starin.

'U rly fink so?' I asked sexcily bitin ma left index finga an lookin dwn at maself.

'Yeee man' He sed, stil a bit amazed.

'Wel den show me hw sexc u fink i am' I sed droppin da lil sweety gurl act an lookin serious. I wnted him.

43

He looked up at ma face an came close 2 me. We kissed deeply. I pulled away an looked at him, a lustful look in ma angel eyes.

'Get off da bed' I told him. 'Sit in ur chair an face me'

He went ova 2 da chair turned it 2 face me while i woz on ma knees on da bed.

'Im all urs, wt do u wnt me 2 do?' I sed lookin at him wit a serious look. I wz serious.

'Put ur hands in ur pantys n finga urself' he sed lookin at ma pussy n shiftin in his seat lyk da look of it gave his dick happy memories.

I took ma hand an put it dwn ma knickers, at first i strted rubbin but den i moved my 2 fingas deepa dwn an found ma hole. I put ma 2 fingas up der an groaned in ecstacy. I knelt der fingerin maself, groanin an callin out ricardos name. He sat der wit his dick redy 2 shoot out da cielin. Afta a gud 10mins, I took ma fingas out an looked at him. I gt up an walked ova 2 him. I wz a cuple of feet away 4rm him an den i bent 4wrd an pulled his chair twrdz me. Ma pussy an his chest were touchin. He strted lickin an kissin ma stomach. Movin his tunge in an out of ma belly button. It made me wet agen. I eased maself on top of him afta a time n strted grindin as he kissed an sucked ma nek. He spun da chair around an b4 i knew it i woz bein put 2 lie on his desk. He woz in frnt of me dropin his calvins den i felt him thrust his enormous dick inside me rawbck. It felt 22 good 4 me 2 complain abat him doin da rawbck. He moved in an outa me wit skill makin me moan an groan his name. He came inside of me 3 times b4 i woz all fucked out.

4

I woz worried as hell. We did da rawbck an he came 3 whole tymz! I wz on ma way 2 a chemist early in da mornin. 'Plz may i av da mornin afta pill?' I asked da stern faced black woman at da counter. She wz abat 45 an jus looked at me wit a rude look. She musta bin disappointed becoz i wz a sista an i had dun sumfin stupid. She kissed er teeth an went in2 da bck. I wz vex an wz rdy 2 cuss er out str8! She came bck out, nostrils flared, wit a clipboard.

'Fill out dis form' she instructed in a jamaican accent, thrustin da clipboard at me nt lookin at me.

'Yuh gtta pen?' I asked in a jamaican accent.

'No, but me gt condoms' she replied lookin up at me an den turnin on er heels an goin 2 da bck of da chemist once agen.

I kissed ma teeth loudly an spoted a pen on da counter. I took it an sat dwn in a chair an filled out da short questionaire. While i woz doin so da bitch came bck outta da bck room an made erself look busy.

'Me finish' I sed stndin up an handin er bck da clipboard.

She cut er eye at me took da clipboard an went in da bck. Abat 10 minz 18r she came bck out an gve me ma pill.

'So yuh cyant gimme no water?' I asked lyk it wz compulsery.

Da woman kissed er teeth loudly an gt bck 2 wt she wz doin.

'U kno wt ye, teens dnt cum ere 2 gt an ear bashin or a stink attitude 4rm ppl lyk u. Dey cum ere in confidence. I made a mistake i kno an i dnt wnt 2 ave 2 cum bck ere agen 4 makin da sme stupid mistake, okay! So i wuld appreciate it if u werent so rude 2 me an treted me wit at least an ounce of respect!' I sed an turned on ma heels an wlked outa da chemist.

I wlked in2 a small newsagents a few doorz dwn, grabbed a botle a wata outa da fridge an payed 4 it. As i sat at da bus stop i took ma pill an wished 4 da best.

A 279 came soon enuff an i jumped on it. I sat dwn on ma j's an daydreamed outta da window, wonderin 2 maself wot it wud b lyk 2 hav Ricardos baby an hw he wud react da day i eva broke da news dat he wud b a daddy. I woz 80% sure he wud b ova da moon but den agen, u neva kno. Ma mind reflected bck 2 da day, da day i wud neva in ma lyf 4 gt, da day dat i had 2 gt serious:

'POSITIVE?!?!?!?!?!' I asked maself in disbelief. It woz da 15th July 2004 an i had been throwin up an fellin dizzy evry mornin i woke up. a gut feelin woz tellin me i woz pregnant but of course i didnt wanna believe it. I woz 14 yrs old an pregnant? Naaa dat cudnt b, i thought. But der i woz wit da white stick in ma black handz tellin me da total opposite.

Da word i prayed dat i wud neva read on dis white stick. I made deals wit da lord dat i wud not hav sex 4 a whole year if god cud jus make sure dat i was not preg- nant, but, of course, god didnt wanna hear dat shit an 'cursed' me wit a nu lyf growin inside of ma smal stomach.

I had been fuckin around wit guys 4 abat a yr an neva rly cared less. I woz raised by strikt west indian parents (Mum, Jamaican an St Lucian, an Dad Trinidadian an Bejan) But of corse wen ur parents r strikt, da kidz dnt listen, which was xactly y i woz in dis mess. I had been fuckin around wit dis guy 4 abat 2 months. His name was Michael an he woz sexcccc. I always lyked him jus lyk all da ova gurlz in da endz. Michael had it all, da money, da gurlz an da respect. He woz a top runner 4 da top shotta on da block. He had evrything at his fingatips. I guess his money an his respect attracted me 2 michael even more. I'd known Micheal 4 a lng tym an had lyked him 4 a lng tym 2 but we had onli gt it 2gva jus b4 summa. I woz jammin around wit sum hoes 4rm da endz, tryna catch Micheals attention wen he finally came up 2 us an sed 'wha gwan' 2 evry1, den, 2 ma suprise, he asked if he cud speak 2 me 4 a while. I woz smilin 4rm ear 2 ear while i folowed him 2 a nearby block. He sat dwn on a step an i stood up in frnt of him. I had ma arms folded across ma chest tryin as hrd as posible nt 2 smile dwn at him while he jus sat der an gazed up at me:

'I lyk u, u kno' he sed out da blu.

'Izit' i mumbled noddin ma hed wit a smile on ma face.

'Ye, it iz' He replied gttin up.

He stepped closa 2 me an put his arms around ma waist. In no tym at all we woz stndin up der toung wrestlin in da block. Imagine dat, abat 7 wordz ago all i cud gt 4rm da [redacted] woz a 'wha gwan' or basic frendly chat. If i woz lookin rlllllllllllly nice on di odd occasion i wud get a 'sexc' shout 4rm evry1 on da estate includin him.

'U wnna cum bck 2 my yard?' He asked afta da wrestle woz ova.

'Ye' I replied lyk a dumb hoe. I folowed him a cuple blocks 2 his yard. He opened da door wit his key. As i steped in da house da strong smell of weed hit. He walked 2 his bedroom as i folowed. He stod in frnt of da bed an pulled me closa 2wrd him until we were touchin. We strted kissin

agen an b4 i knew it i found maself naked
on top of him ridin his dick. Afta da sex
he didnt rly say much. I didnt feel nice
lyk i hoped i wud hav felt afta fuckin
Michael. 4 da 1st 2 weekz i woz fuckin
him he alwayz used a condom bt den we
strted 2 relax an he insisted i wudnt gt
pregnant so we stopped usin dem. At first
he didnt cum inside of me, he wud alwayz
tke it out b4 he woz abat 2 cum, but den
i guess he jus wasent bovad an strted
cummin 2-3 tymz inside of me. An das y i
woz here sittin on ma bathroom floor, da
white stick in ma black handz, tears
streamin dwn ma face an a broken heart.
I decided 2 go round 2 michealz an tell
him the news. He woz at home an wen he
sw me standin der he let me in, he woz
usherin me 2 da bedroom an wen i gt in
der he strted undoin his belt quickly.

'Na na na, i aint cum ere 4 dat i need
2 chat 2 u'

'Can we chat afta we fuck'

'No dis iz important'

'Ite den make it quick init' he sed in
an anoyed tone.

'Micheal, I-I-I'm Pregnant' I shakily
sed, his eyes rose up 2 me an he had a
mad look on his face. Das wen i nu it

woz jus da sex an der woz no more Micheal
an Me.

'Iz nt mine, gt out u hoe' he sed
disgusted. An dat woz all it took, 7 wordz
2 ruin ma lyf strt a bad reputation an
break a young heart even further.

Ma stop came an i climbed of da bus. I
woz jus dwn da road 4rm shanice an
ricardos. I trekked dwn an rang da bell.
Shanice awnsered, she woz on da fne an
jus stepped bck 2 let me in greetin me
wit a smile. I went upstairs folowin her
big bum up 2 da top landin an i continued
dwn da hall 2 ricardos room, leavin her
outside her door. I steped in2 ricardos
room. He woz on his fone also. He greeted
me wit a smile an a smal wave an continued
his conversation on his cellular. I lay
dwn on da bed an jus thought 2 maself hw
much ma lyf had changed afta da 1st eva
tym i had sex.

5

'Oi sket!' shouted a group of boiz as
i walked thru da endz. I woz so used 2

dis i jus caried on walkin wit ma hed held hi. Eva since da day i tld Michael i woz pregnant wit his baby i hav had 2 put up wit dis kinda shit. I woz goin home 2 gt sum fingz den i woz goin bck 2 ricardos yard. I had bin der da whole week. Der woz a pyjama party goin on at aroun 10 an me n ricardo wer gnna go der 2geva. I reached home an as i entered i woz greeted wit an argument between ma brovas. I made ma way up stairs an bumped in2 mum on da way.

'Hello young lady' she sed.

'Hey mum' I replied den heded 2 ma room, as i stepped in i threw da bag i had on ma bed n walked ova 2 ma wardrobe 2 pik out sum clothes. I piked out sum sexc pyjamas 4 da party n garmz 4 da nex day as i woz sleepin at ricardos. I packed dem both in a bag n went bck out ma frntdoor. I walked past da sme group of boiz an dey shouted out da sme shit. I gt 2 ricardos hse an let maself in wit his key. I ran up da stairs in2 his bedroom an threw dwn ma bag. Ricardo woz standin in front of a draw wen i entered. He closed da draw wen he saw me an i wlked ova 2 him. I kissed him an den climbed on2 da bed an switched on da TV.

He lay on das bed bhind me runin his fingaz up n dwn ma bck. I sat der watchin a film. Wen da film finished it woz around 9 an it woz nearly tym 4 da party. I ubrubtly switched da TV off n jumped up.

'Lets hav a showa cuz da partys strtin in a hour' I sed facin ricardo.

'Ite cum den' he sed lazily an gt up.

We walked 2 da bathroom n i turned on da showa an began tkin off ma clothes, ricardo did da sme an climbed in2 da showa while i tied up ma hair. I stepped in an took a scrub in2 ma hand an poured sum soap on2 it. I strted scrubin ma body. ricardo turned around an took da scrub 4rm me an strted scrubin ma body whilst kisin ma lips. He droped da scrub an started rubin ma body wit his handz. His dick woz stndin tall an he tried 2 push me against da showa wall to enter me. Even doe i woz horny i didnt wnna do it 4 sum reason.

'No baby' i moaned as he pushed his fingas in2 me.

'Y not' He breathed on ma neck.

'Plz baby nt nw, wen we gt bck 4rm da party'

'Ite den, but bash me off' he whispered. I took his dick in2 ma handz an gt dwn on ma knees insted. I strted lickin n suckin on his dick until he came in ma mouf. I spat out da cum an gt up. He looked dwn at me an tuched ma mouf an slowly let his fingas glide dwn ma body. He kissed me on da cheek an turned off da showa an gt out. I gt out an put a towel round maself. ricardo left da bathroom an i brushed ma teef an exited da bathroom also. I went bck 2 his room an afta creamin ma skin put on ma pyjama (sum white an pink french knicker an a tyt short boob tube top), wen ricardo sw me he had a 'RAAAHH' look on his face. He had on a pair of nike boxerz an sum nike sockz.

'R u sure u wnna go an nt jus stay hme wit me. We can do it all nite boi' he asked hldin me around ma waist an lookin 4rm ma eyes all da way dwn ma body.

'letz go 2 da party, den wen we gt bck we can do it all day' I sed smilin.

'k den, but, put on ma tracksuit botomz an ma hoody ye' he sed tkin out a nike tracksuit 4rm his wardrobe.

'Okay den' I sed tkin it 4rm him an slidin in2 it. It woz enourmous.

Afta he gt dressed in a avirex track-suit we went dwn stairs an jumped in2 his whip. He drove a couple blocks an we gt

2 da hse dat da shubz woz bein held at. We walked in an wer greeted wit bashment playin an a whole leepa blck ppl dancin an whinin up. I went 2 a toilet wit ricardo an we both slipped out of our tracksuits, i ge it 2 him an den we both went out on 2 landin 2 put da trcksuits in2 a bedroom. We went dwn stairs an strted dancin 2geva. I spotted a group of guyz bop in an den realised it woz a whole leep a boiz 4rm my endz.

'SHIT' i mumbled 2 maself bt carried on dancin prayin dey wudnt spot me. But, yet agen, god didnt wnna hear it did he an dey spotted me n strted starin at me n ma man dancin on da dance floor 2geva. Dey were mumblin an laufin amongst demsleves.

'Oi u sket, u gnna b givin rides n shines 2nite or wot?' 1 of dem called out. I ignored dem an carried on dancin wit ricardo hu woz unaware dey wer tlkin 2 his gurl.

'Oi man im fuckin tlkin 2 u. R u goin 2 b givin headz and fuckin guyz upstairs 2nite, yes or no?'

Ricardo pushed me off of him an moved me out da way.

'Ay blud iz dis da way ur tryna step 2 ma gyal?'

'Ur gyal?? Rahhh boi, r u dumb. Dat stink sket iz URZ?' Da crew of boiz fell abat laufin but stil shocked.

'Oi rude boiz if u call er a sket agen ill fuckin draw 4 ma tool n buss 2 shotz in eacha unu head! Dnt b calin ma gyal a sket ya' Ricardo replied pointin in 1 of da guyz faces n stepin closa 2 him.

'Iz nt my fault shes a sket n has killed atleast 4 babies 4 difrent manz in da endz' 1 of da guyz sed quietly whilst turnin his head n boppin off wit his clique folowin close bhind.

Riardo jus stood der lookin on at dem as dey roled out. I woz scared of wot he mite fink or say but, bcoz i knew he woz such a kind, gentle n 4givin person twardz me, i fort dat he wud let it slide even doe i hadnt tld him abat ma past. He turned around an stood lookin at me. I looked bck at him n i cud c da hurt in his eyes.

'Is it tru?' He asked softly.

'Not here ricardo lets go bck home' I replied nt wntin 2 spred ma buissness in public.

He turned 2 da left n headed 4 da stairs 2 go gt his tracksuits. I folowed him. I didnt kno wot 2 expect. I knew he woz dsapointed an believed dat atleast sum of it mus b tru 4 da guys 2 b sayn dat shit. He went in2 da room an gt da tracksuits. He pased me da 1 he had lent me witout lookin at me. I felt ashemed an durty. I fort dat ricardo didnt hav luv or respect 4 me nemor. I mean, hu wntz a gurl datz had da whole estate drillin up in her shit rawbck? I didnt wnt 2 lose him. Afta all dese yrs of fightin him off i wished i had gt wit him 4rm da beginin. So mny fingz wud hav bin diffrent in ma lyf.

6

Da ride bck home woz so ded. Da silence woz so tense, I ddnt kno if i cud tke it. Wen we arived home i waited 4 him 2 open his door n den i opened minez n climbed out. I wz so nervus. I folowed him up 2 da frnt door n he opened it he held it open 4 me bt wudnt look @ me. I wanted 2 turn around n run away, as far as posible, i wnted 2 run in2 ma past n chnge evryting ... bt dat wudnt hapen. I walked in n jus stood der. He closed da door.

'So, ill ask agen, iz it tru?' he sed firmly.

'Look ricardo, i love u. An i fort u luved me aswel-'

'U kno dat i luv u n hav alwayz loved u, an ill probably love u 4 aslng as i liv but at da end of da day i need 2 trust u n protect u. U kno dat nuffin on dis earth cud eva cause me 2 b unatracted 2 u or fall outa love wit u. Ur ma wifey man n im gnna make u ma WIFE legally as soon as i gt outta dis game. All i wnna do iz save up as much p as posible n den evryting wil b bless, u gt me ... it will b me n u das it' he sed, tears formin in his eyes.

'I luv u 2 ricardo, im jus .... scared' i replied, tears rollin dwn ma cheekz.

'Scared of wot? scared of wot i mite fink? I dnt care ye. Leme tell u a story ye. Has shanice eva tld u y we liv in ds house by ourselves nw?'

'No' I replied. Ricardo n shanice lived in a spacious 4 bedroom house all by dem selves. I jus clocked.

'Because ma mum woz a crack head prostitute n ma dad woz a drug dealin pimp ye. Ma mum woz 15 wen she had me n 17 or 18 wen she had shanice. She met ma

dad at da age of 14. He woz 23. He woz
a drug king pin in da "hood" bck in da
days. Sold evryting u cud fink of. Him n
mumz relationship woz goin gd. She ran
away 4rm hme 2 liv wit him, dey had kidz
n lived happily. She had evryting at er
fingatipz. Money, cars, clothes, Drugz. But
she wernt alowed 2 touch da drugz. But
of course, ppl r fass up n curious n coz
she woz yung n dumb she decided 2 put er
fingas wher dey wernt meant 2 b. On a big
old rock of crack. Nw u kno afta dat first
lik iz nxt 2 imposible 2 stop. So, to
mke a lng story short she licked dat pipe
n cudnt stop. Wen ma dad found out he
went mad n beat her ass until she woz
blck n blu. He locked er in da attic 4
a week. He called it 'king-pin rehabili-
tation'. We cud hear her screamin n cryin.
Tryin 2 scratch her way outta da ropes 2
gt anuva hit.

Afta da week woz up, i guess ma dad
fort she woz sumwot cured n she cme outta
der. A few months went past n den wot
did she do, she licked it agen but dis
time she licked da pipe n shot up sum
heroin afta 2 stop da agitated feelin n
2 relax er. But da didnt work 4 long.
She woz loosin weight by da minute! so

insted of da king pin rehab project, Dad sed 2 er 'U wnna smoke crak, u gonna work 4 it. Dis iz da ghetto bitch. Nufin iz free' N wit dat, he strted pimpin er lyk all his ova hoes. She wud disapear 4 days n cum bck beat up or jus strung out on da drugs. She acted happy but cum on, hu woz happy wen dey had 2 suck dick jus 2 gt a peice of rock cocaine which woz da size of ur thumb nail n dun in 2 or 3 pullz. She kept chasin dat hi 4 yrs. Dad didnt care. Me n shanice woz in skool doin well n evryting. we wud c er on occasions n she wud beg us 4 sum money. I neva gve her a penny but i kno shanice did. So der it iz ... dat woz da begginin of ma lyf so NUFIN u tell me will shock me. Im tellin u, nuthin shocks or suprises me nemor!'

I jus stood der in so much shock. I cudnt believe ricardo woz tellin me al dis. I rememba his dad 4rm bck in da dayz bt he woz so nice n frendly n wotnot.

'So, r u gnna tell me?' ricardo asked cutin in2 ma thoughts.

'Ricardo, i gt 1 abortion an das it. But dat woz da onli abortion ive eva had. I duno wher dat prick woz goin abat 4!! Ive slept around abit aswel, but ive used protection atleast 90% of da tym. I aint proud of da tingz i bin up 2 bt at da end of da day iz al in da past n i luv u so much n ive bin in denial all dese yrs. I wish i cud turn bck da clock soo badly but i cnt n evryting happens 4 a reason. But im so srry dt u had 2 find out lyk dis'

Ricardo stood der starin at me, his face expressionless. I gt scared dat he mite tell me 2 gt ma tingz n step, but sudenly a smile spred acros his face. It wasnt a big smile, it woz kina weak, bt it woz a gd sign.

'Lyk i sed befre b, i luv u 2 def n nuffin dt hapened in da past cn chnge dat. Ur da 1 4me n nufin n no1 cn chnge dat. Ur so beautiful n sexc i cnt wait til we hav kidz n gt maried n mke a propa lyf. I wud drop dwn on ma knee ryt nw wit a ring but i need 2 gt outa dis ting we call da "game". I dnt wnna tie u dwn wit me n ma problemz by marryin u nw. But i wnt u 2 hav dis' Ricardo took off 1 of da mny ringz he had on his fingaz, his favorite ring, 'iz a promise ring, i promise dat i wil luv u n onli u 4 as lng as i liv n i also promise i wil marry u n mke u happy'

I jus stood der speechless, tears streamin outta ma [redacted] eyes.

'Wots rong b?' he asked a lil woried look on his face.

'No1s eva tld me dey luved me b4' i sed lookin up at him.

He kissed ma lips n took ma hand in2 his an rubbed da ring lookin in2 ma eyes. I took grip on2 his hand n led him up da stairs 2 his room, a trail of clothes left n 4goten bhind us. Once we gt 2 his room i turned around 2 face him n all @ da sme tym ma body hit da bed n his body floped on2 me. We strted kissin deeply. He hungrily sucked on ma lips. He reached 4 ma bra fasenin bt stopped in his trackz.

'We dnt hav 2 do dis u kno' he sed lookin in2 ma eyes.

'I wnt 2' i replied n dived bck in2 lickin n kissin his smooth lips.

He undid ma bra n it hit da floor. Since he woz on top of me i moved ma body 2 da side n rolled maself on top of him, our lips neva disconectin in da proces. Afta a few mins of lipsin i sat up. By dat tym ma knickers had joined ma bra n his boxers had joined ma undawear on da floor. He lay der wit me on top of him rubin ma thighs n lickin his lips.

I lifted maself up n sat on topp of his stndin dick. It entered ma soakin pussy n str8 away i rode n wyned ma waist n moved ma

self up n dwn n around, up n dwn n around. He woz moanin n telin me 2 go fasta. I gyr8ed ma hips in a circular n up n dwn motion as fast as i cud. Afta 5minz ma knees wer strtin 2 ache. Jus as i woz goin 2 slow dwn ma legs strted shakin n i strted feelin weak. Ricardo cme jus b4 me. I colapsed on top of his chest. He put his arms around me. I moved 2 lay bside him. Whilst i lay bside him i glanced at da ring n thought of da promises ricardo had made 2 me. I smiled.

'Ricardo, wot eva happened 2 ur mum n dad?'

'Ma mum, shes around sumwher. Herd she gt picked up by sum rich white man hu gve er a place 2 stay n money. So evryting iz bless 4 her init, well, as lng as he gts er "services" weneva he wnts. An ma dad died. He left dis hse n a big ol chunk of drug n blood money 2 me n shanice.' he replied.

I lay der in his arms. I cudnt believe dat da man i luved had bin thru al of dis. I wnted 2 hld his face in ma handz

63

n tel him evryting wil b alrite. I wnted 2 slip off 1 of ma chains n put it around his neck n tell him dat i wud stick by him 4eva n dat ma luv n lust 4 him wud neva eva end. But cud i b sure of dat? woz da milion doller question.

7

I awoke 2 da sound of ma fone ringin @ 11 in da mornin. Ricardo lay asleep nxt 2 me, catchin flies. I laufed 2 maself.

'hello?' i awnsered 2 da withheld caler.

'Im gnna gt u duty bitch!' replied da caler.

'Huh? wot?' i asked bck absolutly baffed bt da person cut off. I disregarded da call n climbed out da bed. I went 2 da bathroom n turned on da showa. I washed maself several tyms ova coz i woz bored. Wen i gt out i dried maself n gt dressed. I opened shanices bedroom door 2 c if she woz up or even in der. She woz sittin up in er bed in er bra wit da covers pulled up 2 er stomach. Der woz a guy sittin on er bed fully dressed on er bed facin er. Dey wer speakin in hushed voices. Wen i opened da door shanice looked up n smiled at me n playfully gestured me 2 basically gt out. i smiled n steped out n went bck 2 ricardos room. I had 2 go hme 2 gt garmz. I woz gnna sleep @ ricardos 4 a while lnga. Probably till tuesday. Wen i stepped in ricardo woz up.

'U ite b' he asked lookin up @ me as i entered.

'ye' i sed.

'leme quickly go do sumfin' he sed quickly walkin past me, hldin ma hips as he slide past. i smiled 2 maself bcoz i knew he woz goin 2 brush his teeth n wash his face.

Wen he re entered 5 mins l8a i woz sittin on da bed. He lunged at me n dove str8 4 ma lips. We lay der, wit him on top of me, 4 a gd while suckin on each otherz lips n tastin eachova. Wen we finally finished ricardo lifted his hed up n lookd in2 ma eyes.

'I luv u u kno' he sed.

'i luv u 2' i replied 'bt i gtta go'

'go where???' ricardo asked alarmed, half way gttin up off of me.

'jus 2 go gt sum clothes, no need 2 hav a fit!' i replied half laufin.

'o skn. do u wnt me 2 cum wit u?'

'Na na iz okay. ill b bck soonish init'

'ite den. Cum' he sed gesturin 4 me 2 cum 2 him. I steped ova 2 him n he held me so nice bt tite. i kissed his lips n turned 2 pik up ma bag.

'soonish ye' he caled afta me.

'soonish' i replied n left da room.

I bolted dwn da stairz n outta da front door. I walked dwn da road n turned on2 a nxt rd. As i walked sum guys wer wlkin a distance bhind me. Dey wer all blck boiz n der woz abat 5 or 6 of dem. Wen i focused ma ears on der rather loud convo, i realised hu dey wer n realised dey knew hu i woz. Dey wer da guyz 4rm da party da ova nite. I speeded up ma pace. Tryna walk as fast as posible but den i buckled n fell flat, nearly on ma face. I herd footstepz run up bhind me n handz grab at me. Da guys lifted me up n carried me dwn a alley. Wen we reached da end of da alley a car sat der. Da cars windows wer tinted n da car woz blck. 1 of dem opened da door n dey thru me in 2 da bck. 2 jumped in da bck n 2 in da frnt. I woz 2 confused 2 mke a sound, evryfin hapened way 2 fast.

'make a sound n die' sed 1 of da guyz dat woz in da bck, i didnt even look at him. I felt sumtin cold against ma hed.

Wen i strained ma eyes 2 look 2 ma left 2 c wot it wz ma eyes caught a glimpse of da barrel of a gun. I quckly snapped ma eyez 2 face da frnt. I woz so scared.

'Wh-wh-what r u gnna do 2-2-2 me?' i shakily asked.

'Dnt wrry. Jus kno ull enjoy it' sed da driver.

Da car carried on drivin. I knew all da places we pased 4 da 1st hour, bt den i gt lost. Afta anuva hour da car stoped in a field type of place. Der woz a motorway abat half a mile ahed.

Da driver n da guy in da pasanger seat gt outta da car n opened da door 4 da guy 2 da left of me hu had da gun 2 ma hed. He climbed out n dey demanded me 2 gt out, so i did so.

'Folow me' sed da guy dat had been drivin. Dey strted wlkin until we gt 2 a bridge. We wer undneath da bridge.

'Drop ur trousers n pantys' da driver demanded.

'W-w-what?' i shakily asked in disbelief.

'U herd me bitch' he shouted n in a flash i felt da wind on ma legz n bum. 1 of da 2 men dat wer stndin bhind me had pulled dwn ma trousers n undawear.

'Gt on ur knees on all 4s' da drver demanded. I did as i woz tld n dropped on al 4s. B4 i cud gt used 2 da damp cold floor against ma once warm skin, a hard lng dick woz thrust in2 ma ars. I let out a scream 4rm da pain. Hu eva it woz woz thrustin demselves hard n fast in2 ma ars at such speed. It hurt me so bad. Ma bum felt lyk it woz bein torn in half. His fingas wer digin in2 ma bum. I thought of da day ricardo doggyed me n thought of hw nicely he held ma bum n hw softly he slapped it, so playfully. Dat woz wen i broke dwn n strted 2 cry. Dat woz wen i knew hw much i luved him.

'Suck it' demanded anuva man, wen i looked up his dick woz danglin in frnt of me. He took hld of it n thrust it in2 ma mouf. I strted suckin wit as litle efort as posible. Afta 10 minz of lazily suckin da guy took a hld of ma hed n thrust it bck n forth. Within a min he came in ma mouf. I spat it out.

'Bitch lik it up now! N swalow it all' he demanded pointin da gun 2 me. I liked up da cum n swalowed it.

Finaly da man @ da bck of me took his dick out of ma ars and kiked me 2 1 side. I lay on ma bck pain rippin thru ma side n ma ars. I felt anuva dick push its way in2 ma body, dis tym abit smaller bt thicker. I woz nt wet atall i woz jus scared. Da man on top of me pounded in2 me wit gr8 force clawin @ ma hips. Wen he came i looked at ma lowa abdoman n sw bleedin scratches. Da driver n da guy dat woz in da passenger seat stood ova me. Da drver stood ova ma pussy n da pasenger seat guy stood ova ma hed. Da guy dat woz ridin in da pasenger seat woz caled Kubez. I had fucked wit him in da past. He looked dwn @ me n unzipped his trousers, as i looked at him i searched his eyes 4 even a litle bit of sympathy. Der woz nun. Ma vision of him woz soon blured as he directed his dick in ma face n pissed on me. Wen he finished i rolled over on all 4s spitin n spluterin all his piss outta ma mouf n throat. I felt a dick tear itself in2 ma ars yet agen n den secondz 18a a dick woz forced in2 ma mouf yet agen. I sucked n sucked on it. wen dat round woz finished i colapsed on ma bck n jus lay der. I felt a hard kik in ma leg n den a blow 2 ma side. I felt a hevy fist blow in ma face. Den dey scatered. Dey ran across da feild 2 da car jumped in it n swerved away. I lay der 4 a gud 10minz b4 i dared

2 sit up. Once i sat up i grabed ma trousers n put dem on. I walked as fast as i posibly cud 2 da motorway. I strted wlkin 4 a while. I didnt kno wher i woz goin. I didnt kno wher 2 go.

'BEEP!!' i spun round @ dat sound. In da car dat beeped me woz a middle aged couple. Da woman in da pasenger seat gestured 4 me 2 gt in2 da car. I gt in da bck. 'Child, wot happen 2 u?' asked da lady as her husband caried on drivin.

'I-i-i wnna i wanna go hme' i stutered starin ahed.

'Well hunny wher do u liv?' da lady asked. I gave er da nme of ricardos rd.

'Curtis, can u drive der?'

'Yes' da old man replied.

'So hunny wot happened 2 u. U hav a bruise cumin up on ur face n ur clothes r all durty n torn' da lady sed lookin me ova.

'P-p-p-plz. Plz j-j-jus tke me h-hme. I-i-i woz ataked. I wnna c-c-c ricardo' i stutered bck. I burst in2 tears. I cudnt stop cryin 4 da whole of da journey. Wen da car finally turned on2 ricardos rd i flew outa da car. I quickly walked dwn da rd. Wen i gt 2 ricardos hse i rapidly knocked on da door. Ricardo opened da door.

'KEISHA!!!!!!!' he shouted n grabed me in his arms n carried me in2 da hse.

'Hu did dis 2 u baybee gurl. Tell me hu did dis 2 u???' ricardo hurridly asked.

'K-k-kubez n his boiz' I managed 2 say.

'SHANICCCCCCCCCCCEEEEEEEEEE!!!' ricardo shouted up da stairs.

'WOT?!' cme shanices shout. full of atitude.

'Bring ma gun n ma fone' he shoted bck. within seconds shanices footsteps dwn da stairz cme. Wen she sw da state of me lyin der in ricardos arms she droped da gun n da fne n ran 2 me.

Ricardo put me 2 lay on da sofa he gt his fne n da gun. He put da gun in da waist band of his trousers n dialed a numba on his fne.

'Yoye. Cum 2 ma yard now n bring all da goonz straped up' he sed in2 da fne. He hung up. He droped on his knees n kneeled by me lookin @ me.

'Keisha keisha keisha. How??' he asked lookin @ me tears formin in his eyes. He brushed ma hair outa ma face.

'I dnt kno ricardo. Dey jus grabbed me' i xplained.

'Tell me wot hapened' he sed. I explained everyfing dat happened. Da frown n da sparkle in ricardos eye ment dat it woz WAR. Soon der woz a knock @ da door.

'I luv u keisha n ill c u soon' ricardo sed kissin me on da forehed.

'B careful ricardo. I luv u 2' i sed bck. He kised shanice on da cheek n left.

8

Abat an hour l8a ricardos keys turned in da lock in da frnt door. He took his gun outa his waist an dashed it 2 1side den he took off da gloves n dashed dem 2 a nxt side. He cme ova 2 me n held me so close n so tite.

'wot did u do ricardo?' i quietly asked afta a min or so.

'da truth?' he asked.

'plz, da truth' i replied.

'da truth iz i killed dem.' he sed flatly. I jus stayed in his armz silently lookin blankly @ da TV. 1000 thoughts runnin thru ma hed. I knew he loved me bt wot if he ended up gtin killed. Wot if da police found out. Wot if he gt life in prison.

'dnt wrry abat it' he sed outta da blu. It woz lyk he cud hear ma thoughts. 'der woz a bag a men @ da scene n it woz in a house abat 10 minz away 4rm here. Plus i gt a silencer on da gun so u cnt hear shit. sum of da guyz took da bodies 2 dump dem sumwhere. an truss alla dem r ded.'

I woz stil silent. Stil partly shocked. Bt i stil lay in his armz. Bt sumhw i knew everyfin woz gnna b alrite.

2months l8a

It had been 2months afta da rape. I had been @ ricardos hse da majority of da tym. Da relationship woz as strng as eva. Even doe we hadent had sex in 2months, ricardo didnt seem 2 mind. Every fing woz gr8.

It woz a friday afternoon an i had jus reached ricardos afta goin shopin. I let maself in wit da key he had given me. I ran up da stairz 2 ricardos room. He woz sitin @ da side of his bed countin sum money. I dropped da bagz on da floor.

'Ill b bck b. Leme go chek on shan' i quickly sed abat 2 wlk bck outta da door.

'Not even a kiss ya na' he muttered.

I ran ova 2 him an kised him on da lips den i ran bck out. I hadent seen shanice properly in a cuple weekz an we wer basicaly LIVIN 2geva. I knocked on er bedroom door an entered. She woz lyin in bed.

'U ite shan'

'ye ye b' she replied 'Keisha? i need 2 tell u sumfin'

'Wot iz it?' i asked lookin @ er.

She had a slight glow in er cheekz. She looked mor radiant an er skin woz barrre clear.

'Im 4 months pregnant'

I woz shocked 'by hu?' woz all i cud ask.

'U c dat boi dat woz sitin on da end of ma bed dat tym u cme in ma room. Well das ma man 4rm abat 7 months ago. An hes da dad.'

'Dus he kno?'

'ye. hes happy n everyfin. he wntz 2 set up hme n all dat'

'Awwww wel das gdgd init. U kno hw moss of dese wayste manz r dees days, dey jus wnna plant der seed n dukle'

'U gt me' shan replied smilin. 'So hws tingz wit u n rico?'

'Der gd u kno. I fort dat afta da rape he wud b actin funni n wot not bt hes da sme as he alwayz woz, if nt betta!' I replied brightly.

'Ok das gd 2 kno. U ite doe b?'

'Ye ye. Im blessical.'

'Gdgd. I need 2 gt ma ars up outta dis bed ya na n go c ma hubbayyyyy!' shan sed slowly gttin outa da bed.

'Ite den ill leve u 2 it. Bt errrmmm, dus ricardo kno. Abat da bby?' I asked cautiously.

'No. Bt im gnna tell him soonish yeye' she sed lookin @ me all traces of smiles or hapiness gne. She knew ricardo wud moss probably hit da roof. Especially if da breh wernt willin 2 step up.

'Ite den. bt mke sure u do. ASAP!' N den i left.

I went bck 2 ricardos room. He woz lyin on da bed. Da money woz in stackz on his desk. I started pickin up da bags n sortin da clothes out wen ricardo sed, 'Oi. Erm excuse me miss, but ehh, whers ma hug?' i went ova 2 him n gve him a hug. 'N ma kiss?' i gve him a kiss on da cheek .'N ma REAL kiss?' i moved ma mouf directly facin his n he brought his lipz 2 mine n opened his mouf. I sat on his lap passionatley lickin n tastin his full lips n warm mouf. Wen we finished (afta a gd 5minz) he looked @ me n sed 'An ma sex?' He asked seductively. It had bin a whole

2 months an i hadent had ne sex wot so eva. Neither had he. Tru say i woz a highly sexed gyal n he woz a highly sexed man so 2months iz a lng lng tym 2 of nt had sex. I woz mor dan redy 2 do it nw. Despite da rape. He slowely strted 2 gt up 2 indicate 2 me dt he wnted 2 stand. I wrigled of his lap n stood, he gt up n stood infrnt of me. He lifted ma top ova ma hed n strted caressin ma perky breasts thru ma bra. I unbuckled ma belt n drped ma trouserz. Ricardo stoped caresin ma breasts n pulled me closa 2 him by ma small waist. Wen our chests wer tuchin i looked up n ma eyes hit his lips n i strted kissin n suckin dem. He slid his handz dwn ma frenchies n strted caressin ma bum n bngin ma groin against his. Afta a min or so he gently pushed me bck on 2 da bed n took ma legz n spread dem apart. I closed ma eyes expectin his thick solid dick 2 thrust in2 ma achin pussy bt i felt somethin else. It woz litle n warm n wet n it woz gently strokin ma clit. It felt soo gd. I struled 2 open ma eyes bcoz of da ecstacy i felt. Wen i managed 2 open dem, i looked dwnwrd n sw ricardos hed inbetween ma legz his

tounge lickin n strokin ma clit. Ma eyes
shut agen n i took ahold of his head n
pulled it twrdz me so his tounge cud go
deepa in2 me. I woz so suprised dt he
woz lickin me out. I knew it had bin a
lng tym bt ... RAH! Afta a cuple minz of
pleasure, i came. He stopped lickin n woz
jus abat 2 thrust his dick in2 me wen i
pushed him away.

'Sit on da bed' i ordered. I gt up n
stood infrnt of him. I knelt dwn. I took
his lng solid manhood in 2 ma handz n
placed it in2 ma mouf. I sucked on it
lyk a pro. Lickin n suckin in a rythem.
A pattern. Ricardo woz moanin n breathin
faster. He came in ma mouf n i swaloed.
I gt up n sat on top of him. He lay bck
n i lifted maself on2 his dick. I strted
ridin his dick hard n fast. It felt so
gd! Afta all of dis tym i kept thinkin
2 maself. I felt weak, quicka dan usual,
n i cme. As i cme he strted 2 gt weak
n cum aswel. I climbed off of him n lay
dwn nxt 2 him pantin. We jus lay der 4
a few minz. Den i felt his hand strt
rubin ma thigh.

'Redy 4 round 2?' He asked n i smiled
a 'yes'.

9

Da nex mornin i awoke wit ma legz achin me sooo badly lyk asif i had dun 3 hrs trainin @ d gym. All 4rm 1 orgasm filled nite wit ma sexc hubby. He lay der nxt 2 me fast asleep. It woz 12pm n he woz stil asleep.

'Lazy ass' i smerked 2 maself.

I climbed outta d bed feelin a satis-fiying ache inbetween ma thick thighs. I smiled. I crept 2 d ova side of his room. I noticed a drw dat woz a lil bit open. Nw for 1. im blck 2. im his gurl an 3. im a nosy shit any way so i opened d drw further. Wot met ma eyes shocked me. Der woz enuff money in d drw 2 feed all d hedz dat lost all der tingz in d tsunami 4 a month. Der woz also 2 strapz n pure crack, weed n wt lookd lyk heroin.

At dt point i woz vexxxxx! Hw cud he b sellin alla dat shit afta dem sme tingz fucked up his own muddas lyf. An hw cud he put me n shanice in such danger by sellin dees kina drugz on his fuckin doorstep. I woz rdy 2 blast his raas as soon as he gt his big hed outa da bed. I went 2 d bathroom 2 d showa. I quickly showerd, climbed out gt dressed n did ma hair. Afta i did ma hair i opened da curtains n cleared up a few of ma fingz cz i wernt expectin 2 sleep der anuva nite until all dem drugz wer shifted. Wen i finished poterin around n dat i decided 2 look thru a nuva drw. It woz full of money n der woz a shank in der aswel. I shook ma hed n closed bck d drw.

Soon ricardo strted stirrin n he woke up.

'wha gwarn b ...... y u screwfacin?' he sleepily asked.

'wt da FUCK iz alla dis?' I asked hldin up 1 of da mny bagz full of crack cocaine.

'Iz crack' he sed. He sounded cool n calm bt in his eyes i cud sense abit of alarm n shock. He climbed outta d bed n headed 4 d bag.

'Wt d fuck u doin wit all dis kina shit in da house ricardo. Ur da sme person dt tld me dat story bout ur mudda an father n ur sellin d sme ting dat made ur own blud mudda giv up on u n abandon u! Fucks rong wit u?' I shouted.

'Wt d fuckz rng wit u. Y u goin thru manz drws n screamin all up in mans face aswel? Dis iz 4 a fuckin futre my dear. Do u undastnd? FUTURE?!?!?! Dnt cum scream

up in ma fce in ma yrd lyk dt agen ...
imma bad man. U neva kno?' He sed tkin
d bag 4rm me n stufin it bck in d drw.
I woz in 22 much shock 2 sy a wrd! Wt
woz RONG wit him? I jus looked @ him,
kissed ma teef, picked up ma bag n left.

I ran dwn d stairz n outa d door.
Ricardo cme afta me.

'Shanice gyal cum ere! Y ya gwan so? U
kno i do ma ting 2 mke a livin, giv u
d tingz u wnt n 2 mke a decent future!'

'Yess ricardo. Wteva ye.' I replied
wlkin off. I walked, ricardos shouts
folowin me. I gt 2 mahse n let maself
in wit ma key. I went str8 2 ma bedroom
n threw ma bags 2 1 side. I chnged in2
a pair of shortz n a tshirt n went bck
2 bed. I slept 4 a gud lng 5 hours. Wen
i awoke i strted unpackin ma bagz. Ma
fne had 23 missed calls 4rm ricardo. Der
wer 12 voice messages n 9 txts. All of
dem sayin basically d sme ting. 'I luv
u bby'. 'I miss u bby', 'Im sorry bby',
'Keisha pik up ur fone'. I jus kised ma
teef. I went dwn stairs 2 wher ma mum
woz cookin.

'Hello madam. Lng tym no c n da las
tym i checked u wer ma daughter' ma mum
casually sed wit er eyebrws raised.

'Hi mum' I breathed. She woz dishn up sum food. She dished up a plate n i yammed it dwn. I woz board. I went bck 2 ma room n looked in da mirror. Ma hair woz jus-psed-ma-shoulderz-lng, curly n jet blck, ma nose woz smal n so wer ma eyes n mouf. Ma eyes wer [redacted] as eva. Dey wer a niccce lite brwn color. Ma stomach wz flat n ma bum n chest woz big. Ma thighs wer thick-ish. U cud c all ma shape in da tite short tshirt n shorrrt tight-ish shorts i wore. I smiled 2 maself. I took a dvd off d rack n went dwn stairs 2 d sittin room 2 watch it. Half way thru da film der woz a long an loud car horn blow rite outsidde ma hse. Den der woz shoutin. I decided 2 look by da window 2 c wha gwan wen i sw ricardo stndin outside his car wit a biggg bunch of mixed flowers n sumfin else in his hand.

'KEISHHHHHHHHHHHHHAAAAAAAAAAAAAAAA!' he shouted.

I jumped up n went outside. Wen i strted cumin dwn da path he cme 2 me. Wen he gt 2 me he handed me d flowers n droped on 2 his knee. Der woz a big sparkly diamond ring. Ma eyes grew.

'Keisha, will u b ma wife?' He asked wit a tear in his eye. I woz speechless.

Afta a min i replied 'N-No ricardo. I cnt wen ur doin fingz lyk dat on ur doorstep!'

'I sold alla dat shit keisha baby. I wnt me n u 2 b 2geva 4eva. Ur ma wifey 4 lifey. Plz say yes i love u soooo much baby i cnt liv wit out u. Wen i left 2day i cried lyk a bitch. Den i shotted all d drugz. I had 4 straps n i shoted 2. I had bare shamkz n i shoted dem all now i onli hav 1. I wud do enyfing 4 u.'

'An how did u shot ala dat in da space of lyk 7hourz?' I asked unimpressed.

'I shotted moss of da stuff 2 ppl dat wer big tym shottas so dey cud buy tingz in bulk n da rest i gve 2 Badda, 1 of da goonz, n hes gnna shot it 4 me n gimme me da money init.' he sed.

I looked dwn @ him, d hard look in ma eyes softenin.

'So imma ask agen, Keisha will u b ma wife?'

'Yes ricardo' I replied smilin, tears of joy streamin dwn ma face. He put da ring on ma finga n jumped up. He woz huggin n kissin me. Squashin da flowers n soakin ma top wit his tears of joy.

'Baby, i love u.' he whispred.

'I love u 2' I whispered bck.

20mins 18a

I woz lyin on da bed spread eagle waitin 4 ricardo 2 enter me.

'Uhhhhhh' I sighed wen his thick manhood entered me slowely. He strted 2 thrust himself in fasta n fasta. Ma breathin gt fasta n ma moans bcame louda. I wz reachin ma climax n wen i reached i let out a lng hard moan. Ricardo colapsed bside me strokin ma stomach. I rolled on top of him inbetween his legs n jus rested der. Ricardo fel asleep. I looked @ d ring on ma finga n up @ ma sleepin hubby. He woz so sexc. His skin woz so clear n soft n a sexc brwn dt made him look mixed wit indian jus slightly. His lips wer thick n full n so smooth. His eyes wer blck. Which woz sooo unusual n sexc. His hair woz cut in a sharp shape up. He had both ears pierced twice wit fat sparkly diamondz shinin n twinklin. He woz my definition of PERFECT. So i thought!

10

Da summa holidayz woz ova n i woz goin in2 ma 2nd college yr. Evryting woz

diffrent. I woz married. As i walked thru
da 2 doors in2 d foyer i sw d old faces
n sensed hardly ne chnge in pplz attitudes. sme old ignorant shits. I went 2
ma common room n woz greeted wit a cuple
nu faces. Der wer 2 nu gurlz n 1 nu boi.
dey wer stndin infrnt of d class waitin
2 b introduced by d teacha dt woz rege-
stirin us. Mrs Barkley woz in frnt of d
class also tryin 2 mke evry1 quiet so dey
cud b introduced 2 d nu arrivals. I walked
in2 d class n sat dwn inbetween ma 2
frendz.

'OMG. Iz dt a ring on ur finga?' asked
kayla shocked.

'Yup. it sure iz' i sed smilin.

'hus d lukki cunt den?' asked alisha
grabin ma hand 2 examine d ring.

'ricardo'

'ricardo hu? shanices ricardo?' asked
alisha droppin ma hand in shok.

'Yep' i nodded.

'Dnt lie.' dey sed in unision.

'swr dwn' i sed.

'wher is shanice neway?' asked kayla
lookin round.

'shes pregnant. 5months' i tld dem.

'awwwwwwwwwwwwwwww!' dey both squeled.

'CAN ALL OF U JUS SHUT UR EFFIN MOUTHS' screamed Mrs Barkley ova all da chatta.

Every1 buss out laufin bt stayed quiet.

'Now, we hav 3 nu students joinin our form dis yr. We hav Rhianna and Eliza' she sed pointin 2 d 2 blck gurlz stndin awkwrdly infrnt of d class. 'And here we hav Malachi.' she sed pointin 2 d sexc blck yute stndin away 4rm d gurlz. He lookd restless n woz screwfacin. It woz hot an he had on a white nike t-shirt wit a white string vest cumin out 4rm d bottom. He wz busin lw batty wit sum grey nike tracksuit botomz n sum grey n white crep, he had ona black n grey era cap. He looked sexxxxc. He woz starin @ me der in da bck wiv ma gurlies. As Mrs Barkley introduced him our eyes met n he licked his soft thick lips. I smiled. He smiled 2, showin perfect pearly white teef.

'Keisha man, newaiz, wenz da weddin?' asked Kayla totally snapin me out of ma trance.

'Huh ... O d weddin ... i dunno' I sed.

As we continued 2 chatta, da nu boi malachi cme n sat dwn nxt 2 Karl an Pablo, da 2 out of d 3 guys dat me, kayla n alisha usually jammed wit.

'Wha gwan' sed Karl, a 100% jamaican bredda.

'Kool kool kool' replied malachi, his voice woz so deep n sexc. He spudded both Karl n pablo. 'yo fam, whers jamal?'

'I duno man. U kno hw dt fool iz, gt 2 much p 2 worry wit bein on time 4 no bludclart EMA @ d end of d week' Karl sed.

'tru say, tru say' malachi replied.

'Oh ye lemme introduce u 2 d laydees of dis crew ting' pablo sed turnin 2 face me, lisha n kay 'Oi fat hedz, cum ere'

'Wot?' kayla replied in an anoyed tone.

'Ders sum1 i wnt u 2 meet abat "wot"' pablo sed bck strtin 2 screw. 'abat shes tryna boy manz' he mumbled.

We wnt ova 2 da table dey wer on. I ended up wit a seat nxt 2 malachi. He woz lookin @ me as i sat dwn. I wnted 2 burst out laufin.

'Dis iz malachi u lot' sed karl.

'Hi' lisha sed.

'Hi' Kay sed.

'Hey' i sed.

'Kool kool kool' he sed bck.

Der woz an awkwrd silence an yet agen i wnted 2 burst out laufin. Malachi sat bck in his chair n looked ova @ me slouched in ma chair. He woz watchin me up n dwn. If i cn say so maself i looked mighty fine. It wz a hot day n i had on sum white shortz, blck shoes an a nice blck an white rocawear top. I had ma hair up in 1 ponytail an had a large hoop earing in every hole dt had eva been peirced in ma ears. I had on a gold chain wit a diamond crucifix an ma 5 favorite ringz on. Wen i clocked malachi woz watchin me up n dwn i looked at him. His eyes met mine an he smiled sexcily n den looked away. He put his arm around da bck of ma chair n slouched further dwn in his chair. He put his hand in da front of his trou-sers. 'Rahhhtiddd. Hes sexxxc' I thought 2 maself.

'Whers jamal?' Kay asked 2 break d silence.

'Duno boi. Probly tkin his tym. Alie dt guys 22 loaded 2 giv a fuck abat EMA. Dat £30 iz dust 2 him man.' Pablo sed.

'U gt me' I sed.

'Ye i gt u' malachi mumbled, tryin 2 b funny. I laufed quetly n looked at him. He had hazel-honey eyes an woz a bit drk skinned. He woz tall (6ft 2) an had sum sexc strng arms. His teef wer perfectly white. His lips wer thick n juicey n he kept lickin dem n bitin dem. He had a professional shape up dt u cud c unda his tilted era.

'Arrr man im slippin 2day i swr dwn' he sed outta d blu snapin me outa ma malachi trance. 'I jus wernt bovad dis mornin man'

'Ayo jamal. cum ere fam' shouted Pablo ova d noise.

Jamal cme ova n spudded n hugged evry1. Da bell went n it woz tym 2 move 2 1st lesson. I gt up n went ova 2 ma bag. I picked it up n den went 2 ma locker. As i rumaged around in ma locker, da common room began 2 empty. Son der woz onli da 7 of us in da comon room (me, pablo, jamal, kay, alisha, malachi and karl).

'We all gt ict init' karl sed.

'Ye wot teachas hav u gt?' i asked.

every1 looked at der nu timetables after a while we realised we all had da sme teacha, except me n malachi. Me n malachi had Mrs jet an every1 else had Mr white. Mrs jets classrom woz all d way on da ova end of da corridor.

'Ite cum den keisha' Malachi sed as i looked ova ma timetable.

'Ite. Bless u lot c u all 18a' i sed. I woz nervous boi. Wot if i slip trip buss up ma lip. Dat wud b ova embarrasin. Na man. We walked outta d common room an on2 a corridor.

'Lead d way' malachi sed. 'Im nu here init'

We strted walkin. Me leadin wen suddenly i felt a hand on ma arm.

'Keisha?' I turned around 2 face malachi 'Ur a peng ting u kno. Pengest ting ive seen in a while. Ur wifey material man. Definatly. So man us wnts 2 kno r u on a linkin ting?'

'Um ... N- ... Im engaged' i sed.

'Ur wot??' he asked in shock grabin ma hand. 'Rahhhhh' he sed wen he clocked d ring.

'Ye' i sed. I felt bre bad coz dis guy woz d real perfect 4rm wt i cud c.

'r u happy?' he asked afta a cuple secondz jus starin @ me.

'I fink so' i sed. i didnt kno. i guess i woz coz i sed ye bt den wen i sw ds guy, it woz lyk, look wot im missin.

'U fink?' he sed steppin closa 2 me. He placed his handz round ma waist n puled me closa 2 him. I moved his handz away 4rm ma waist.

'No' i sed shakin ma head.

'y?' he asked, tryin 2 put his handz bck wher dey wer.

'im married' i sed quietly as he tryed 4 d 3rd tym 2 hld me close.

'no ur not. an ur nt happy.' he sed.

'get 2 class now d pair of u! no hanky panky in d corridorz!' shouted mr thorn outta d blu. We quickly bopped off wit malachi folowin ma lead.

11

As d yr progresed Malachis passes seemed 2 b mor frequent n mor heavy evryday. He knew i had a man n he knew hu he woz bt he didnt seem 2 care. I thretened him tym n tym agen dat i wud tel ricardo abat his passes.

but he alwayz sed 'no u wnt' ... n i neva did.

Me n ricardos relationship woz goin gd. We hadent planed d date or nefing 4 d weddin bt it had 2 b wen i left college doe. I had 2 admit i did hav doubts abat d weddin lyk 'wt if i cnt stay loyal' or 'wt if i fall 4 malachi'. I felt confuzed at tymz lyk i woz rushin fingz bt i woz determined 2 turn ma lyf around. Afta bein a sket 4 so lng dis woz lyk d onli chance 4 me 2 calm maself dwn. Iz sooo easy 2 bcum a sket coz it woz lyk d day dt i lost ma virginity i didnt fink i wud crave sex or wnna do it ona regz, i fort i cud control maself. Bt i woz rong, jus ova week afta loosin it i woz horny as eva, out 2 fuck ne random boi. Exactly 2 weekz afta loosin it, a boi 4rm round ma endz churpsed me, Reece his nme woz. He had bin on me 4 tym n kept on tryna link bt i nva even waysted ma tym. Newaiz 1 day i had a P.I.D. (pussy in distress) n needed a lash. So asusual i wud wlk thru d endz n der wud b a group of boiz.

'Oi. Keisha. Cum ere 4 a sec' shouted Reece.

I went ova 2 him, 'Ye?'

'Manz bin watchin u 4 tymmmm lyk n i wnted 2 kno if i cud gt ur numba init' he sed lookin me up n dwn.

Reece woz a tall light skin boi wit wavey hair n drk eyez. He woz aboit on d skinny side doe.

'Ye ite den' I sed as i took his fne in ma hand. Boiz always lyk it wen gurlz r 4wrd.

'So wher u goin nw?' he asked afta i sved ma numba.

'Nowher. Gt ne ideas?' I asked as i looked at him sexily n licked ma lips.

He gt d message loud n clear. 'My place?' he asked.

'Soundz gd' I replied quietly.

'Folow me' He sed turnin around.

I folowed him 2 his yard. He opened d door wit his keys n led me in. I walked in n he closed d door bhind us. He sliped past me lookin @ ma perky breasts. He walked 2 his room wit me folowin. He dashed dwn his keys n took off his tshirt. He took off his crepz n turned around. He walked ova 2 me n held me around ma waist n we strted kissin. He lifted ma top ova ma head. He undid ma bra n it drped 2 d floor. He moved his lips 4rm mine n strted on ma breasts. He bit ma nipples 2 mke dem harden. I unbuckled his belt n undid his butonz on his jeanz. Dey droped 2 d floor n he steped out of dem. He strted kissin ma lips agen n caressin ma breasts, he moved his handz dwn ma stomach 2 ma shorts n undid dem. Dey droped 2 d floor n he pushed his hand dwn ma knickers n strted touchin up ma alredy wet pussy. He moved his fingas bck, leavin d clit n headin 4 ma pum. He pushed his 2 fingas in2 me. I started moanin loud as he pused dem up in2 me fasta n fasta. He took dem out b4 i cme n took hld of ma hand. He led me 2 d bed. He lay dwn n i mouted on top of his rock hrd dick. I wnted sum dick soo much it didnt matta HU i woz fuckin. I lowered ma wet n starvin pussy on2 his skinny but lng dick. As it entered me i let out a lng sigh n strted bouncin up n dwn on his dick. He woz moanin n he woz close 2 cummin so i strted goin fasta n fasta n he cme within a min.

Afta dt day i woz dick hungry. Gagin 4 an orgasm. Das hw i gt ma title Top Sket.

Even doe i woz a freak n a half i woz bein satisfied by ricardo. He knew hw 2 hit it. His dick woz so thick n lng. Perfect blck manz dick. It woz 1 of d biggest i had eva had.

1day at college i woz wlkin 2 class wen Malachi cme runnin up bhind me. He slapped ma bum.

'Ict init' he sed lookin dwn @ me.

'Yup' i replied.

'Oi. Cum we bunk. Hav u even dun her hwk?'

'wot hwk???' i gasped. Mrs Chester woz 1 of d strictedt most bitchiest tchas in d whole skul. If u failed 2 do her hwk even 1nce dat woz u styin bhind 4 half an hour 2 complete it.

'exactly. I onli found out 2day so i aint dun it either.' malachi sed.

'Ye we beta jus bunk 4 real' i sed.

We went in2 a special class room dt woz bein dun up on 1 side of it. Da room woz used 4 special needz usually bt der woz wrk goin on in der dt wz nearly finished. Wen we entered der wer no wrk men in der. Malachi closed n locked d door bhind him. I sat maself ona a table.

As we jammed der chatin abat muzik n listenin 2 tracks on our fnez, malachi asusual gt on2 d subject of 'me n him'.

'U kno i propa lyk u init keisha'

'so u say' i replied rollin ma eyez. I woz fed up of hearin d sme line ova n ova.

'Na im bein ova serious. Y dnt u jus b ma wifey?'

'Coz im in love n im engaged 4 d 100th tym' i sed bck lookin @ him.

'Ye bt i love u aswel doe. Ona level keisha. Im slippin rite nw bcoz im propa spilin out ma feelinz n shit rite abat nw n man lyk me dnt usually do dem 1z u gt me. Bt das hw much im feelin u n das

hw much i wnt u as ma wifey init.' He
sed. I cud c in his eyes dat he wernt
messin abat.

I jus looked @ him n afta a while i
sed 'I cnt'

'U can' he shot str8 bck. 'U can do
neting if u put ur mind 2 it keisha'

'No nt dis Malachi.' i sed.

He didnt say nefing. Afta a lng while
he sed 'U kn wot ye fuck d "feelin lyk
a pussy hole flex". Im jus gna telin it
hw it iz ye str8. I love u off ye ur
wifey material gyal. Me n u belong 2geva
truss i can feel it in ma chess al da
tym. At first ye i did wnt u 2 b ma wifey
bt i wernt on no lng relationship ting
wit u. Mayb jus a 5 month ting u gt me.
Bt now iz a lifey ting man. I cn c me
n u 2geva in d futre, lyk in a lnggggg
tym. Ur jus soo perfect u dnt undastnd.
U gt 1 biggg sexc batty n sum nice big
breasts dem. Ur nice n thick in all d
rite places, thighs, batty n breasts. U
woz blessed in d body n lookz department
4 real. Ur nt buff or peng or sexc ur
beautiful n das soo hrd 2 find. I cn tell
dt ur d kinda gyal daat wen u wke up in
d mornin ur stil ur sme beautiful self.
Ur jus natural. U gt a gd personality ur

carin, ur kind, u gt sum attitude which iz wt i lyk. An i cn c d frak in ur eyes. Dnt fink i dnt c dt. Man ly me cn read gurlz lyk a nursery book. Dnt gt it twisted. Ur ovaly perfect n i kno u gt ur man n everyting bt plz leme show u dt i can plz u n treat u 10 tymz betta dan him r ne ova man. Gimme a week 2 sho u'

I cudnt say nufin. I woz jus shocked n baffled. I knew dt ricardo loved me n dt he had sed sum swt fingz bt neva dis!

'malachi i-i-i ... ' i stammered.

'Shhhh. No wrdz needed' he whispered n put his fingas on ma lips. He moved closa n closa n i knew wot woz cummin. I cud of stopped it if i wnted. But i didnt wnt 2. So i alowed his lips 2 touch mine. I alowed his tounge 2 enta ma mouf.

I alowed him.

Jus dis once.

once?

12

'Oii! Keisha!' malachi shouted dwn d corridor as i cme outa ma last lesson.

'Oh shit' I mumbled unda ma breath. I didn't want him to hav caught me buh he did! I hadent seen him since yesterday n i felt awkwrd n didnt kno wot 2 say.

'Wha gwan sexc' he sed wrapin his armz around me.

'ye, hi, u alrite' i sed wiv a fake smile as i took his armz 4rm around me.

'woz rong wiv u?' he asked lookin puzzled.

'everyfing. lok wot happened yes2day' i sed.

'ooooo wot did ricardo tke d break up badly or sumfin? look bbz dnt wrry bout it ok he'll get ova it. I mean i wnt blame him gtin vex or walleva look @ u. Perfection boi. Ur my wifey nw nwwaiz-'

'WOT? Wot break up? m8 u gt it all rng' i sed absolutly baffed.

'Ur ma wifey doe. I swr das wot d kiss ment'

'Noooooo!!!!' i basically shouted out of fustration 'No malachi i aint ur wifey me n ricardo r stil 2geva n d kiss woz a bigg mistke n i wnt us 2 4gt abat it'

He jus stred @ me wit a scary look in his eyes. It woz a mixture of rage, dissapointment n confusion buh it woz all scary aswel. It woz a mad look. It woz d kinda look dat psychos had in der eyes.

'w-w-wot?' he sed quietly.

'look ill speak 2 u l8a' i sed n quickly power walked off. I dived in2 d toilets n let out a deep sigh. big mistake woz all i cud fink.

Suddenly malachi cme stormin in2 d toiletz.

'So u mean 2 fuckin tell me dt kiss yes2day didnt mean shit 2 u? iz dat wot ur fuckin tryna say?' he screamed.

'Malachi stop keep ur voice dwn' i tried 2 say as firmly as possible.

'Wot d fuck u mean abat keep my blud-clart voice dwn?' he shouted n lifted his fist 2 hit me buh @ dt instant a group of 3 chinese gurlz cme in. Malachi quickly droped his fist n rushed out d toilet.

'everything okay?' asked 1 of d gurls.

'Ye ye im kool' i sed. I waited a whole 10 minz b4 i exited d toilet n went 2 d front office 2 sign out. I jumped ona bus n gt off @ ma stop. I opened d frnt door wiv ma key.

'Shanice?' called ricardo 4rm d sittin room.

'No. Iz me' i sed n sat dwn nxt 2 wher he woz lyin.

'Wot u doin bck hme b?' he asked lookin concerned.

'I wernt bovad wit college 2day' i replied lookin @ d TV.

After a while of watchin TV n huggin up on d sofa ricardo sed 'Whers ma kiss?' I looked @ him n he moved his lips 2 mine n we sat der lipsin 4 a bit. He strted tkin ma top off. I moved ma lips 4rm his 2 pull ma top ova ma hed. I gt up n took off ma trousers. Ricardo took his bottomz off. I climbed on topp of him n sat on his erect dick. It didnt enta doe. I strted grindin on him n started moanin. His dick gt harda n harda undaneath me. afta a while i lifted maself up n sat bck dwn n let his manhood enta me. I let out a sigh n slowly n gently gyr8ed ma hips in a pattern. His breathin gt fasta n so did mine. I woz moanin n den i felt his hips jerk n he cme.

'Ok. U gt urs. Now i hav 2 get mine' i sed as i climbed off of him. He gt up n wrapped his armz around me. He stroked d arch in ma bck.

'I love u' he whispered.

'i love u 2' i sed. We stood der 4 a gud 3minz huggin up 2geva ass naked. I den lay dwn on d sofa n spread ma legs.

Ricardo took his fingas n strted strokin d inside of ma clit I strted moanin. Beggin him 2 fuck me hard n fast. After a while of teasin me n mkin me soakin wet ricardo put his lng hard dick in n strted fuckin me hard n fast. Jerkin ma body up n dwn. After a few minz of bein bnged out i cme. I felt exhausted n ova satisfied.

Ricardo sat @ d end of d sofa as i lay der tired. He rubbed ma thigh.

'U kno ur 18th iz cummin up init' he sed outa d blu.

'Ye' i sed.

'Wot do u wnt init' he asked lookin @ me.

'Errrr ... a car' i joked.

'sknizzle' he sed.

Afta dt he didnt say enyfing. Mayb he didnt gt d joke i thought. O well i thought. I lay der finkin abat wot had happened @ college wit malachi. Dt woz ova scary. I didnt wnna go in d nxt day wotsoeva. He myt beat me or tell every1 abat d kiss. I rly fucked up boi.

Later dt evenin @ around 9 ma fne rang.

'Hello?' i awnsered 2 d withheld caller.

'Keisha im so so so so so sorry abat 2day plz 4giv me. Buh i love u so much n i cnt b seein u wit no nxt brehs coz iz ment 2 b me n u nt u n sum nxt boi. Plz can it jus b me n u lyk iz ment 2 b plz by gurl if u b ma wifey den i promise 2 treat u rite. 100 tymz betta dan dt nxt boi, woz his nme, ricardo. Plz keisha ill giv u d world plz i love u 2 much 2 let u go n i wnt stop until i get u. U hav 2 undastnd ma actionz 2day man buh wen i kissed u fort dt ment it woz me n u init buh den wen u jus boied it i woz lyk, boii. I woz shocked. I woz propa lookin 4wrd 2 goin college 2day 2 cum c ma wifey i wnted u 2 cum afta college wit me 2 move ur fingz outa dt hse n in2 mine'

Shock. das all i felt. I quickly hung up ma fone. Wot d fuck woz rong wit dis guy? No iz No n u dnt gwan lyk dis. I mean cum ON! As soon as i hung up ma fne rang agen. I jus switched it off. I defin8ly wernt goin college d nxt day 2 c dt nutta!

Fuckin fruit cake!

13

'Babez wake up' sed ricardo shakin me 'Iz 8:45 ur gna b 18'

'I aint goin in' i groaned.

'y not?' he asked lookin puzzled.

'coz im gna spend d day wit shanice' i sed lookin @ him.

'okay. sknizzle' sed ricardo. I gt up outa d bed n rushed 2 d toilet 2 pee n brush ma teef. Wen i left d bathroom ricardo woz standin outside d door. I smiled @ him n wlked bck 2 d bedroom. Wen he had finished in d bathroom he cme bck 2 d bedroom. I woz stndin up in frnt of d wardrobe wen he cme in, he pulled me from bhind on 2 his lap n he sat on his leather swerve chair.

'So ur goin out ye. n leavin me here on ma jz' he whispered in ma ears wit his deep sexc voice.

'yup' i sed.

He bit ma neck n sucked oon it. i wz laughin n squrmin.

'gellof u animal' i shouted. Wen he stopped he held me round ma waist n lifted me up hi in d air. I screamed.

'Put me dowwwwwwwwwwwn' i screamed @ him. He put me n slapped ma bum hard. I quickly took ma towel, fne n clothes n left d room. Wen i gt 2 d bathroom i locked d door n sat on d toilet seat. I switched on ma fne. Der woz 30 missed calls, 26 voicemailz an 12 txts. I jus switched ma fne bck off. I gt undressed n climbed in2 d showa. While i scrubbed ma skin i burst in2 tears. I had fucked up so badly dis tym. Dis guy woz nt on leavin me alone 4 a lng lng tym. After a gd 10 minz of stndin unda d showa jus finkin, ricardo knocked on d door.

'Oi gyal, u kno dat london iz runnin outa water init'

'Im cumin' i sed smilin. I climbed out n gt dressed. I fned shanice on d hse fne.

'Im cummin 2 pick u up 2 go shoppin rite' I sed.

'okay den. I need sum fingz 4 wen i go in2 hospital newaiz' she replied.

'Ok ill b der in lyk half an hour yeye' i sed n hung up.

'BABES IM GNE YE' i shouted 2 ricardo.

'Oi excuse me wait a sec' he sed bck. His voice woz so deep dt he didnt even need 2 shout. He cme dwn d stairs wit money in 1 hand.

'Whers ma hug?' he sed. I gav him a hug.

'N ma kiss?' i gave him a long kiss on his thick sexc lips.

'N ma sex?'

'It aint gna work dis tym round negro'
I laughed.

'Na im jkin buh heres sum money, couple
hundred, i dnt even kno. Buh giv half 2
shanice ye n half 4 urself yeye' he sed.
He kissed ma forehead n i turned 2 go.

I gt 2 shanices house 20 minz l8a. I
knocked n she opened d door. I stepped
in n gve er d money.

'Here 150 boof 4rm ricardo ye' I sed.

'Awww. He alwayz lookin afta us init'
she sed grinnin up er teef.

'yup' i sed smilin. He woz always lookin
afta me. I duno wot i wud do witout him.
I loved him soooo much n i felt sooo
shame n so DUMB everytym i fort of d tym
dt i kissed anuva breh. Kmt. Bt i had 2
4gt abat it. It woz all in d past now.
Tym 2 gt on wit lyf n jus look 4wrd 2
d futre. Well ... das if d past didnt
cum bck n haunt me!

We set off 4 shoppin. West end woz d
PLACE. It woz kinda quiet as every1 woz
@ work, skool, or college. Da shopz wer
burstin wit all kina unique clothes n
un-bait fashion.

'Do u dare me 2 get a tatoo?' i sed 2
shanice as we passed a tatooin parlour.

'Ye ... double dare' she sed grini teef.

'Ite den'

Wen we stepped in der woz sum freaky ppl der boi. I went 2 d counter n asked hw much it woz 2 gt a tatoo.

'£25' sed d punk lookin women @ d counter.

'Ok kool can i gt 1 dun 2day?' i asked.

'Ye sure. Folow me' she sed gttin up. I folowed er in2 sum lil bck room wher a man sat wit a tray nxt 2 him wit needles n all kindz a containerz n shit.

'Sit der n tell me wot u wnt init' he sed. His voice a low rumble. He looked lyk 1 of those Hells Angels kinda pplz.

'Can i hav a red heart n the name ricardo around d top of it'

'Ye wot size heart' he asked tkin out a book.

I picked out a heart dt woz biggish n asked 4 d tatoo 2 b on d frnt of ma waist so wen i wore hippsters u cud c d tat. Da tatoo took a gd hour 2 do. Shanice sat nxt 2 me hldin ma hand thru out d whole fing.

'I hpe ur gnna b holdin up ma hand lyk dt wen dis bbys rdy 2 pass thru' she laughed.

'Ye defin8ly' i sed wincin in pain. Wen d man had finished he put a big peice of coton wool on it n taped it dwn wit speshul tape. I gt up paid d woman n left. It stung abit bt it woz alrite. As we walked bck 2 d bus stop 2 jump on n tke a gd lng bus ride bck 2 d bitz, caught a glimpse of a guy dt looked soo much lyk malachi. Jus as i sw d person, a tall man wlked past d malachi look a like, den he woz gne. I quickly gt on d bus n tried 2 gt d thought outa ma mind.

Imagine if he wz folowin me, i thought 2 maself.

Wen i gt hme ricardo woz in d livin room on d fone thankin sum1. I stood der lookin @ him.

'Fank u soo much. Fank u. U wnt regret it.' den he hung up.

'Wot woz all dt abat?' I asked.

'Arrrr dt woz sum BMW car show room. I gt a job der b. Gnna b bussin out suits everyday, test drivin d hottest cars.' e smiled.

'Das gr8 bby. Y didnt u tell me u applied 4 dt job?' i asked givin him a big hug.

'I wnted it 2 b a suprise init. So ... SUPRISE!!!' he sed throwin his armz up mkin himself look [redacted].

I strted laughin 'Ur so silly'

'Ye but u still luv me' he sed.

'Ye i do' i sed givin him anuva hug.

He strted kissin ma neck n bitin it. He strted rubbin ma inner thigh n took hld of d waist band of ma trousers.

'SHIT D TATOO' i thought.

I moved his handz away bt it woz 2 l8, he had felt su of d tape.

'Woz dat?' he sed lookin dwn. He pushed me dwn so i woz layin on d sofa n pulled ma trousers dwn a lil bit. He sw d coton wool n tape.

'Wot happened 2 u' he asked lookin baffed.

'Nuffin' i sed pullin ma trousers bck up.

He pulled dem bck dwn n ripped of d tape n sw d tatoo. He stared @ it 4 a few secondz.

'U kno i ova love u keisha init' he sed quietly lookin in2 ma eyes.

Ye. I knew ...

14

It woz monday mornin. I woke up bright n early 2 tke ma showa find summink 2 wear n do ma hair. Wen i left ricardo woz stil fast asleep. I had on ma blck n white adidas respect me tracksuit n blck n white krep n ma blck jus do it bag. I got 2 college early n met kayla n alisha in d common room.

'KEISHAAAA!' dey both shouted in unison.

'wher hav u bin man???' kay asked wen i gt closa.

'At hme ennit. I wenrt bovad 2 cum college so i jus stayed hme wit ma hubby' i sed smilin.

'mmmmm' smiled lisha.

We all buss out laughin.

'So hw iz shanice?' asked kay.

'shes kool. I woz wit er on friday we went up west. I gt a tatoooooooooo. U wnna c?' i sed.

'Ye man leme c' sed kay.

I gt up n shwed dem.

'AWWWWWWWWWWWWWWWWWWWWWW!!!' dey bothed cooed in unison.

I smiled n coverd up ma hip n sat bck dwn.

'U kno malachi aint doin 2 good' alisha sed lookin serious.

'U gt him WHIPPED' kay sed tryna lighten up d situation.

'No u gt him CRAZY in love wit u. Literally' alisha sed wit er eyebrows raised.

'Cum bruv leme chat 2 u' he sed firmly n quietly.

Karl took malachi away 2 d ova side of d room n woz tlkin 2 him. He lookd ova @ me a few tymz bt his face woz expressionless. 5 mins 18a Mrs Barkley entered, shouted @ us 2 shut up n took d register den hurried out, all flustered n stressed asusual. Wen mrs barkley left malachi gt up n strted 2 wlk 2wardz me, agen ma hart strted beatin fast out of fear an agen karl grabbed his shoulder, whispered sumfin n malachi turned around n left d common room. Karl cme ova 2 me.

'Keisha we need 2 tlk' he sed lookin @ me.

'Karl wot did he say? wotz rong wiv him? i mean-' i sed all breathless.

'Keisha look ye hes in love wit u n love can mke u do sum dumb fingz truss me i kno. But he sw u on friday, dwn westend. Hes pure confused keisha n ur jus fuckin his head up by doin d fingz ur doin. Ur ma gurl 4 life, ur lyk a sista 2 me. I wud shank dt prick in his eye if he eva tried 2 hurt u bt iz u aswel. Ur sendin out d rong signalz. I kno abat d kiss bt d fing iz u hav a hubby der @ hme, ur engaged. U need 2 set malachi str8, if u had dun dt 4rm d begining u wudnt b in dis shit right now.' Karl sed.

'I kno karl, bt i lyked him im nt gnna lie, bt i fort it woz jus abit of fun. I didnt kno it wud cum 2 dis. I mean ricardo loves me bt he dnt go on all crazy lyk dis.' i sed, tearz formin in ma eyez.

'If u gt up n left ricardo 2moro u wud c anuva malachi allova. U betta go 2 ur lesson Keish.' karl sed givin me a big bear hug. He woz such a gd person, he woz beta dan ma real flesh brotherz.

'Alrite karl. I luv u karl ur lyk a big bro 2 me' i sed.

'I love u 2 keisha gurl u kno dat ur ma likkle sis bt u need 2 listen 2 advice. But ill speak 2 u l8a on yeye' he sed turnin 2 leve, he held da door 4 me n we walkd in opposite directions.

Afta ma mornin lessons it woz lunch. I went 2 da common room 2 gt ma hoody outa ma locker n met up wit kay n lisha. We went out 2 lunch jus lyk normal. Wen i gt bck 2 college n signed in malachi woz standin der lookin outta da big windw at da entrance watchin me as i cme in. I avoided his eyes n walked past him n pretended i didnt c him. I signed in chatterin away bt stil anxious 'whers karl man??' i woz askin maself. I walked bck 2 ma afternoon lessons. I onli had 1 den i cud go hme wher as every1 else had 2 lessons b4 dey cud leve. Wen ma class finished i went 2 da main entrance n signed out. As i turned 2 leave da premesis malachi stood der. Our eyes locked. 'Oh shit oh shit' woz all dat woz goin thru ma head. I woz scared 2 def n didnt kno wot 2 do. I quickly walked past him bt he grabbed ma arm.

'Keisha wot kinda SHIT u tryna pull?' he spat. He looked crazy. I woz terrified. ma mouff woz paraliysed.

'N-n-n-nuffin.' i ova stuttered.

'so y aint u cum 2 mines 2 cum wuk man?' he sed gettin up in ma face. Dat scared me even mor. I didnt kno wot da fuck 2 doooo.

'Plz d-d-d-dnt hurt meee' i pleaded tears swellin up in ma eyes.

'No baby i aint gnna hurt u. Neva. I love u rememba. But if u try pul ne dumb shit i mite hav 2 discpline u ... if u kno wot im on abat' he sed.

'Plz let go of me' i mumbled, stil scared.

'So u can go hme 2 dat prick hu put dat peice of stink ring on ur finga? Galang, but imma gt u. Kno dat' he sed lettin go of me.

I walked away as quick as i cud. Jumped on da first bus dat cme n went hme 2 ricardo. No1 woz hme doe so i jus put on da TV, kiked bck n relaxed. It had bin a lng shitty day i thought.

2 hours l8a ricardo cme hme wit food n a suit on. I gt up wen i herd him cum in. I smiled grinin up all ma teef wen i sw him.

'Wot u smilin @? me or da food?' he asked smilin bck.

'U' i laughed goin ova 2 him 2 gt ma kiss. We stood der lipsin, wit his free hand placed happily on ma bum.

'We gtta disscuss wha gwan 4 ur 18th u kno b' he sed as we sat dwn 2 eat.

'Ok' i sed.

'So do u wnt a shubz or wot?'

'Ye i wnt a house shubz. Dat wud b live, alie?'

'Ye soooo u wnt a hse shubz ye. Rite. So das DJ, food, drink ... das it rly. I fort u wnted sumink big lyk 1 inna a fat hall or a limo an resturant' ricardo sed.

'Na, a hse shubz iz gd' i sed.
'Ite il gt da invitationz printd 2moro.'

WEDNESDAY

I stood der wit kayla n alisha handin out invites.

'Shud i invite malachi?' i asked dem.

'NO dat crazy ass fool.' kayla shot bck.

'But hes gnna find out abat it newai den he myt gt even mor vex coz u didnt invite him' alisha sed.

'Ye das tru' kayla sed finkin.

'Ok so ill invite him den. He mite not even show up' i sed tryna convince maself bt i knew full well he wud mos probly b da 1st der.

Malachi wlked in 2 da common room 18. I gve an ivitation 2 kayla n she went n gve it 2 him. I watched as he opened it n afta readin it he smiled, lookd ova @ me n nodded. I smiled bck politly n lookd away avoidin ne eye contct.

He woz stil strin @ me, i cud c outa da corna ov ma eye.

Wot woz he finkin?

Onli god knos.

15

It woz da day of ma 18th bday shubz n i woz ova excited. Da party woz set 2 start at 8:30 and it woz 6 alredy. All day i had been restin n beein pampered by my sexc hubby.

'U lookin 4wrd 2 2nite?' ricardo asked 4rm his desk wher he sat lookin at me lyin on da bed.

'Ye' i smiled, lookin at him.

'Gt tym 4 a quickie?' he asked wit a mischevious smile on his face.

'Noo der aint no tym 4 no quickie u horney child' i sed laughin n gettin off da bed headin 2 da bathroom 2 get in da bath.

'U kno u wnt alla disssss' he sed imitatin jay 4rm 'my wife n kids'. I buss out laughin at his stoooopidness.

'Ur so silly' i sed turnin 2 leave.

'Dnt hate. appreciate' he sed in a womans voice. I shook ma head, he alwayz knew hw 2 mke me crak up! Das anuva fing i loved abat him. I made ma way 2 da bathroom n slipped in2 da relaxin bath ricardo had ran 4 me, on top of directin n instructin da party planners dwn stairz whilst i rested n relaxed lyk sum kinda queen. I smiled 2 maself. Ricardo rly did mke me feel lyk a queen n i knew his love wud b evalastin no matter wot happened. Dat thought n knowin woz a comfrt which caused ma smile 2 widen. An hour n a half later i woz slippin in2 da small black dress i had picked out 4rm a store up west. It hugged ma body, bringin out ma curvez, big pert titties n apple ass. I slipped ma well pedicured feet in2 sum blck 'killa' heels. I looked in da mirror n lyked-no-loved wot i sw. Ma hair woz out n curly an abit wet so i jus put sum moisturizer in it n put it up inna clip. I neva wore no makeup except 4 lip gloss but i made da effort by putin on sum eyeline n mascara. Picture perfect.

'Ohhhh shit! Ma wifeys tryna gt pregnant 2day!' ricardo sed as he walked thru da bedroom door.

'Shullup. No babies yet' i sed playfully.

'U sure u dnt wnt 2 hav a quickie?' he sed stndin bhind me n holdin ma small waist n pressin himself up on ma bum.

'No definatly not. Ur gnna mess up ma hair n everything' i sed, turnin around n smoothin out da shirt he woz wearin wit sum dark blue jeanz n black timberland bootz. Ma man looked n smelled GOOD.

'U kno u look beautiful' he sed lookin in2 ma eyes. He kissed ma lips.

'Thank u baby. Ur lookin very nice urself' i sed smilin broadly.

'Gurrrrrrl, u kno i look betta dan u' ricardo sed soundin lyk 1 of dem american chickz. I laughed agen.

'Ur crazy' i sed.

'In love. Ye, i kno' he sed. Ma smile faded along wit his cos it woz serious.

'I love u 2 ricardo. U kno dat' i sed strokin his face.

'But not as much as i love u keisha, neva as much as i love u' he sed. Jus den da doorbell rang.

'Guests r here' he sed jus above a whisper. He kissed ma forehead n went dwn 2 let da group of ppl in. I stared at da door he had jus left out of.

Ma fone strted ringin, i snapped outta ma trance lyk state an awnsred.

'Hello?'

'Hey, kiesha? Its me karl'

'Oh u kool'

'Yeye, jus doin me, look buba im gnna be abit late. Ill b der by 9:30'

'Ok das kool'

'Ite ill c u den. Bless'

'Safe bro'

I herd da loud bass of musik n da faint rumble of vioces. Ricardo cme bck up.

'Ready?' he asked smilin.

'Ye' i sed smilin bk as i went over 2 him n took his extended hand. We walked dwn da stairs n in2 da busy-ish livin room.

'AWWWWWWWWWW' cooed alicia an kay as dey cme rushin ova 2 me. I giggled at dem. We all hugged. As i hugged kay, over her shoulder i sw malachi starin at me. His face woz expressionless bt soft. Wen i finished wit ma gurls he approached me.

'Excuse me miss' he sed tappin me on da shoulder. I turned around n smiled a frendly smile.

'Oh, hi. Fanx 4 cummin.' i sed givin him a short n frendly hug, tryin 2 go on as natural as possible.

'U look ... beautiful' he sed steppin bck n lookin me up n dwn.

'Thanx' i smiled turnin 2 walk off. Malachi tightened his grip on ma arm. I turned 2 look @ him an his face looked serious. I woz automatically scared. Wen he sensed ma fear he let go of ma arm n slowly walked off.

For da rest of da night i tried 2 ignore it. But i cud feel his stares. I danced an laughed an smiled, but deep dwn i woz afraid n knew dat sumfing wud spoil everythin. By 9 everybody woz at ricardos. Dancin, eatin, laughin, talkin, jus havin FUN! Ricardo tapped me on ma shoulder n sed 2 follow him. I followed him through da crwd 2 wher d dj woz set up, da dj cut off da music n gve ricardo da mic.

'WHA GWAN EVERYBODY?!?!?! Welcom 2 keishas 18th birthday party im glad u all cme. I jus wna say', he turned 2 me 'happy birthday bby, n i love u' he took a box out of his bck poket n handed it 2 me, wen i opened it, it woz a key. Wen i took da key outta da small box der woz a key ring which had da letters BMW on it. I looked at him n he nodded.

'A-a-a-a car?' i stutered

'Ye bby' he sed. I gasped n threw ma arms around him huggin him, hangin on 2 him 4 dear life. I kissed his face n da crwd jus 'oooohed' n 'awwwwwed'.

'If everybody cud jus mke der way out 2 da front' he announced. Once i gt out da frnt door ma eyes hit da dream car. It woz silver an da roof woz dwn; it woz sooo peng. Jus gleemin der. I hugged n kissed ricardo once agen. He laughed n beemed wit happiness. We all mde our way bk inside 2 enjoy da party.

I stood in da middle of a circle wher a few of ma close frendz surrounded me, dancin n laughin. Den malachi made his way 2 da middle of da circle n handed me a card n a small box. I looked up at him n he smiled, wot looked lyk a genuine smile.

'Can i hav a dance?' he asked.

'Ummm ... y-ye' i sed, relieved dat he looked lyk he had kinda gtton ova da fact dat me n him cud neva b an item. I slipped out of da circle n malachi led me 2 a corner wher der woz a table. He took his gifts 4rm ma handz n placed dem on da table n slipped bhind me n strted winin n grindin up against me.

I laughed n sed 'haha vry funny, i kno u dnt fink ur gnna be grindin up on me lyk DAT!'

His face dropped n a serious and sinister look consumed his face.

'Ill do wot i wnt 2 u' he sed in a low yet audible voice. Da feelin of fear n betrayle set in n i woz frozen in sheer shock. Before i knew it a set of handz wer closin around ma nek n anuva set of handz wer draggin me twards da floor den ma whole world went black ...

16

I woke up n all i cud c woz black. I cud here da faint rumble of voices deep in da darkness. I let out a faint whimper.

'Help!' I wept into da darkness hopin sum1 wud cum n help me. I ran ma handz ova ma body. Ma dress woz still on but it woz torn, exposin ma stomach abit. Ma nose woz runnin n ma hair woz inna curly mess! Ma jaw n head woz poundin an it felt lyk i woz either experiencin a bad hangova or a killa beatdwn. I cud feel warm liquid oozin outta ma leg. Blood. I let out anuva soft whimper. 'Help!'

Suddenly der woz a click and der woz light. I woz in wot looked lyk a warehouse or a derelict factory. I looked around tryin 2 gather ma surroundingz. Der wer big tall windows dat wer covered in dust. No light cud pass thru da windows. Da room woz enormous. The floor woz dusty and dirty. As i looked around i spotted a figure stndin in da huge doorway.

Malachi.

I let out a gasp n tryed 2 scramble up 2 get away 4rm him. He strted 2 walk toward me but i woz 22 weak 2 even get up quickly enuff. Wen he got 2 me he knelt dwn.

'Awww poor bby. Here. Have sum water' he smiled. He took out a bottle of water an un-capped it n gave it 2 me. I drank, greatful 4 da water an not carin wether it rly woz even water.

'P-p-plllzz, d-dnt h-h-hhhurt me-eee.' I heavily stuttered.

'Shhh' he sed strokin ma hair and smilin. 'U hav bin an evil bitch doe'

'P-p-pllzzz, i-i'm sorry. But plz dnt hurt meee!' i whimpered frantically.

'Dnt worry. I'l take care of u. Den we'll go bck 2 ricardos, get ur stuff n start a new life' he smiled. He spoke 2 me lyk i woz a 4yr old child. He took da water 4rm me. Even doe i woz tired n feelin weak i knew da look in his eyes woz not da look of sum1 sane. He woz not mentally well. Atall. He had a scary, sinister kinda look in his eyes dat gave u da chillz if u stared 4 2 long.

'Plz' woz al i cud whimper.

'Shhh. Shh. Now, take off dat dress n lets c wot ricardos bin gettin n wot ive bin missin out on all dis tym eh' he sed.

'N-nooo'

'What? I sed ... TAKE OFF UR FUCKIN DRESS!!!!' he screamed. I jumped n struggled 2 pull it off as fast as possible. He unstraped ma bra n ripped ma knickers off of ma body. Ma fone skid across da floor. He ignored it den he smiled n reached in2 his boxers n took out his dick.

'N-n-no ... Pleaseee NO!' i pleaded.

SLAP! I felt dizzy ...

'Shut ur fuckin mouth' he spat. And he raped me. Over and over.

Meanwhile ...

'Wher da FUCK iz keisha?' ricardo screamed. Ova nite he had gone almost mad tryin 2 find keisha. He woz all ova da place lookin 4 her askin every n any1 buh no1 knew anything. It woz sunday mornin n dwn stairz woz a mess 4rm da party last nite but ricardo had no desire 2 clear it up. He woz sittin on da sofa in da middle of all da mess askin himself a million questions. Wher da fuck iz she? Why wud she leave? Why didnt she take ne clothes or atleast da car? He called her fone over n over which was the only thing which belonged 2 her dat woz missin. It jus kept continuously goin 2 voicemail. Ricardo woz past angry an frustrated ... he woz heartbroken. Wher woz she? Ricardo didnt believe she had gne booz she wanted 2. He provided 2 much love n support at home.

'DING DONG' da doorbell went.

Ricardo raced 2 da door hopin keisha woz on da ova side. Wen he opened it a hench blick ugly man woz standin on da ova side.

'WHAT?' he screamed.

'U ricardo?' he asked in a deep bari-tone.

'hu wants 2 kno?' he asked screwin.

'Im here 2 pick up keishas tings. Shes gone away wit malachi n wont b comin bck' he informed.

'W-What?' ricardo asked absolutly shocked yet confused.

'Look man ive jus bin sent n payed 2 pick up keishas tingz u get me. I aint allowed 2 say nufin abat her wheraboutz coz she doesnt want u 2 kno but wot i do kno iz dat shes makin a new life wit malachi' he sed.

'No ... No ... NOOOO ... dis cannot be. She cudnt of left me man. Ur chatin shit.' ricardo shook his head. He couldnt believe wot he woz hearin. Keisha left him? NO! It cudnt b.

'Can i take da stuff n b on ma way plz?' da man asked wit an attitude.

'No ... r u dumb?' ricardo sed n slammed da door in his face. He stomped bck 2 the sofa frantically ringin keishas fone even more confused and agitated as b4. After 20 mins of continuously callin keisha 2 no avail, he decided 2 fone karl.

'Yo ricardo'

'Kool, yo keishas disappeared'

'Wha u mean??'

Ricardo explained all of what he knew.

'Im on ma way ric' 10 minz later karl was at the door.

'Karl man what we gnna doo?? I cant leave da house jus incase she cums bck. But i need 2 go on da rd n find her.'

'Ite look, call shanice tell er 2 cum over wit her man and me n u will go n find keisha'

Within 20 mins shanice was there ... belly and all.

'What da rass u lot callin me ova here like say u got any food?!?!?!' shanice asked goin thru da cupboards.

'We can't tell u man jus shut up n order pizza or sumfing' ricardo awnsered annoyed. Shan culd get on his nervesss at times.

'Who ya tell fi shut up?' shanice asked.

Ricardo jus kissed his teef. 'Yo im out ye safe'

'WHATEVER I EAT IS ON YOU BITCH!!' shanice shouted as ricardo made his way 2 da door wit karl.

'Whateva u piq' ricardo mumbled bck.

'I HEARD DAT!'

Ricardo n karl jumped in2 karls car and drove around.

'Where shud we go 1st?' ricardo asked.

'Dat prick, malachis yard' karl awnsered n zoomed off.

Elsewhere ...

I was awakened by sumfing cold bein poured ova ma head. Water.

'Get up' malachi snarled.

'Can i go home plz???' i begged.

'Ye. Of course. Home with me' malachi sed sweetly.

I started cryin.

'Were goin now. You can get all cleaned up and make urself at home.' he dragged me up. When i got on to my feet i tried my best to keep up with him. When we got outside the cold air whipped around my body and made goosebumpz erupt all over me. Outside a car waited. Malachi opened a backdoor n threw me in. He got into the passenger seat and, 30 secs later a guy came joggin towards the car, got in and drove away. All i could do was sob there in the bck seat.

'Why u cryn baby? Are u that happy?' malachi asked ova his shoulder. I swr i culd of ripped his head off his shoulders at dat point. I didnt even hate him, i had passed that, i just pitied him and hoped he culd gt help and leave me tha fuck alone after this ordeal.

'No' i sed quietly 'im jus tiredd'

25 minz later we got to a block of flats. There were a couple of cars scatered here n dere but 1 in particular stood out. it was black wit rims, neon lights and a jamaica flag on da numba plate. I knew that car all too well.

That was karls car ...

KEISHA REVISITED

1

'Turn that racket down!' Mum screamed. She was only saying that because there was nuff swearing in this tune. Sometimes she annoyed me to death, because when she was drinking, smoking and acting an eediat, no one else's opinion counted. I turned Vybz Kartel's 'Picture This' down and got back to chatting to Ramel on MSN.

'Yeh so wot u on?' Ramel alerted me. Ramel was one peng boy that I had been chatting to for time. I met him on 321teenchat and he actually had a webcam so I knew I weren't chatting to no buttaz guy.

'Arrrr nuttin much ya na . . . kinda bored ya na . . . need sum entatainment in my lil borin lyf!' I typed out my reply, smiling to myself, knowing he would reply with something funny or something dutty. I pressed enter.

'Arr skn skn, I need a likkle excitement inna my lyf, inna my bedroom, inna my bed!' he replied bare quick.

I bussed out laughing. 'LOOOL, joka, naa gyal lyk me ain't loose u knw,' I wrote back.

'Iz jus a likkle fun init, no1 needs 2 kno.'

'Mmm.'

'Mmmmm . . . so das a no den.'

'Scroll up da convo . . . did i type da word NO?'

'Mmmmm . . . man lyk da way u tink.'

'LOL! N e wayz ima b off now I mite chat 2 u 18r yeh.'

'So . . . Can man fone u 18r 2 c if I'm gna get n e excitement ina mi bed 2day?'

'Yeh, u can fone 18r . . . Bless x.'

'Yeh, bless xxx.'

That boy is too too peng, I swooned to myself spinning round in my desk chair. He was born in Jamaica and came to England when he was eleven. He didn't have an accent no more but he could drop into patois when he was ready and it sounded too sick. Everything about him was over sexy. He had long black hair. His skin colour was like chocolate, he had some peng hazel eyes and I swear they had a green circle around the iris, and the sexiest and softest lips like the rapper LL Cool J. And not to forget his body. He showed me his pecs on webcam and I swear down, I wanted to drop on the floor. And to top it off the boy could spit! He sent me his mixtape that had 322 plays on MySpace and counting. Did I mention he's from Jamaica and just over sexy?

I moved from my computer and plonked down on my bed, momentarily grinning at my flirty conversation with Ramel before wondering to myself why the fuck I came off MSN? Like I had anything better to do, but I didn't bother to go back online because then I'd just look like an eediat!

My phone started ringing next to me. The screen flashed 'Private caller' and I debated whether I should answer it or not. Maybe it was the sexy ting Ramel. I took the risk and answered and was instantly disappointed when I heard that stupid fool Michael on the line.

'Wha gwarn, Keisha?' he said. I wanted to just kiss my teeth bare loud. How could he be phoning me after everything that had happened? Michael was my ex that broke my heart properly. Not like cheating or two-timing. All boys did that shit, alie? Nah, Michael did something I never expected anyone to do.

'Hello,' I said sharply sitting bolt upright.

'Yeah, wha gwarn, so wot u can't return ma txts?'

'I told u alredy, dnt fone ma fone or txt ma fone agen you stupid eediat. Ur a eediat dat tinks dey can gt piece outa evry gyal in Hackney,' I spat, gun fingers poised.

'Hu u chattin 2 lyk dat?'

'Hu iz on ma line?' I retorted, rolling my neck.

'Listen likkle gyal—'

'NO, u listen u prick! If you fone ma line agen I'm gonna make sure u neva c ya likkle limp dick agen, u stupid dickhed!'

I dropped the line. I was proper vex now and really needed some 'excitement' to help my mood. It was the first week of summer and I wasn't starting it like this. I'd prepared for this holiday *properly*. We had three and a half months off and I'd saved my wages from my Saturday and Sunday morning shifts at the Caribbean Bakery on Kingsland High Street since finishing my GCSE's the summer before. I'd decided to quit in time for the holidays, plus, I was tired of arguing about the size, shape, smell and freshness of the Harddough bread. I wanted a job in central at a clothes shop next so I could get discounted garmz. I'd start thinking about that after summer though.

I lay back down on my bed and my phone rang again. This time Shanice's name flashed up.

'Yeah, wha gwarn gyal, I jus gt a cal 4rm dat eediat u know,' I exclaimed, ready to launch into the story.

'Wot did dat wasteman want?' Shanice spat, kissing her teeth in disgust.

'I don't kno, but I neva gave 'im a chance 2 tlk rubbish inna me ears, ya MAD?'

'Ahh, ya dred gyal! Gimme nuff joke, so wot u doin 2day den?'

'Duno boi, dat sexc boi Ramel iz invitin me 2 his yard to lash init, but I duno if I'm gna reach it or not.'

'Go, man! 4rm wot I've seen dat bwoi iz 22 buff!'

'I knooooooo! Oh my dayz! Wot u on 2day doe?'

'Nuttin rly, u kno. U wanna jam an den I'll follow u 2 Ramel's yrd?'

'Yeah, ite den. Arrrr I jus gt 1 gully idea! Ramel sed he'll fone me, wen he dus I'll ask him 2 bring his bredrin 4 u.'

'Wot bredrin?'

'Sean, hes nufffff peng aswel!'

'Wot dus he look lyk?'

'Lite skin, peng green eyes, canerow, nuff tall.'

'Yesssssssssss – wait, how do u know?' Shanice asked, bare suspicious.

'JOKA! I saw him on webcam 1 time wiv Ramel.'

'Swear down! Okay, n e wayz, cum 2 ma yrd in lyk half an hour?'

'Yeah yeah, kool.'

'Bless.'

I jumped up and looked in the mirror to check myself out. I wasn't going to see that peng ting looking like this! I still had on my houseclothes: an old bleached-out velour tracksuit. It was a sunny day so I opened my wardrobe, and took out my short white rah-rah skirt and a pink vest top. I got my brand-new Converse out of the box. They were all white and folded at the ankle to show pink swirls on the inside. I completed my outfit with a pink Nike wristband, and my white rosary beads around my neck. I looked in the mirror and thought to myself, 'Oh rasss.' I sprayed half a bottle of pink Charlie body spray all over myself, and then I ran downstairs and told Mum I was going to Shanice's yard and that I would be back around eleven. It was three o'clock in the afternoon and, if my timing was right, I was catching Mum at the best time.

As I approached the kitchen doorway, I heard the clink of the whisky bottle against her glass – I had caught her pouring what was probably her first drink. Perfect! She wouldn't care what I had to say.

'Mum, I'm goin 2 Shanice's. I'll be back 2nite or something. I'll text you,' I said confidently.

'Yeah alrite, c u 2moro,' she said, not bothering to look up as she carefully poured some Freeway Coke into the generous helping of Whisky in her glass.

'Byeeee.'

I skipped out of the house and walked briskly down the road, feeling bare relieved to have caught Mum when she was feeling good because in a couple hours it'd be a different story. I turned onto the busy high road and walked past the shop where Mum always got her drink. One of the eediats that stood outside everyday with tins in their hand, chatting shit, called out 'Hello pretty girl!' to me. I just kissed my teeth. I passed the Dixy, smelling the crunchy oily chips through the open doors. There was always a group of boys from endz sitting on the wall jamming when it was hot, and today the sun was blazing in the sky. I knew I looked and smelled nice, and that one of them would try to churps me. I walked by, trying not to smile, as they began to make a cacophony of noise at me: 'scuse me darlin', 'chung ting', 'big batty gyal' I made out amidst their juvenile laughter and the horns blaring and music playing from passing cars. All of a sudden, one of them jumped off the wall and marched straight up to me. He was buff and he knew it.

'So can I gt ya numba, darlin?' he said, taking out his phone. I knew all too well what to do. I took it from him boldly, and began pressing the silver buttons. I smiled, typing my number into the Nokia 6230 he handed me as he took a sip of his Supermalt and licked his lips.

'Arr I'll fone u 2moro or l8r init,' he said, looking me up and down before turning back to his boys, who started a new, affirmative cacophony of noises as he returned to the group, with my number in tow.

I bopped off, smiling, continuing the walk to Shanice's yard. It was typical summertime in Hackney. Cars were blazing bashment and UKG, boys were bussing wheelies with ice poles hanging out their mouths, and girls were rocking their bright matching outfits for summer. I reached Shanice's yard, and knocked on her door. It wasn't long till the door opened and I was greeted by her big brother, Ricardo. He was bare tall, kinda hench and a CHUNG ting. Forget Ramel and Supermalt boy for a minute. *Every* girl was on Ricardo, and *no one* could chat to him in the ends. Ricardo was on a next level.

'Rarrrr . . . sure ur lookin 4 Shanice an not me!' he said, looking me up and down.

Ricardo was always running jokes and flirting with me like this. I'd never forget how on the day of me and Shanice's Year 11 prom, when he saw me with my hair and make-up done, he said, 'Mind I don't wifey you, Keisha,' and I swear down I smiled for a whole month!

I laughed, and just moved him out of the way gently with my hand and walked towards the stairs. As usual, he took the palm of his hand and gave me a sharp slap on my bum as soon as my back was turned. 'Oi man!' I said, laughing, and jogged up the stairs. I didn't give him a serious reaction like he was any breh; it was *Ricardo.* Not only was Ricardo like the chungest boy in Hackney, he actually had my back. Anytime I felt down and I came over to vent to Shanice, he was there to listen too, and he always reminded me: any time I had trouble with a dickhead boy on road I should call him!

I followed the rumble of bashment music playing from Shanice's room. The sound hit me as I swung open her door and starting whining to 'Goodas Mi Back Mi Back' in her doorway. Shanice cackled as I pushed up my lip like a true yardie, ready to give a serious whine. Me and Shanice always knew the latest bashment since we'd made friends with one yardie man in Ridley Road Market who got CDs straight from his 'link' in Kingston. I was actually messing about until I sensed someone behind me. I knew it was Ricardo, so I made sure to start bruk-king out *properly*, imagining him getting close to me, dropping his chin onto my neck, resting his hands on my hips and grinding on my batty. He needed to see how I could gwan!

'Gwan, bad gyal,' Ricardo said, obviously watching me hard. I started grinning bare teeth and then Shanice started to turn the volume down. I pulled down my skirt that had been riding up with all the movement, and looked over my shoulder flirtatiously at Ricardo. His eyes were glued to my batty and I started bussing up laughing as I walked over to Shanice to finally hug her.

'Close da door, man!' Shanice called to her brother. Ricardo kissed his teeth at her but obeyed her command.

'U kool, gurl?' Shanice said, reaching to hug me from her chair.

'Yeah gurl, im gud. Ur bro iz on me hard doe, did u c him!' I said, hugging her back, laughing.

'I kno, dnt take no notice,' Shanice replied.

I laughed again.

'Ay, stay here one sec,' Shanice said, pausing the music and getting up from her desk. 'I'm gna go dwnstairs 2 get sumfin, yeah?.'

'Okie doke,' I said, sitting on the edge of her bed.

I heard her loud footsteps running down the stairs. Suddenly her bedroom door opened, and Ricardo stood in the door frame. I took one look at him, rolling my eyes but grinning teeth.

'Soo, wha gwarn, sexy?' he said casually as he joined me on the bed. Ricardo was a flirt, we'd played this game before: Shanice was gonna go downstairs to either bill it or get a drink, and Ricardo would come and find me to flirt. But this time he wasn't playing, because he started to stroke my thigh.

'Wot, you tryna show me how you can move in MY room?'

'Mayb 2moro init,' I replied, playfully rolling my eyes and grinning uncontrollably.

'Mmmmmm,' he groaned.

The space between our faces began closing. I could smell his Versace Blue Jeans and the Juicy Fruit in his mouth.

'Did I tell u hw sexc u b—'

I interrupted Ricardo's words with my lips. I just had to! He was too sexy, and ever since he opened the door, he had been seducing me so slowly, I couldn't handle it! We sat there lipsing and I had to stop myself from smiling and knocking my teeth against his mouth, but I, Keisha, was finally lipsing Ricardo! His lips were so soft and he was holding my face, which I'd only seen them do on TV. Maybe this was how boys who were over eighteen lipsed, I thought to myself.

Then he pulled away, looking me in my eye and positioning himself on his back. He lay there, propping himself up on his elbows and staring at me, as if to say 'come here den'. I didn't give myself time to think! I confidently swung my leg over his stretched-out buff body. My bumper was in the air, and my lips were on his, kissing him gently, pulsing my tongue in and out of his mouth. I was feeling it. All of a sudden, I remembered where I was. Shanice was downstairs; we were on her bed. Instantly, I stopped.

'Wot abat Shanice?' I hissed.

'Wot abat her, baby? Wen me an u r gettin it on she ain't gna b der.' Ricardo continued to reach for my body.

'Na babe, let's go 2 ur room or sumfin, b4 she finds us lyk dis,' I said, climbing off and pulling down my skirt.

'Come to my room. Go tell 'er I've got u 4 a bit.'

I nodded obediently as Ricardo rose and stood in front me, reaching behind me and stealing a feel of my batty.

'Wait a little bit,' I said, playfully pushing his hands away. He was biting down on his bottom lip, looking down at me like he wanted me so bad. He took a final deep breath like he was accepting defeat, and I turned to leave the room.

I ran down the stairs to find Shanice at the dining table in front of the garden door, billing a zoot.

'Oi, Shan, I'm gna b wit ur bro in his room 4 a bit, yeah?'

'Urmm, why?' she said, frowning, as she concentrated on rolling the zoot as tight as possible.

'Nuffin man, jam. He asked me. 5minz,' I said, trying not to smile like some ediat.

'Ur sum dutty freak u kno. N e wayz, dat boiz bin on u 4rm dai . . . jus b careful doe,' she said as she licked the rizla.

'Safe, gyal!' I said, relieved she wasn't trying to chat shit about how Ricardo should leave her bredrins alone.

I ran back up the stairs and hesitantly pushed open the door to Ricardo's bedroom. I had never been in there before. It was such a boy's room. The walls were blue, he had a double bed with blue sheets, and some dark blue curtains. They were completely drawn, and the sun shining brightly that day, gave the whole room a cool blue glow. In the corner of his room stood his wardrobe. He had a small desk with a computer on it. I spied a stash of condoms poking out the desk drawer. At the foot of his bed he had a television connected to a PlayStation 2, with a stack of CDs and DVDs on either side. Ricardo watched me take his room in as he sat patiently on the bed.

'Finished?' he said, smiling cheekily.

He stood up and came over to me. Ricardo was so tall that he towered over me, and had to tilt his head forward to look into my eyes. Looking at him, I didn't know why it hadn't got to this earlier. This was bare easy; all I had to do was wear a tight skirt and dance in front of him.

He leaned in and laid his lips on mine and we just stood there lipsing for *ages*. I just wanted to feel him hold my face and smell his after-shave forever. Our bodies were pressed so close, I could feel his dick start to harden.

He took my hand in his and walked me over to his bed. He laid back again, his legs hanging over the edge, and I took my cue to climb on top of him. This time, I pulled my vest top and bra over my head in one swoop, and felt his hands move up my torso towards my breasts.

He leaned forward to lick them and caress them with his lips. I started rocking back and forth, grinding against his crotch as the tingles from my nipples moved down to my clit. After a while, I moved his hands away from me and got off of him, keeping eye contact, indicating I wanted him on top. I inched my body up the bed as he got up, making room for him to mount me, and pulled my skirt up over my hips. He ran his hands over my legs and crotch, and I felt myself getting hotter and wetter.

Ricardo positioned himself on top of me, propping himself up on his knees and one arm, skilfully playing with my nipple between the fingers of his free hand and planting kisses along my neck. Usually I was scared of boys trying to give me a love bite as all hell would break loose when I got home to my mum, but I wasn't moving my neck away from Ricardo's lips for anything! By that point, I could've sworn there was a puddle underneath me because I had never felt like this before.

Ricardo had his rock-hard crotch expertly resting against me, which I couldn't help but grind against as my groin developed its own pulse. He was squeezing and pulling at my nipple, which was standing to attention and sending light tingles surging through my body, and he was kissing my neck so passionately, I caught myself whimpering like a dog.

Suddenly, I started pulling at his tracksuit bottoms, I wanted him so badly! He pushed my hand away to move back towards the foot of the bed. He stood at the edge and dipped his hand into his pocket, pulling out a body bag which heightened my anticipation even more. He took out his big, veiny dick. As he tore open the packet and carefully shook out the slimy condom, I wondered if Ricardo's dick was the biggest I'd ever seen in person.

I snapped out of my thoughts and hurriedly pulled off my skirt and very wet knickers, carefully hanging off the edge of the bed and placing them on the floor, hoping he wouldn't spot the massive wet patches on my pants. Ricardo's hands reached for my thighs, travelling further up the inside of my legs. His soft touch and rhythmic fingerwork instantly intensified what I was already feeling. I responded by lifting my head to kiss him, biting his bottom lip. At that, he slid a second finger inside of me. It felt so good that I let out a long, quiet moan.

Ricardo responded by sliding his fingers in and out, each time going deeper and deeper. This breh was a pro, and I was going to be so disappointed that I couldn't report back to Shanice with the details of this! He slid a third finger in, and I started to moan his name. I felt weak, and the tingles were getting intense. My legs started to shake uncontrollably as I squeezed Ricardo to keep me stable while I came. I knew it pleased him, because he slid his fingers out and continued to kiss me deeply. I noticed that he didn't squeamishly wipe my juices off on me, but steadily went back to rhythmically pulling and squeezing my nipples between his fingers, apparently not grossed out by how I'd soaked his hand.

I was lost in the way he was making me feel, but it was my turn to impress. I pushed him away from me and slid off the bed, perching on my knees on the floor in the gangway between his bed and the wall. He knew exactly what I was suggesting and sat himself at the edge of the bed in front of me. I slid my hand over the length of his dick and began playfully licking the shaft. He closed his eyes, savouring the pleasure. After a few moments, I gripped the base of his warm dick and took him in my mouth. I confidently worked my hands and mouth rhythmically up and down the length of him, which drove him wild, making him moan my name. His hand met the back of my head and he began to set the speed, letting me take more of him in my mouth, faster and faster, until he came. When I finished, I pushed myself up from the floor and sat next to him as he removed the condom and cleaned himself up. I sat there expectantly, unsure of what to do. I watched him scoop up his boxers from the floor and step into them.

He looked at me. 'U need to giv man 10minz or suttin,' he said, laughing.

I giggled, taking that as my cue to put my clothes back on. I reached over and discreetly pulled my damp knickers on, along with my skirt, bra and top. Ricardo was switching on his PlayStation as I pulled my top over my head and turned to look in his mirror and pat down any parts of my slicks and side bun that may have moved out of place. As I smoothed my perfectly in-place hair, my mind raced, contemplating what I should do next. 'Should I watch him play his game? Should I just say bye? Maybe he wants me to wait till he's ready to go again?'

'So, I'll c u agen, yeah?' he said from behind me, instantly soothing my panic.

I turned to look at him sitting on the bed, looking me up and down. I smiled and rolled my eyes, masking my relief, 'Umm, yeah.'

'Ite. Dnt leave Shanice waitin 4 u, b4 she starts chattin shit,' he said.

I turned around and walked out of his room, closing the door gently behind me. I wanted to jump up and down. I just had Ricardo all over me *and* he wanted to see me again! I practically skipped back to Shanice's room with a smile on my face. She was sitting at her PC with her MSN going off as usual, and slow jams playing in the background.

'So, lil miz freak, r we gna go 2 dis Ramel boiz hse or wot? I wanna see this Sean guy, u know I'm tryna get over Kareem.'

Kareem was Shanice's on-again-off-again hubby, but this time she'd given him back all the Me to You teddies, cards, and the promise ring he got her for her sixteenth. We were sure this was for real.

I laughed. 'Yeah, dnt worry, were gna reach dat! Jus wait 4 him 2 ring me.'

'R u sure u can handle all dat in 1 day?' Shanice said with her eyebrows raised.

'I am lil miz freak, aren't I?' I said, staring straight back at her with a dutty grin on my face.

2

Me and Shanice left her house at seven o'clock. Ramel had phoned at six to check I was still coming. I asked him if he could bring Sean along for my friend and, as fate would have it, Sean was already at Ramel's yard! So I suggested we go on webcam quickly so Sean and Shanice could see each other, which turned out to be bare jokes! So we jumped off webcam, I slicked my hair again and Shan got ready. She put on her all-black Converse, black rah-rah skirt and a black vest top, with the thick gold chaps chain and bracelet that Ricardo got her for Christmas.

We left the house and hurried to the bus stop. The sun was still shining and the high road was busy with cars and buses and people. Me and Shanice waited at the bus stop for any bus to Stokey so we could get a 349 to Ramel's ends. He lived in Enfield, and it was going to be quite a journey from Hackney.

'So, u gnna cum spend da nite at minez?' Shanice asked.

'Gud idea ya na,' I replied. I took my phone out of my pocket to text Mum like I'd said I would: 'Im gna sleep ova at Shanice's house'. I made a point to never call or pick up any of Mum's calls while I was out trying to have fun, in case she weren't in a good mood and started shouting at me over the phone. Long!

An hour later, we got off the bus after what felt like forty-five stops, and walked towards Ramel's road. It was quiet except for cars and buses driving along. No one was cotching at the corner shop, no music blaring from cars . . . not even the eediats with their tins!

'He sed it woz on Croyland Road,' I said, looking around.

'Derz Croyland Road rite der,' Shanice said, pointing to a street sign.

'This road is bare dark,' I said, looking down the silent street.

'Come, man, lets quickly go,' Shanice said, scooping my arm with hers.

We walked down the long, silent street until we reached number 14. When we got to his door, I knocked quietly, suddenly feeling really shy.

'I shoulda smoked before we left, u kno,' I whispered to Shanice as we waited.

Seconds later, the door opened and Ramel stood there with a big smile, eager to greet us. He was shorter than I thought he would be, but he was wearing a vest that showed off his arms and pecs. He looked me up and down, smiling like he liked what he saw.

'Cum in,' he said, standing back.

Shanice walked in first, making her way through the passageway to her new 'friend', Sean. I followed her, slipping past Ramel who grabbed my bum. I turned back and gave him one of my dutty grins, and walked into the house a little further. Ramel closed the door behind him quickly, coming up behind me and placing his hands firmly on my bum as we all stood in the corridor. I kept my eyes on Shanice, waiting to see if she'd make eye contact with me to signal for me to stay with her. That was our thing when we went to link brehs. But she seemed to be okay with this Sean breh, because she didn't make any eye contact with me. He wasn't her usual type, but he was definitely very buff: he was so tall and slim, like some basketballer, and had long hair which he wore in two cainrows. He was holding Shanice's hand and looking into her eyes, asking her bare questions.

'Wot, iz dat ur real hair den, beautiful?' I heard him asking before Ramel started whispering to me.

'Ur body's lookin rite in dis skirt ur wearin u knw. Ur turnin me on,' he said in my ear. I giggled.

'Am I?' I teased.

'I'm abat 2 show u hw much ur turnin man on,' he warned.

'Ay, cum we play sum music,' Sean suggested, pushing the living room door open and inviting Shanice to step inside.

Sean and Shanice took a seat on the dingy cream leather sofa in the smoky room. Ramel led me over to one of two worn fabric armchairs. He sat down and pulled me onto his lap.

I giggled. 'Why you laughing?' he asked me, leaning in to kiss me before I could answer. I could taste that he'd been smoking.

Either Sean or Shanice had begun playing slow jams from their Walkman phone, and when I came up from my lip-lock with Ramel, Sean was busy billing it while Shanice was laid back on the sofa, chilling, waiting patiently to be offered a toke.

'Cum we go upstairs,' urged Ramel, whispering in my ear.

'In a minute,' I giggled, unsure if I wanted to. He couldn't kiss like Ricardo, and he smelled a bit sweaty.

Ramel was squeezing and grabbing my thighs when Sean asked, 'What, do u lot smoke, yeah?' addressing me and Shanice.

'Don't ask dem dumb questions, blud!' Ramel reprimanded before we could respond. I shot a look at Shanice, confused by Ramel's slight outburst, but she didn't catch my attempt at eye contact before Ramel proceeded to usher me up onto my feet.

'Cum, let's go upstairs. Jus me an u,' he said, getting up from the old seat, grabbing my hand and leading the way towards the door.

'Imma be upstairs, yeah?' he said to Sean.

'Yeah, cuz,' Sean replied. 'So we're gonna have down here yeah, sexc,' he said, turning to Shanice.

'Yeah, definitely.' She smiled, licking her lips.

I left Shanice downstairs in the living room and Ramel led me upstairs to the floor with his bedroom.

'Ur breathin bare hevy,' he told me over his shoulder as we climbed the second flight.

'Wat? No I'm not,' I said, confused.

'I'm jokin man, jam,' he said, laughing.

At the top of the staircase, we got to his room. He opened the door for me and I walked in, holding my breath just in case he heard me breathing for real! He closed the door gently and spun round, pulling me to him by my arm and lipsin me more aggressively than he had downstairs. He took hold of the hem of my vest top and began trying to lift it over my shoulders. His quick and hostile advances took me by surprise, making my reactions slow, and my arms remained by my sides instead of compliantly rising above my head for him to lift my top off. He very quickly stopped trying, instead pulling off his own vest.

He proceeded to pull me by my waist towards his unmade bed, and guided me to sit down next to him. I whipped off my vest top and bra, and untied my shoes before lying back and waiting. Ramel hovered over me, propping himself up on his knees, slobbering all over my chest and my breasts. I couldn't help but notice the smell of his saliva as it dried on my skin. He worked his tongue down my body and used his free hand to pull my skirt over my bumper and off, and parted my legs. Moving the thong I'd changed into at Shanice's aside, he shocked me when he began to glide his tongue over my clit. It took a moment for me to register how good it felt because I was so taken aback. No one had ever done this to me before, and according to every boy everywhere: man didn't do dem tings! But Ramel was flicking his tongue back and forth so gently. Juices started flowing out of me and meeting his mouth, and I was soon trembling and moaning quietly as he continued to pleasure me confidently.

When his head popped up between my legs, the sides of his mouth were gleaming with my moisture, and I secretly prayed he wouldn't try to kiss me again. He kissed my inner thigh, then he moved to hover on top of me. Propped up on one arm, he used the other hand to pull my thong off and began rubbing my clit impatiently. I closed my eyes, trying to adjust to the contrasting aggression he was now showing and relax into it, when he suddenly pushed his middle, index and ring fingers into me. He immediately tried to start pumping them in and out, but my body stiffened and my legs closed a little. He pushed them back open and tried to continue pumping his fingers deeper and deeper. Through the floor, I could just about make out Shanice moaning downstairs, which distracted me from the discomfort of what was happening up here. Ramel abruptly took his fingers out, grabbing my legs and pulling me towards him. This was nothing like how it had gone with Ricardo, I thought to myself.

Ramel pulled his dick out of his tracksuit bottoms and spat on his hand, rubbing the stringy saliva across the head, and pushed it into me. Worry started to creep in to my mind – he hadn't put on a condom, but I didn't feel able to say anything. He began pumping hard and fast, and I clenched my jaw to stop myself from screaming in discomfort. He lifted one of my legs onto his shoulder and continued to pound me, crying 'Ahh shit' into my ear. It didn't feel the same as with Ricardo because Ramel didn't go slow or touch my legs or hold my face when we kissed, or even look at me. I took hold of Ramel's face and, although I didn't want to kiss him again, I tried to bring his face in to peck him on the lips and establish some eye contact, but he grabbed my hand and threw it away from his face. He took my leg off of his shoulder and got off the bed.

'Cum 'ere,' he commanded irritably. I obeyed, moving to the edge of the bed. He yanked down his bottoms and aggressively pulled one of my legs over the other trying to twist me on to my stomach, insisting, 'Get on all fours.' He steadied himself, gripping my waist with one hand and guiding himself into me with the other. I closed my eyes as he pumped in and out, placing his now-free hand on my boob, and tried to imagine Ricardo. I pretended that Ramel's lazy kneading of my breast was Ricardo's rhythmic fingerwork, and the unmade dingy floral sheets beneath me were Ricardo's crisp blue ones. Before I knew it, I was pushing back on Ramel's dick, feeling myself turned on by the slap of my skin against his. I began to stroke my hand against the nipple that wasn't getting any love, and after a few moments I was crying out, 'Ricardo!'

Ramel stopped right there behind me. My eyes flew open. He'd definitely heard me because he hadn't climaxed.

'R u fuckin dumb or sumfin?' he spat, as I sat up, reaching for my clothes and avoiding eye contact. This was too embarrassing!

'My name ain't Ricardo, iz RAMEL. Gt it rite, u slag!' he said, kissing his teeth. He pulled up his boxers and sat down on a chair across from his bed. I continued pulling on my clothes and shoes. I could sense his eyes on me but I dared not look over at him. He chuckled and mumbled stuff to himself under his breath that I was sure was about me, but I just ignored him, trying to get the fuck out of there. I finished lacing up my right Converse and jumped up to head for the door when he suddenly called from behind me, 'Oi, ur 4gtin sumfin,' throwing a 50p coin at me and falling about laughing. I saw red. I weren't no prostitute! My feet glued in position in front of the door, I looked to my right and my eyes caught his nunchucks. I grabbed them up and took a series of blind, lucky swings from a distance, not knowing where the heavy wooden handles struck him. I ran out of the room and down the stairs, nunchucks in hand.

'SHANICE, SHANICE, PUT YA CLOTHES ON NOWWWW!' I screamed as I descended the stairs, dragging the chain across the railings. By the time I got to the top of the last flight, Shanice was stood at the foot of the steps looking worried. 'Come! I sparked dat bowcat with the nunchucks!' I shouted, grabbing her hand and running towards the front door.

I could hear Sean behind us calling up the stairs, 'Ramel, cuz?' as he pulled on his trousers. I yanked open the front door, hearing Ramel tumbling down the stairs way behind. We ran down the quiet road, the sound of our panting, our Converse tapping against the pavement, and the jingle-jangle of the nunchuck chain heavy in my ears, and Ramel's shouts far in the distance.

When I began to see the high road in the distance, I chucked my weapon into someone's front garden and slowed down slightly, confident that Ramel and Sean couldn't catch us now.

We jogged over to the bus stand where several buses were lined up, and climbed onto the first one in line, taking the stairs two at a time and lying down on the top-deck seats until the bus started moving away. Only then did we even dare to sit up.

'O my dayzzzzz. Keisha, wot did u do?' Shanice shouted at me.

'Nah Shan, he try boi it! Guess wat he sed 2 me?' I flew up from the seat and stood in the gangway on the empty top deck, clapping the back of my right hand in the palm of my left to punctuate the story.

'OMDZ wot?' Shanice lunged forward in her seat.

'He called me a slag, Shan,' I said, getting hot.

'Naaaa . . .' she tilted her head up, drawing out the word in her disbelief.

'Yeah, so I sparked him in his dumb head with the nunchucks!' I shouted, and we buss out laughing.

The journey was long! We changed buses in Haringey twice, and after over an hour and three different buses we arrived back in Hackney.

'U ite doe?' Shanice asked when we finally stepped off the bus in ends.

'Yeah, I'm bless,' I said and smiled mildly.

We walked up the high road and turned onto Shanice's road. There were a group of boys whistling at us and Shanice stopped to chat to the one that pulled her arm.

'Excuse me, miss, cn I chat 2 u 4 a sec,' he said confidently. I continued walking and waited for her to finish; I couldn't be bothered to chat to no one.

'He sed y u movin stoosh, Keish,' Shanice said when she finished with the boy and came back over to me.

'I'm ova tired, man,' I said.

'Ar skn.'

We walked the rest of the way back in silence. As we arrived at Shanice's front door, I remembered I should really check on Mum. She hadn't texted back and I expected she was just very drunk, but I wanted to check in anyway.

'I'm comin, yeah, I'm jus gonna ring ma mumzy. She didn't text me back.'

'Ite, cum in wen ur ready,' Shanice said, opening the door with her key and placing it on the latch for me.

I walked a little distance from the house. Even though Shanice was my best friend and knew almost everything there was to know about me and my mum, I still got embarrassed. I couldn't predict what mood my mum might be in – or, worse yet, what situation she might have gotten herself in, so to stay on the safe side, I walked to the corner to make the phone call. As the phone rang and I waited for Mum to pick up, I noticed several police cars pass.

'Keisha,' Mum slurred on the other end of the phone.

'H-hello, Mum? You alrite?' I asked, slightly distracted.

'What d'yu mean, am I alrite? Who you talkin to like that? I'm not your friend dem,' she berated me, slurring heavily. I was too distracted by what I was seeing ahead to react to Mum's rubbish. The silent convoy of police cars had stopped right outside of Shanice's. The officers in their riot gear were making their way over to the house with a battering ram, and the fucking door was on the latch!

'Mum, Mum! I'll call you back,' I hissed as they piled into Shanice's front porch.

I called Ricardo. He picked up on the second ring as the police started knocking.

'Jakes are comin to raid you. Throw it out the back window. I'm outside!' I squealed urgently. In the background I could hear the faint pitter-patter of footsteps and Ricardo rustling around in his room.

I ran round to the back, my heart beating so hard and fast I could hear it. Just as I reached the back and looked up, something came flying out of the window, landing in the gutter. I ran over and bundled the black plastic bag up into my arms and made my way through the dark back roads to my house.

I let myself in with my key.

'Mum?' I called. I hoped she was asleep.

I heard the rumble of a man's voice from the living room and rolled my eyes. Mum had company, and that always meant foolishness. I really could've done with being at Shanice's right now. Since their grandparents died when Shanice and I were in school, Ricardo and Shanice had lived alone, and their house had become a bit of a safe haven to escape my block and my mum's madness. I checked my phone, willing either her or Ricardo to have called me, but the coast might not have been clear just yet so I had to sit tight.

'Keisha. Go shop for ur mudda, I beg yuh please,' I heard Mum slurring. She was seriously drunk, and I hated it when she was like this.

I opened the living room door to say good evening and then disappear to my bedroom.

'Hello, good evening,' I said dryly, before my eyes could even adjust to the state of my mum and the living room. Mum was slumped on the floor and her company was sat on the sofa bolt upright, looking bug-eyed. The room was slightly smoky and Mum's whisky bottle was on the coffee table. I stepped into the room when a funny smell that almost smelled similar to the nail shop hit my nostrils. I stopped in my tracks.

'Mum? Mum? What's going on?' I shouted.

'Why you shouting?' she blubbered, just about audibly and unable to open her eyes.

At that moment, my phone started buzzing in my bra. I pulled it out and 'Ricardo' flashed on the screen. I ran upstairs to my room.

'Keisha! You alrite?!' he panted into the phone.

'Y-yeah, I'm bless. I've got it,' I said, closing my door behind me.

'Wait, r u alrite?' he asked, detecting something was up.

'I'm bless, I'm bless,' I tried to reassure him.

'Oi, you saved man, Keisha blud. U don't understand! Fuck! D'yu know how lucky I feel, blud. Nah, ur a rider u know,' he babbled on the other end of the phone. As Ricardo went on and on insisting on how much he owed and appreciated me, I just wanted to beg him to let me come back.

Beneath me, I could hear a little commotion in the living room, and prayed Ricardo would get off the phone in case it started kicking off. I tried to listen to both Ricardo and the situation downstairs, but I must have been failing miserably because the next thing I heard over the phone was: 'Keisha? Keisha? Keisha? You there?!'

'S-sorry Ricardo,' I stammered.

'Ay, wots dat in da background? Where you?' he asked. I wanted to die. I didn't think he could hear.

'I'm at home. It's nuttin. My mum's jus bein dumb,' I said, as tears unexpectedly began to spill out of my eyes.

'Keisha? Y u cryin?' Ricardo questioned, sounding concerned.

'I'm cool. I've got ur tings init, so bell me 2 bring it.' I tried to get off the phone before my sobbing got unmistakeable, failing miserably.

'I'm booking you a cab now. Pack ur overnight bag. It will b der in 5 minz,' he said sternly.

Five minutes later, I was climbing into a minicab with my overnight bag on my shoulder.

Ricardo was waiting at the front door. He leaned in and paid 'boss', opening the back door to help me out. He grabbed my bag and put an arm round me, bringing me into the house. The house was a state after the police had rifled through every crevice looking for what Ricardo had thrown out the window.

'Let me get you a drink,' he mumbled, heading into the kitchen and re-emerging seconds later with a tall glass of juice. 'Cum' he said, leading the way upstairs to his room. I followed behind him, noticing how my bag balanced on his broad shoulders and how he held my drink carefully in his other hand. I felt relieved and taken care of. I felt safe.

I sat down on his bed and Ricardo stood in front of me, handing me the juice. He stared down at me.

'What was happening at home? Is your mumzy alrite?' he asked, his brow furrowed with concern.

'I dnt even know, Ricardo. I think the breh dat was drinkin wiv ma mum was smokin white or suttin. He was buggin and the room smelled all funny,' I replied, exasperated.

'Wot? Wot was ur mum doin?' he asked, still concerned.

'She was jus on da floor lyk . . .' I said, at a loss for words.

'Rah, boy . . .' Ricardo sighed.

We sat in silence as I sipped my juice.

'Keisha, u saved man 2nite. I swear down. I could've bin ridin a big boi bird from 2nite,' Ricardo said very seriously.

'Iz minor, man.' I shrugged. I just wanted to sleep.

'Na, I can't thank u enuf, Keisha. Wen I rang u an u sounded all sad, I was bare paro dat sumfin happened 2 u coz u helped man,' he persisted.

'Oh, nah nah. Iz minor, trust me,' I tried to reassure him. 'Fank u 4 gettin me away from mine. I needed it,' I added.

'Anyfin 4 u, Keisha. Swear down, after wot u did 4 man 2nite, I got u.' He reached over, took my free hand in his and gazed into my eyes. I couldn't help but smile. He was so buff, but also I'd never felt so appreciated by a breh before.

A moment of silence passed.

'I'm gonna go sneak into Shan's and go bed. Iz bare late,' I said awkwardly, draining the rest of the juice into my mouth so I could avoid his eyes on me.

I stood up, keeping my eyes on the glass in my hand. I felt so shy, my heart was pounding. Even though we'd done what we'd done earlier that day, I felt more nervous in this moment, fully clothed.

'Stay wiv me. I want u 2,' Ricardo said quietly. I looked at him, almost doubting what I'd just heard, but his eyes – fixed on me – confirmed in themselves that Ricardo wanted me to stay.

He reached for the glass and put it down on his desk, then turned to open his wardrobe, retrieving a t-shirt and handing it to me before he whipped off his tracksuit and got into bed to wait for me. I stood at the end of his bed, awkwardly peeling off my clothes and processing what was happening: I was getting in bed with Ricardo. I hesitated as the hem of his t-shirt hit my thigh and I was ready, undeniably ready, for bed.

'Cum b,' he encouraged me.

I climbed on the bed nervously and laid on my back next to him, staring at the ceiling as butterflies flapped around in my stomach. I couldn't believe I was in bed with Ricardo.

'Wot u finkin abat?' he asked after a long silence.

'Bare fings,' I mumbled. I heard him turn his head on his pillow to look at me, so I turned on my side to face him. I couldn't believe this. Way back when I was like thirteen and he was fifteen, he'd had a bit of a crush on me. Ricardo would always put his arm round me when he saw me about, or tell me I looked buff or make jokes about beating up boys that liked me. Now I was seventeen and he was nineteen, and in one day things had gone from childish crush to serious.

This was real.

I leaned in and kissed him on his soft lips. He kissed me back and we laid there kissing each other till the early morning.

3

I awoke at 10 a.m., with Ricardo sound asleep next to me, his mouth hanging open catching flies, which made me smile. I thought about the events of yesterday. It was the first week of summer and I'd already sparked someone with their own nunchucks, and saved and won Ricardo. I needed to jam! I got myself up and out of bed finally, and to the shower. Shanice's house wasn't my house but it was my home away from home, from school days when my mum would get too drunk and tell me to get out or when I just needed to get away. I changed into one of Ricardo's Ecko t-shirts and went to see Shanice. She was lying in her bed wide awake looking at a *Young Voices* magazine.

'Hey gyal,' I said, closing the door behind me.

'U cool?' Shanice replied, her voice still a bit husky.

'So . . . wotz on da agenda 2day?' I asked.

'Dunno boi. Cum we go shoppin!'

'Yeeeeah!' I said.

Shanice jumped out of her bed and went to the shower. When she came back, we got dressed together. Shanice let me borrow her tight blue jeans, which I wore with my short white Nike t-shirt and my Converse. Shanice put on her blue velour tracksuit with the diamanté crown on the back pocket and her new white Air Force 1s. I went to say bye to Ricardo, but he was still asleep. I wrote him a quick note, 'Wha gwarn babez, naa i aint jus left u hangin lyk dat im goin shopin wit shanice, dnt wrry ill pik sumfin sexc jus 4 u nuff luv xW!FEYx' and left it on his desk.

Shanice and I decided to hit up Wood Green.

We walked through to the busy high road and up to the bus stop to catch the 243 bus, which would take us the longer, scenic route. We rode the bus through Tottenham, peering out the top deck window at the bustling Bruce Grove, anticipating what Tottenham heads we might spot at the McD's or the bus stop across the road. The sun beamed through the grease-tainted windows where we rested our heads to face one another on the back seats, and yesterday's worries felt far away.

We bopped off the bus at Tops, where it instantly felt like everyone was out in Wood Green either doing shopping or going to the cinema. The high street was buzzing; there was standstill traffic on the main road, and every other shop was blazing music from speakers as we made our way practically one Piccadilly line stop on foot.

'Let's go JD Sports first, den da tracksuit shops,' Shanice said.

'Ite den.'

As soon as we walked into JD Sports we spotted a group of boys swooning over crep. We made sure to bump past them to get to the women's trainers, and, like clockwork, we heard the whispering and then the chants: 'Chung tings, chung tings.' As I was following behind Shanice, my arm was grabbed by a particularly assertive one, insisting, 'Ay, let man chat to you,' to which I beamed: 'Sorry, I've got a man!'

We made our way over to the Air Force 1s so Shan could get her all-black ones, then we continued our journey on foot towards Turnpike Lane to the tracksuit shops to try on the Lot 29 and Akademiks tracksuits on display.

'Wots new here, boss?' Shanice exclaimed, strutting into the shop.

'Everything, darlin. Look, pink Akademiks for you,' said Bossman, amused. Shanice loved bussing jokes with shopkeepers, and often it meant a little discount or something free.

We'd bundled a mountain of the latest garms into the changing rooms to try on when Ricardo phoned me.

'Hello?'

'Wha gwarn sexc, u stil out?' his morning voice rumbled through the phone.

'Yeah babe.'

'So u cumin bck 2 mine 2nite?'

'If u want me 2,' I flirted back.

'Obviously man want u 2. Ay, make sure u pik up sumfin 4 me 2 enjoy doe.'

I laughed. 'Yeah, dnt wrry.'

'Ite sexc, c u l8r yeah?'

'Ite den, bye.'

I cut the call, grinning. 'We hav 2 go 2 a nxt shop. I need 2 buy a sexc bra n thong,' I called over to Shanice in the changing cubicle next to me.

'Errr man!' Shanice laughed. 'I know you helped my bruva n dat but low it!'

After trying on almost every tracksuit in the shop leaving with nothing but a free lighter and the flirty well wishes of a South Asian uncle, we headed to Bardo where I picked up one sexyyyyyyyyyyyy thong and bra set. It was pink and lacy, and I couldn't wait to see Ricardo's face when I put it on!

'Let's get food, man!' Shanice groaned as we left Bardo.

'Yeah man, I'm starvin!'

McD's was heaving with families and young people cotching, food long digested. We shouted our orders at the cashier over the din of trays clattering, kids screaming and Walkman phones providing unsolicited entertainment. We grabbed our identical 'McChicken Sandwich meal, Sprite, and BBQ sauce, please?' orders and hopped on the 67 bus back to Hackney. We shovelled down our meals at the back of the bus, chatting over the echo of Shanice's phone playing grime against the dusty bus window.

We hopped off the bus and I took the opportunity to suggest, 'Cum we go minez 4 a bit so I can pak sum garmz.'

'Yeah, cool cool.'

We bopped towards mine. 'I hope Mumzys tipsy so she dnt start chattin shit u knw. But ur wiv me so she mite b bless, alie?' I said as we approached my road, apprehension creeping in.

'Yeah, I got ur bck doe, gyal,' she reassured knowingly.

'Safe, gyal,' I said, glad that Shanice understood the situation with my mum.

When I was in primary school, Mum had started drinking every day. I was too young to understand but I was aware of how her moods shifted, how I went from having a 'happy' mummy to an 'angry' one. She would come to pick me up from school drunk, or regularly forget to pick up food shopping and I'd have buttered bread with cereal for dinner. When I was allowed to walk home from school by myself, I started going to Shanice's house and letting Ricardo walk me home when it got dark and I could just go to bed.

I could hear music playing from inside. I let myself and Shanice in with my key, and Mum met us in the passageway in a playful mood, drinking a Special Brew. She was in good spirits.

'U lot dnt know tune!' she cooed, dancing around. We laughed with her, then excused ourselves upstairs to my room.

As soon as the door closed, I exhaled, 'Fank God, man! Shes inna good mood, alie!'

I packed my shit quickly mindful of my time sensitive luck, and we shuffled back down the stairs before anything changed. I found Mum still prancing round the living room.

'Mum, wer goin, I'm gna stay at Shanz for anuva night,' I let her know gently, in case she flipped.

'Alrite. Cum, giv mummy a hug,' she slurred. Confusion washed over me and I froze before going to hug her – we never really hugged.

'Okay, bye Mum,' I said and ushered Shanice out the front door.

We got to Shanice's to find boys cotching in the living room. A breh with short plaits stood holding up his bike, looking on while another two sat on the sofa addressing Ricardo. Shanice and I craned our necks in far enough to spot a breh with an afro lounging on the sofa next to his boy, who wore a black New Era cap, sat on the edge of his seat talking in hushed tones to a focused Ricardo, who sat across the room in an armchair. Me and Shanice scurried upstairs, clocking on to what Ricardo was up to: 'business'.

He came to find me in Shanice's room when everyone left.

'Let me chat 2 u 4 a minute?' he said, pushing the door open and looking straight at me.

'Ur soo bate man, u can hav 'er 4 aslng as u lyk, man,' Shanice jumped in.

I got up to leave, making sure I had the shopping bag with the very important lingerie inside, and closed the door behind me. Ricardo greeted me on the landing with a kiss and I followed him to his bedroom. Once inside, I placed the bag on his desk chair as he lay down on his bed, propping himself up on his elbows to see me clearly.

'Did u hav a gud tym?' he asked.

'Yeah. Wot abat u?' I said.

'I jus took sum money off my yungas 2day,' he said, sitting up and taking out a wad of notes from his tracksuit pocket. Peeling off a few notes, he extended his hand to me. I looked at the money and then at him, hesitantly. I was taken aback.

'Wot?' Ricardo said innocently. 'I kno hw 2 treat gyal, u knw!'

Thoughts surged through my head as I accepted the money. He'd just said he knew how to treat gyal, I thought. He didn't say *his gyal* but he basically meant that. Was I Ricardo's gyal? I had written 'wifey' on the note earlier and now he was giving me *money* . . .

'So, show me woz in da bag den,' he said, interrupting my 101 thoughts.

I shook the underwear set out of the plastic bag, holding it up against my body while I looked at him, grinning, waiting for him to say something.

'Mmmm, so ur nt gna put it on 4 me den?' he asked, licking his lips.

'Nope, nt until 2nite,' I teased, putting it back in the bag, climbing atop the bed and straddling him.

'Ur tkin da piss,' he grumbled, kissing his teeth and feigning annoyance.

I giggled, climbing off to lie beside him and stare up at the ceiling.

'So, did u lyk me all dis tym?' I asked.

Ricardo started laughing. 'I fort u wer sexc init. Naughty doe.'

'Wot do u mean by dat?' I asked, laughing.

'Lyk naughty, init. Lyk ur nt shy n dat, I could see u knw hw 2 tek control an dem tings,' he said more seriously. I smiled, feeling shy.

'Do u lyk dat abt me?' I asked him, feeling uncertain.

'Yeah, man lykz dat,' he said.

Before I could ask my next question, Ricardo's phone started ringing.

'Broski!' he exclaimed. I reached for the remote, flicking through to the music channels and zoning out of the chat about Hackney beef. As video after video played onscreen, my mind floated elsewhere. I had proper proven myself to Ricardo, saving him from riding a big bird for whatever was in that package. And Ricardo had proven himself to me. He knew how to look after me. He wanted to look after me. He was gonna save me from my mum, from Michael, from everything.

From where I lay, I zoned into him. He sat with his back to me, his whole body punctuating his sentences as he explained how he knew Creepa was a pussy'ole and why man had to watch out for Samson. I propped myself up on my knees behind him and started running my hands up his back and along his arms. I started kissing him softly and licking his muscular arms seductively, my eyes on him as he turned to look at me. I took out the hand he often kept in the front of his trousers when he was concentrating on something, and slid mine down. Gliding my hand teasingly over the front of his boxers, I felt him harden.

'Yeah, but broski, hear wot, man gtta go.' He started to stutter as I took my hand out of his trousers. Encouraged by the reaction I was getting, I took my top off. I was sure before 'broski' could respond, Ricardo had hung up the phone to gawp at me.

'Dnt jus look at me. Cum an get me,' I teased, enjoying this.

I lay back topless as Ricardo stood up over me. He slid off my jeans and climbed onto the bed between my now-propped-up legs. This was about to be our proper first time, I wanted to gush out loud. Instead, I met his hungry kisses with enthusiasm, grabbing his hand and placing it on my naked breast. He got to work caressing my skin and sending waves of heat flushing through me. Then he penetrated me. I let out a long moan mid-kiss, which echoed in his open mouth. He pumped steadily, working a precise rhythm. As he savoured the moment and focused on his steady movements, his mouth stopped kissing me and hung open. The intensity made me tremble and cry out his name, just as I had with Ramel.

Ricardo stopped and, as if in sync, I went to straddle him as he moved to lay on his back and lent me a hand as I lowered myself onto him. He let out an almost pained sound as he entered me, which I'd learned long ago signalled something good. I rocked and ground my hips into him, determined to make him explode. Ricardo caressed my legs and bum hungrily with his soft hands, sucking in his breath intermittently. The sound of the bed creaking, along with our movements and SLK's 'Hype Hype', filled the room. Moments later, Ricardo gripped my leg and bit down on his lip. I got off from atop him as his breathing slowed down. His eyes were closed, and some beads of sweat had formed on his forehead.

I sat next to him, expectantly waiting for him to open an eye or something. I never really knew what to say after sex.

'I'm goin in da showa . . . u comin?' he suddenly asked, opening one to look at me.

Before I could contemplate what I was about to do, I was following behind him. I headed straight to the mirror over the sink to ground myself, staring myself in the eye before I stripped off to shower with a breh for the first time. I pretended to finish tightening my side bun as Ricardo pulled the shower curtain over the forceful water and pulled off his boxers. It heated up and he helped me in before stepping in himself. I got under the water and Ricardo just stood there, in the steam, his muscular body catching flecks of hot water. I got down to rubbing soap onto my body, feeling Ricardo's eyes on me. He reached out and slapped my soapy bum and I shot him a rude gyal 'wot u doin?!' look. He laughed before taking a shuffle towards me and reaching for me, kissing me as the water hit our bodies and ran down our backs. With my nakedness pressed against his, he looked down at me lustfully.

'Have you ever fucked in da shower?' He smiled cheekily.

'For me to slip and buss my head!' I exclaimed. He burst out laughing. I'd never showered with anyone. The truth was, this was the closest and most intimate interaction I'd had. I'd never properly slept over at a breh's yard, and I'd certainly never shared a shower with one. I felt comfortable and shy all at the same time. It was Ricardo – who on the one hand, I'd known since we were little, but on the other, it was *Ricardo*, my untouchable, unattainable crush who I'd daydreamed about lipsing before I'd started lipsing boys.

Ricardo shut off the water when we were done, pulling back the shower curtain and handing me my towel.

'Ur forgettin sumfin,' he said randomly.

'Wot am I forgettin?' I retorted, blinking at him. He wrapped his towel round his waist and left the bathroom without another word. I listened out, trying to understand what he'd meant by that as I dried my legs off. I heard some rustling as he made his way back to the bathroom, Bardo bag in tow. He thrust it at me, looking proud of himself, and I laughed out loud.

'Okay, u go 2 da room den,' I instructed. He obeyed without a word, going to his room while I finished drying my body, moisturised my skin with cocoa butter and carefully put on the thong and bra, praying silently that I looked good in it. I carefully studied myself in the mirror, sucking in my stomach. As I inspected my maturing body, I thought back to when I was twelve and thirteen, when I was convinced my developing figure was unacceptably fat and disgusting and I'd hated how I looked. I turned slowly, less repulsed by how the tops of my thighs curved, able to appreciate how the waistband of the thong rested neatly above my hips. I was growing to like my figure, and being told I'd been blessed with a 'big bum' and 'nice thighs' more and more the older I got definitely helped.

I emerged from the steamy bathroom with Ricardo's robe on, ready to prank him. As I shuffled into the room, Ricardo looked over expectantly. Spotting me in his robe from where he stood in front of his desk, his expectant look soon turned into a puzzled one.

'I came on ma redz,' I lied convincingly, holding the heavy robe round me.

I climbed on the bed, trying to keep a straight face.

'Oh, serious?' Disappointment in his tone.

I lay down and he came and lay next to me, closing his eyes as the music channel played in the background. After a minute, trying my hardest not to disturb him, I got up on my knees and undid the dressing gown, letting it fall around me and graze Ricardo. He opened an eye to look at me, and surprise, then delight washed over his once disappointed face.

'Raah, yuh look sexc,' he said in a soft voice, all mesmerised.

'U rly fink so?' I asked sexily, biting my left index finger and looking down at myself.

'Nah, fully man,' he said, taking me in.

'Sho me how sexc u fink I am,' I said, confidently holding eye contact.

He reached for my face and kissed me hungrily. I was falling in love.

4

I was worried. I laid awake thinking to myself, 'We did it bareback and he came three whole times!' I don't know when I fell asleep finally, but as soon as I woke up, I got out of bed, brushed my teeth, put on my clothes and made my way to the chemist to get the morning-after pill. Only pride wouldn't let me sprint to the bus stop on the high road. I marched to the backdoors of the 76 bus and waited impatiently for my stop so I could hurry up and get off. I was going to the chemist in Stoke Newington to avoid anyone I knew, I'd reasoned.

I peered into the window of the chemist, feeling relieved that no one was waiting at the counter and I could feel less ashamed. 'Please may I av da mornin afta pill?' I sheepishly asked the stern-faced black lady at the counter. She was anywhere between forty-five and fifty-five, and didn't look impressed by my request. She must have been disappointed, and assumed I'd done something stupid.

The woman kissed her teeth in response, and went into the back. My sheepishness left instantly – now I was just vex and ready to cuss her, straight! I didn't know who she thought she was. She re-emerged from the back with a clipboard, nostrils flared.

'Fill out dis form,' she instructed me in a thick Jamaican accent, thrusting the clipboard at me and not making any eye contact.

'Yuh av a pen?' I asked, matching her patois.

'No, but we av condoms,' she replied, looking up at me and then turning on her heel and going into the back of the chemist once again. I kissed my teeth loudly and spotted a pen on the counter. I snatched it and sat down in a chair and filled out the short form. As I did so, the bitch reappeared, making herself look busy at the shelves.

'Mi finish,' I called louder than was necessary, standing up and handing her back the clipboard with one hand, my other hand on my hip.

She cut her eye at me, taking back the clipboard and disappearing into the back again. About ten minutes later, she came back out and handed me my pill.

'So, yuh cyant gimme no water?' I asked, like it was compulsory.

The woman kissed her teeth loudly and turned back to potter around at the shelves again.

'U kno wt yeah!' I started, dropping my Ja-fake-an accent. 'Teens dnt cum ere 2 gt a stink attitude 4rm ppl lyk u. Dey cum ere in confidence. I know dat I made a mistake an I don't want 2 ave 2 cum back ere agen 4 makin da same mistake! So I wuld appreciate it if u werent so rude 2 me an treated me wit a little piece of respect!' I said, turning on my heel and walking out of the chemist.

Cars were flying up and down the high road, and the day was only starting to warm up, but I couldn't feel the chill because I was vex! I walked into a small newsagent a few doors down, grabbed a bottle of water out of the fridge and paid for it, then crossed the road to get to the bus stop. As I sat perched awkwardly on the bus shelter bench by myself, I took my pill and hoped for the best. I scrunched up the packaging and leaflet in my hands and threw it into the road. It rolled into the curb, then the bus came and I jumped on board.

I sat down on my J's and gazed out of the window in a daydream. I caught myself wondering what it would be like to have Ricardo's baby and how he would react the day I broke the news that he would be a daddy. I imagined him being over the moon, lifting me up off the ground and spinning me round in glee. I found myself smiling at my daydream like it was real.

As the bus passed through Dalston and I took in the everyday bustle of Kingsland High Street, I spotted two girls, arms linked, strolling out of

Boots. They wore matching grey Nike hoodies, and sported curly slicks that snaked round their foreheads. One of them was clutching a paper bag in her hand and I imagined a pregnancy test knocking around inside as my mind went back to a day that I would never forget.

'POSITIVE?' I said to myself in disbelief. It was July 2004 and my last days of Year 9, and I had been throwing up and feeling dizzy every morning for the past few weeks. A gut feeling was telling me I was pregnant, but that was too scary to contemplate, so I'd tried to ignore it. I couldn't be fourteen and pregnant.

'You need to take a test, Keish,' Abi had whispered through the cubicle door in the girls' toilets.

'I can't be pregnant, Abs,' I'd mumbled.

Two days later, there I was with the white stick in my hands telling me the total opposite. Leading up to taking the test, I'd made deals with God, negotiating in exchange for a 'negative' result, saying I'd abstain from sex for a whole year if God could just make it that I wasn't pregnant. I sat on the loo feeling cursed as the second line undeniably appeared. 'Of course you'd be pregnant,' I told myself, full of anger and regret. I had been fucking around with brehs for the last year.

*

In the beginning, condoms were a must. The rules as soon as I started secondary school were a non-negotiable NO boyfriends, NO sex, NO pregnancy. When I started my period, my mum had handed me pads and said, 'Don't make no boy run up in yuh, coz a big problem goin ketch unu.' I'd made sure to stay safe until I met Michael. Everyone in ends knew Michael was sexcccc. I'd had a crush on him since the very first day I'd sighted him, when I was playing out on my bike at nine years old. From then I always insisted on riding or walking past the cage or Dean's house, where Michael could always be found cotching. Michael was Dean's younger and his runner. Of all the youngers, people rated Michael. No one sent him to the shop or tried to prick him. Michael was sure of himself; he wore shabby garms and he could kick ball.

During the Easter holidays in the same year, I was jamming with some of the girls from my block. We were sitting on a wall playing music from Cleo's Nokia leaf phone, trying to catch Michael's attention by laughing and dancing to the music when he finally came up to us and said 'wha gwan' to everyone. To my surprise, he lingered for a moment, looking at me, and then asked if he could speak to me! I was smiling from ear to ear as I followed him to a block nearby. He yanked open the block door, leading me inside to have this conversation out of earshot. I could hear my friends behind me muttering excitedly, anticipating a rundown of everything he said.

We climbed a few flights of stairs and settled on the fourth floor. He sat down on a step in the middle of the staircase, leaning back on his elbows, legs confidently spread open. I stood on the bottom step in front of him, leaning against the banister with my arms folded across my chest and my eyes cast down at my shoes. My mind raced. There was nowhere to hide – what if he looked at me standing here in front of him and decided I was buttaz? I kept my eyes on my fresh crep, reassuring myself that, at the very least, they were box fresh – and that had to count for something.

'I lyk u, u kno,' he said, cutting into the silence.

'Izit,' I mumbled, nodding my head as an uncontrollable smile crept onto my lips.

'Yeah, it iz,' he replied, getting up.

He stepped towards me and reached for my waist. In no time, we were standing there tongue-wrestling in the pissy block. Imagine that – about seven words ago all I could get from the breh was a nod or 'wha gwan'. On the days that I was venturing to the cinema or to link a breh and I was looking reallllllllllly sexy, I'd get a barrage of 'sexc' and 'chung ting' shouted at me from everyone on the block as I bopped through, including him.

'U wnna cum bck 2 my yard?' he asked, momentarily yielding in our wrestle.

'Yeah,' I replied too eagerly. I knew it was too eager immediately, because I noticed his eyebrows raise slightly, but that doubt soon diminished when he shrugged, saying 'Cum den' and wrapping his arm round my shoulders. I didn't know where Michael lived, I thought, as he gently steered me with the weight of his arm.

We weaved through the tan-brick houses that all looked the same. We crossed the main road and he finally led us into a tower block over-looking the high road. He untangled his arm from around me and took the stairs two by two. I jogged behind him, hyper-focused on not missing a step. On the fifth floor, he opened the door at the end of the landing with his key. I stepped in the house and the powerful smell of weed hit. I waited as he kicked off his shoes in the hallway, noticing the mint-coloured paint on the walls and the soft lino flooring beneath the firm soles of my trainers. I followed him to his bedroom and closed the door behind myself.

He stood in front of the bed in his box room with his arms outstretched, welcoming me into an embrace. I stepped over to him, welcomed by more tongue-kissing. Before long I was lying on my back, naked, waiting for him to finish rifling through his drawers for a condom. I heard him tear open the packet and the muted squelch of the condom being rolled on.

'I hate dis shit,' I heard him mutter, and I wondered what he was talking about.

He mounted me and I welcomed him with spread legs. He silently pushed his manhood into my newly experienced body, his light brown skin going slightly red around his neck as he entered. After he finished, he scrambled off, leaving the room without a word. I lay there in silence. I didn't feel like I'd hoped I would after fucking Michael. I'd expected to feel like I had something to brandish at the girls back on the block. I couldn't think of much to say, aside from that I knew where Michael lived because he'd taken me to his house.

From that day, Michael would often get me to meet him at the cage or at Dean's, and we'd walk over to his house. We didn't talk much, but he always walked me back to my block after and gave me a hug as we parted ways.

'Bless,' he'd say before bopping off.

In the first few weeks, he always used a condom, until one day, when I lay back on his bed and he sat at the edge, maneuvering his fingers between my legs. As he pulled them out of my knickers, I anticipated him moving as he routinely did to take off his trousers and retrieve a condom. I obediently wriggled out of my red velour track-suit bottoms when he hesitated and said, 'I hate wearin 'doms, u know.'

'O-okay,' I stammered. I hadn't agreed to no condoms, but I didn't speak up either. That day we had sex without protection.

'It feels better alie,' he breathed into my ear mid-pump.

He made sure not to come inside me. 'Man don't want no yutes,' he'd mutter to himself as he cleaned himself off after pulling out. But after a while, I guess he got lazy, and I didn't say anything.

And that's why I was sitting here on my bath-room floor with this white stick in my hands, tears streaming down my face and panic rising in my chest.

I didn't wait for Michael to call or text me to link him; I decided to go round and tell him the news after school the next day. When he opened the front door and saw me standing on his door-step, he looked surprised but let me in anyway. He ushered me into the bedroom like always and, as soon as the door closed, he scrambled to undo his belt.

'Na na na, I ain't cum ere 4 dat. I need 2 chat 2 u,' my new-found stress giving me confidence.

'Let's chat afta we fuck,' he said, trying to hold my hand.

'No, dis iz important,' I insisted.

'Ite den, make it quick, init,' he said, irritated.

'Michael, cn u sit dwn doe?' I said, fear creeping in.

'Wot? Y? Talk man,' he tutted, standing with his hand on his belt.

'Pls Michael. Wot I need 2 say iz bare serious,' I pleaded.

He flopped down next to me on the bed, and sensing how annoyed he was getting made me feel uneasy. I wanted to burst into tears. I tried to breathe them away.

'Blud, say it man,' he insisted. Turning to face me on the bed, he frowned at me, confused as to why I was acting like this.

'I-I-I took a pregnancy test,' I said, looking up at him, my voice shaking. His eyes opened wide.

'So, w-wot did it say den?' he said, more slowly and calmly.

'I-I-I'm umm . . . I-I'm pregnant,' I said, feeling scared and sick.

He rose up from where he sat on the bed and slowly turned to face me. I looked up at him, anticipating a look of shock on his face, but he stared down at me expressionless.

'U need 2 leve,' he said quietly. I was confused, what did he mean? My confusion had me frozen in my seat on the bed.

'Blud, u need 2 go!' he said, raising his voice, his irritated disposition returning.

I was shocked. In that moment, I fought any considerations of 'me and Michael', and rage replaced the tears I had been struggling to breathe back.

'Wt da fuk, Michael, wot abt da baby?' I shouted.

'Hu u shoutin at? Get out, man. Iz nt even mine, u sket!' he spat.

That was the day that ruined my life, I'd decided. That was the day and that was the statement that ruined my reputation.

My stop came and I climbed off the bus. I decided to pass by the corner shop and buy a fag and a lighter. I hadn't smoked a fag in ages, but every time I thought about the Michael situation and its consequences, I felt tight and frustrated. I walked the long way back to Shanice and Ricardo's yard so I could smoke in peace.

I strolled through the quiet residential roads and felt better puffing the fag and feeling the morning breeze. I reached their yard, rang the bell and Shanice answered the door. She was on the phone and stepped back to let me in, greeting me with a smile. I followed her big bum up the soft carpeted staircase to the landing, and continued down the hall to Ricardo's room without a word.

Ricardo was on his phone too. He greeted me with a smile and a small wave, and continued his conversation on his cellular. I lay down on the bed and thought about boys and sex and relationships and love. They all brought me so much happiness in the beginning, and so much trouble later.

I rolled on to my side and gazed at Ricardo's profile as he animatedly told the story of his near miss with a bus on Morning Lane two days ago, and hoped he always brought me happiness.

5

'Oi, sket!' shouted a group of boys as I walked through my block. I was so used to this I just carried on walking with my head held high. Ever since the day I told Michael I was pregnant with his baby, I'd had to put up with that kind of shit. It was either bruddas trying to move to me to see if they could get piece, or shout 'sket' after me as they huddled in a group, so I couldn't tell who it was.

I was going home to pack another overnight bag and a fit for that night after spending the week. The day before, Mighty from Ricardo's block had invited everyone to his cousin's pyjama party. 'Blud, iz gna b live-o! All u lot shud come,' he'd boasted to the mandem and Shanice and I. Shanice declined straight away and later told me she was getting a link to sneak over while she had a free yard. So me and Ricardo were going together, and I was excited because this was gonna be my first pyjama party and my first time going to a shubz with my man.

I let myself in at home and was greeted with silence. Mum wasn't playing music, no clink-clink of glasses, no friends round. I popped my head into the kitchen to no sign of Mum drinking. I made my way upstairs, relieved that Mum was either out or asleep. As I planted my foot on the top step, I heard Mum faintly calling my name from the bathroom. Concerned, I ran over to the bathroom door at the end of the corridor and knocked.

'M-Mum? R u ite?' I said nervously. I wasn't sure what to expect.

'I-I'm not feel—' Her sentence was cut short by her heaving into the toilet.

I sighed deeply and opened the door to find my mum with her face in the toilet, throwing up. The bathroom stank of drink, and even though it was a Saturday, Mum still had on her work uniform from her Friday-morning shift in the kitchen at the old people's home.

I went over to Mum and pulled her soft, stray curls from out of her face, and retied her low ponytail for her. I filled the trusty tan bucket that was almost as old as me, with a little water and took it to her room, placing it beside her bed. I fried three rashers of bacon and two slices of bread, and put it on a tray with two paracetamol and a cup of Andrews. I left the tray on her bedside table and returned to the bathroom. Mum was lying on her back on the floor.

'Go 2 ur room wen ur redy, Mum,' I said from the doorway. She grunted and I left to pack my bag for the shubz.

Mum had been drinking for years. I didn't remember how old I was when it started, but I remembered learning how to make her cure when I was eight – fried bread, bacon and an Andrews.

Refocused on the evening ahead, I stepped into my room, dragged my Nike gym bag from under my bed and walked over to my wardrobe to pick out my PJs. I picked out the sexiest pyjamas I could find for the party – a set I'd bought in the sales one Boxing Day. Every year religiously, me and Shanice would hit Oxford Street with Christmas money. That year we'd ventured into La Senza and both picked out lingerie in the hopes that we'd one day put them to use, to tantalise a deserving hubby.

I stuffed the bag with a change of clothes and the PJs, and closed my bedroom door behind me. Before heading down the stairs, I paused to listen out for Mum in her bedroom and heard the clink of the cup against the plate. I jogged down the stairs and out the front door.

I walked past the neighbours' houses – the white elderly couple, the Turkish family and the Somali family, then turned right and walked past the playground and the basketball court where the same group of boys were jamming. They shouted out the same shit and I ignored them like I'd learned to.

I got to Ricardo's house and let myself in with his key, which he'd told me to take because I was going to be quick. I ran up the stairs to his bedroom and threw down my bag on his bed. I kissed him, standing at his desk doing something that I paid no mind to, and then climbed on the bed and switched on the TV. I was lying there catching up on *Big Brother* when Ricardo came to join me, lying behind me, running his fingers up and down my back. When his dusty alarm clock showed 9 p.m. I abruptly switched off the TV and jumped up. 'We're havin a showa cuz da party's startin in an hour,' I instructed enthusiastically, facing Ricardo.

'Ite, cum den,' he said lazily, pulling himself up.

In the bathroom, I turned on the shower and took off my clothes. Ricardo climbed in as I tied up my hair then followed him in. I took a scrub into my hand, pouring soap onto it. I propped my leg up on the side of the bath, scrubbing the length of my body. Ricardo reached for my scrub, taking over scrubbing me, and kissed my lips. He dropped it and began rubbing the lather into my body with his hands. I felt his dick pressed against me, standing tall. He tried to push me against the shower wall, lifting my leg to enter me.

'No, babe,' I moaned. He pressed his erect dick against my slippery skin instead.

'Y not,' he breathed into my neck.

'Not now. Wen we gt bck 4rm da party.'

I'd never felt like I was allowed to decline sex with brehs. Saying no always felt like I was at risk of losing their interest or affection or attention. I'd gritted my teeth through painful sex, gave in when I didn't feel comfortable, and been worn down by brehs I'd not even wanted to have sex with. But I felt sure that 'no' wouldn't carry any consequences with Ricardo.

'But my blue balls.' He pretended to wince in pain. I started laughing.

'Wot blue balls, let me see,' I joked.

'Low it.' He laughed, turning back to finish scrubbing himself.

He kissed me on the cheek, turned off the shower and got out, leaving me alone to get myself ready. I creamed my skin and put on my pyjamas – a lacy pair of white and pink French knickers with a matching bralette. I wiped the steam off of the bathroom mirror to inspect myself. I looked good. I walked into the bedroom coolly, but deep down, looking forward to Ricardo seeing me.

'R u sure u wanna go? We can stay here, boi' he said, licking his lips and smiling.

'Letz go 2 da party, den come back and stay here,' I said, giving him a grin.

'Ite, ite, but put on ma tracksuit doe,' he said, taking out a black Nike tracksuit from his wardrobe. I took it obediently and stepped into it, getting swallowed up by the thick material. Ricardo pulled up the hood on his grey Nike tracksuit and we were ready.

*

We drove over to Mare Street, through to Homerton then Hackney Wick, and arrived in Stratford, where we seldom ventured, for the shubz. We stepped inside, greeted by bashment music thumping and a whole heap of people dancing and whining up in what I'd guess was the living room. Ricardo and I disappeared to the toilet where I slipped out of the tracksuit, then folded it up tight and found a bedroom to stash it in until we were leaving.

We followed the bass of the bashment music down the stairs. The DJ dropped 'Wickedest Ride', and me and Ricardo looked at each other and started grinning. The chorus started playing and I started giving him a little slow whine, sensually grinding my bum into his groin. He held my waist and I could feel him hardening. From our spot in a corner, I had a view of the whole room. I loved the carefree and sensual energy of parties, and being with Ricardo felt like the icing on the cake until I looked up and spotted a group of guys bop in and almost instantly realised it was a bunch of brehs from my ends.

'*SHIT*,' I mumbled to myself. If I kept my head down and carried on dancing, I reasoned that they probably wouldn't spot me. I'd almost successfully reassured myself that spotting me was practically impossible – it was dark, my head was down and we were dancing in the shadows of our corner – but then they spotted me. I noticed a growing group milling around a few paces in front of me and Ricardo, clearly amused. I tried turning around and dancing front to front on Ricardo.

'Oi u, sket, u gnna b givin rides n shines 2nite or wot?' one of them eventually called out. I ignored them and carried on dancing with an oblivious Ricardo, praying he couldn't feel my heart pounding in my chest.

'Oi, Keisha, mans fuckin tlkin 2 u. Wot u on tonite? Ders bedrooms upstairs u know,' one laughed.

I felt Ricardo suck in a short sharp breath at the mention of my name and freeze as he listened for more. Suddenly, he pushed me off of him, clocking what was happening behind me.

'Ay blud, iz dis da way ur tryna chat 2 ma gyal?'

'Ur gyal? Rahhh boi, r u dumb. Keisha da sket iz UR ting?' Several of them were falling about laughing.

'Oi, call 'er a sket agen I'll fuckin draw 4 ma tool n buss 2 shotz in ur head! Dnt b callin ma gyal a sket,' Ricardo replied, pointing in one of the guys' faces and stepping closer to him.

The guys backed off when they realised Ricardo wasn't joking.

'Man didn't know cuz, lyk—' one of them said, trying to reason.

'Nah, fuck dat! Wat r man rly sayin? Man fink dey can chat shit 2 ma gyal wen I'm der n dat?' Ricardo was getting mad. I had never been this close to him when he was this vex.

'Broski, mans sor—' Eman attempted to reason with Ricardo. I knew him well, and he seemed to be present often when someone was shouting 'sket' from a group.

'Who's ur broski, blud? Man will fuck you up!' Ricardo shouted, grabbing Eman. Mighty and Corey appeared and held Ricardo back, whispering in his ear, trying to pacify the situation.

'Iz nt my fault she's dashed her belly bare times 4 da mandem,' one of the brehs said loud enough for Ricardo to hear as they turned to bop off. Ricardo stood, feet glued in place, looking on as they rolled out. My heart was pounding so hard I could've sworn the whole room could hear it. Even though I'd learned to pay the talk about me no mind, I was scared of what Ricardo might think or say, and whether or not he'd believe me. I was so numb to the names the brehs on my block called me, and the truth was so far from the stories they told. He turned around and looked at me, and I could see the hurt in his eyes.

'Is it tru?' he asked quietly.

'Not here, Ricardo, let's go bck home,' I replied, not wanting to spread any more of my business in public.

He walked through the crowd of partygoers and climbed the stairs two at a time. I followed behind, not sure what to expect. He silently passed me the tracksuit. I couldn't fight the thoughts tumbling around in my head. He had to believe me. It wasn't like that. It hadn't been bare brehs. They were lying.

Ricardo didn't make any eye contact with me as he waited for me to pull on the tracksuit. Mighty came looking for him and they spoke in hushed voices as I pulled my trainers on. I felt ashamed and dirty. Who wanted a girl that people said had had the whole estate having sex with her, raw? I didn't want to lose him. I wanted him to believe me. After all these years playing around, I wished we had happened earlier. Before Michael and the others . . . So much would have been different.

6

The ride back home was dead. The silence was so tense, I didn't know if I'd survive it. Ricardo revved and swung the car aggressively, giving the steering wheel and pedals his tension. When we arrived home, I waited for him to open his door before opening mine and climbing out. I was so nervous. I followed him up to the front door, and he opened it and held it open for me but still wouldn't look at me. I wanted to turn around and run away. I wanted to run into my past and change things.

I walked in and stood in the hallway, waiting for him to close and lock the door.

'So, I'll ask agen, iz it tru?' he said firmly from behind me.

I'd always wondered if Ricardo had heard anything about me through the grapevine. Shanice and I were mutually sworn to secrecy – I'd never tell her secrets and vice-versa, and Ricardo's block was beefing mine, so technically, he wouldn't be privy to the gossip. Although my paranoia still anticipated a day he might hear something, I didn't ever anticipate the stakes being this high when that day came.

'Look, Ricardo, I luv u. An i fort u luved me aswel—' I began to plead, turning around.

'Iz not about dat, Keisha man! I'm askin u about wot happened 2nite lyk . . . wot were dey talkin abat? Ur my gyal, I need to trust an protect you, Keisha,' he stressed, and I swear I saw tears forming in his eyes.

'I'm jus . . . scared!' I replied, tears rolling down my cheeks.

'Scared of wot? Of wot I mite fink? I dnt care,' he bellowed frustratedly. 'Do u know y me an Shanice liv in dis house by ourselves?'

'No,' I replied, not understanding where this was going but also contemplating the fact that Shanice and Ricardo did live alone in a four-bedroom house.

'Coz our mum couldn't look after us no more. She started smokin. Trus, man ain't got no judgements, Keisha blud,' Ricardo said passionately.

Minor details began making sense. Ricardo and Shanice's grandparents had lived here, and I remembered their parents vaguely, but I'd never asked questions because, by the time I was eight, I didn't want anyone asking questions about my mum.

'But isn't this ur grandparents' yard?' I asked, really wanting to ask about his mum.

'Well, it was my grannny and grandad's yard, but my dad basically paid off the mortgage for them. He was a shotta in Hackney, that's why you see all them yardies in Dalston and Shacklewell Lane calling me "son" or Shan "daughter" and shit. That's my dad's people from back in the day.'

'Oh.' A moment passed before I asked, 'Where's ur dad nw?'

'Dead,' Ricardo replied shortly.

'Oh. That makes sense.' Another moment of silence passed, then I hesitantly said, 'Rest in peace to him. Iz your mum still alive?'

'Yeah. She's at some rehab ting off endz. She started smoking white when we was little,' he answered, staring at his feet.

I couldn't fight my shock. Ricardo and Shanice's mum was a cat?! My eyes must have been double their size because when Ricardo finally looked up at me, he said, 'Yeah, I know. Iz bare mad.'

'Do u go c her?' I asked, attempting to cover up my shock.

'Man go sumtymz bt da drivez bare lng n I dnt rly lyk seein ma mum in a rehab lyk, u gt me.'

'Y-yeah, na, I hear dat,' I said, trying to wrap my head round what he was telling me. 'I'm bare shocked,' I finally admitted, even though I was sure he knew.

'Yeah, I knw,' he replied. 'Bt I'm showin u so u knw nuffin u tell me cn rly shock man.'

Shanice had always insisted that her mum 'got sick' when conversations about mums came up, and I'd never asked what that meant because my mum was sick too, and I didn't want anyone to ask what that meant.

'So, r u gnna tell me?' Ricardo asked, cutting into my thoughts.

'Ricardo, I got 1 abortion and that's it. That's the only abortion I've eva had. I duno wher dat prick woz goin abat bare! I aint proud of everyfin I've bin up 2 bt at da end of da day iz al in da past . . . I know everything happens for a reason but I wish fings were different doe.' What felt like an awkward silence passed. 'I'm so srry dat u had 2 find out lyk dis,' I added.

Ricardo stood looking at his feet. I willed him to move, react, say something! I must have been staring at him with all of my thoughts flashing on my forehead because he looked at me and reached out, pulling me into an embrace.

'I've got u, Keisha, I told u,' he said, holding me tight. I felt him fidgeting with his fingers as his hands rested against my arm in the embrace.

'Here. Wear dis. I promise u I got u.' I looked down and he was offering me one of the many sovereign rings he wore on his fingers. My heart thudded with overwhelm.

'Fank u, Ricardo,' I mumbled, thanking him for much more than the reassurance his ring symbolised. I put the sovereign on my thumb, the only finger it wouldn't fly off of, and leaned deeper into the embrace.

'Ricardo, did ur dad still luv ur mum wen she startd smokin?' I asked him, still nestled in his arms.

'Yeah, he did u knw. Lyk, in his own way. No1 cud disrespect ma mum even doe she woz a cat, n he neva lyk kicked her out da yard or nuffin

202

lyk dat. But he defo started slappin her up. I dnt condone dat,' he replied.

I listened carefully to what he said and pondered the unconditionality of Ricardo's love. This was very different, but I wondered if his capacity to love and accept me had been modelled on his dad's capacity to do it for his mum to some extent. I wondered if love ran out, and whether I was worthy. I wondered if Ricardo was lying about his true feelings and if he might abruptly have a change of heart.

This felt risky . . .

7

I awoke to the sound of my phone ringing at eleven the next morning. 'Private caller' flashed up on the screen. Ricardo lay asleep next to me, catching flies. I smiled to myself.

'Hello?' I answered.

'Im gonna get u, dutty bitch!' replied the caller.

'Huh? Wot?' I stammered back, but the person cut the call. I climbed out of bed, quickly forgetting the strange call as I wiped the sleep from my eyes, and went to have a shower. I stood under the hot water for ages thinking about last night. How the guys from my block had lied about me, but also how Ricardo had believed me, and what I'd learned about him, and how safe yet vulnerable I'd felt. I dried myself, got dressed and crept over to Shanice's room. I opened her bedroom door a crack to see if she was up or even in there. I hadn't seen her since yesterday during the day, and I wondered if she got her link out before me and Ricardo got back – I was meant to text her when we were on our way. In the crack in the door I saw her sitting up in bed with the covers pulled up to her stomach, and a breh sitting with his back to the door. I could tell from the curly afro that it was Kareem. They were speaking in hushed voices. Shanice made eye contact and blinked bare fast, gesturing for me to get out. I smiled and stepped out, returning to Ricardo's room. He was up and awake now.

'U ite b?'

'Yeah, I'm alrite,' I said, thoughtlessly making my way over to him for a hug.

'Lemme quickly go do sumfin,' he asserted abruptly, sliding by me, bypassing my attempt at a cuddle, and hurrying out the room.

'Mornin bref!' I shouted after him, laughing and shaking my head.

'Shut up, man!' he shouted back. He came back five minutes later, lunging straight for my lips.

'I luv u, u kno,' he mumbled mid-liplock.

'I luv u 2,' I said, pulling away and looking at him searchingly, trying to be sure he meant what he'd just told me. It felt like Ricardo had put words to the events of last night. 'But I've gotta go.'

'Go where?' Ricardo asked, alarmed, reconsidering if he was letting me out of his grip.

'Jus 2 go gt sum clothes, no need 2 hav a fit!' I replied, half laughing at how he hesitated to let go of me.

'O skn. Yeah, bring bare of ur clothes here,' he told me. 'Do u wnt me 2 follow u?' he asked.

'Na na, iz okay. I'll b back soonish init.'

'Ite den.' He reached for me again, holding me in a tight embrace for a few moments longer than usual. I kissed him and turned around to pick up ma bag and leave.

'Soonish, yeah?' he called after me.

'Soonish,' I replied and left the room.

I bolted down the stairs and out the front door. Just as I got to the end of the terrace, it started raining and I contemplated turning back to get an umbrella. 'Fuck it!' I reconsidered, and rushed down the road, wanting to hurry up and get out of the rain – but more importantly, back to Ricardo. I turned the corner and decided against walking through the muddy Fields. I was treading the soaking pavement, regretting not turning back for an umbrella as the rain fell more mercilessly, when a car pulled up next to me.

'Oi, Keisha. Wha gwarn?' It was Smerkz, an older from my block who I hardly saw anymore. He turned down his music and smiled. He had a beard now, and wore a grey hoodie over a navy New Era hat. He had always been so serious. His smile was throwing me because up until then he had never opened his mouth wide enough for me to notice that he had a gold tooth.

'Ar, u-u ite, Smerkz?' I said, kind of surprised to see him *and* that he was being friendly to *me* of all people. Though it was generally the youngers that gave me aggro and shouted dumb shit after me, I still remained sceptical of any and everyone that chilled on my block. For that reason, we barely spoke beyond 'hi', and he was proper older than me anyway.

My awkwardness was surely coming across in the moment, because all I could think about was how many conversations about me he had probably been present for – plus, I was getting soaked here as he grinned at me.

'Jump in init, iz bare rainin,' he insisted.

That threw me again. I didn't want to get in, but I didn't wanna look dumb and stoosh by declining. And then who was I, the block's jezzy, to reject an older's genuine offer of a lift to shield me from torrential rain?

*

After hesitating for a few seconds, I got in. The car stank of weed and the seats were grimy. Though I didn't really know Smerkz, I wouldn't have expected him to drive a dirty car like this. I imagined Smerkz in a nice whip that you couldn't eat or drink and certainly not smoke in. Looking at the state of this though, I would've been confident it was a dinger if he hadn't been driving it barefaced in the daytime *and* stopped for me. As he drove along past the length of the Fields, I studied the clothes he was wearing and wondered why he was wearing those garms. He had on gloves that were a bit small for him, because the wristband sat closer to the palm of his hand, and a mismatched tracksuit that looked like it had met the washing machine too many times. Though I'd not seen him in a while, Smerkz had definitely always been one of the ones who was always shining, so I didn't understand what was going on today.

'Keisha, u knw. Wha gwarn? Man ain't seen u in tym. Where u goin?' he said, bare hype and over-friendly.

'I'm bless,' I said. I was bare confused. Why was he being so over-nice? 'I'm goin 2 my mum's 2 gt suttin quickly.'

'Ar seen. Wot, u in a rush? Man will drop u, lemme jus drop suttin 2 J-man. U memba J-man init? Yeah fuckinnn J-man jus cum out u knw?

Yeah yeah yeah, wot can u smell dat? Yeah mans jus gna drop a 3–5 on my brudda, u knw lyk dat?'

Smerkz was talking so much, I couldn't even butt in to say 'jus drop me here' or 'I'm in a rush'.

'Wot, u smoke alie?' He looked at me expectantly and I nodded. 'Ite, man will roll suttin quick wen we pull up.'

'Ite den but I need 2 hurry up doe,' I managed to get in when he finally stopped to breathe.

The rain was beating against the pavement and the windows as we zoomed round corner after corner on back streets I'd never seen. The way Smerkz whipped the old car and the frantic rain made the journey feel like a blur.

'Arr, what, where u goin afta ur marjays?' he asked.

'My manz yard,' I said.

'Ar swr dwn? Who's ur man?' he asked, his brow furrowing with inquisition.

'Ar I-I duno if u knw him, u knw.'

'Wot, iz he frm Hackney?'

'Yeah.'

'Yeah, wot of course man wil knw him. I bet I could even guess. Wot is ur man Moses?'

I started bussin up. 'No, low it man,' I said. Moses was a shop boy that everyone used to laugh at.

'Manz jokin, obviously nt. Wot iz ur man Showa?' he asked.

'Naaaa, I'm shook of him!' I exclaimed.

Everyone was scared of Showa because of what they had heard about how he got his name.

'I knw who ur man iz. Ricardo init,' Smerkz guessed again.

'Yeah,' I said, smiling bare, not considering it a bit strange that Smerkz guessed someone from another block.

'Seen. Yeah, I fort so. I need 2 chat 2 u still abt ur man u knw, iz kinda important as wel,' Smerkz said, seriously.

Now I was really baffled – Smerkz went from being over-friendly with me, then serious and needing to chat to me about Ricardo.

We had come to a stop at a red light. The rain outside was easing up and every other drop that landed on the bonnet of the car was echoing in my ears as we sat there with the tension creeping into the car with us.

'Wot abt him?' I finally asked, hoping it weren't beef and nothing no one thought I knew anything about.

'Ur man badded up my cousin and my yungas u knw,' he said, looking at me.

'Wot? Wen?' I asked, trying to understand why he was trying to talk to me about it. I knew Ricardo weren't a dickhead but, at the same time, my context for him was that he didn't really have any beef. I wondered who Ricardo was badding and why.

'At da shubz in Stratford last nite,' Smerkz said bluntly. He'd stopped smiling and he wasn't moving hype anymore.

I tried to understand what Smerkz was saying to me. I didn't know Smerkz had youngers, let alone a cousin. He was so stoosh; I couldn't even recall him saying much more than 'wha gwarn' to the younger lot. I wondered which one was Smerkz's cousin.

'Ohhh. Das ur yungas? Ar, na lyk Ricardo jus tld dem . . .' I insistently tried to explain the situation but started getting hot all over again, remembering what they'd tried to say about me. Forgetting about what I had started trying to explain, I found myself getting a bit hype and recalling the night before. 'Coz u knw wot dey sed, Smerkz? Dey sed I had bare abortionz u knw! Lyk, wot kind of dumb lie iz dat?'

Smerkz didn't say anything, and continued to drive along in silence. I gazed out my window paying no attention to what was outside, just feeling embarrassed that he hadn't responded to what I had told him, realising I had expected him to match the shock I'd felt since the night before.

We turned onto a high road when it occurred to me that we had been driving for a little while and that this couldn't be Hackney because I didn't really recognise this high road. I looked out for the next street sign and made out 'N17' printed in red. We were in Tottenham. I looked back at Smerkz to ask him where we were going and why we were in Tottenham, but he didn't look like he was in the mood for answering questions anymore. He looked like old-school serious Smerkz, with his jaw clenched and the emotionless look in his eyes, so I left it. After a few more minutes he turned into a car park, below a tower block. He drove to the end and parked in a bay between two walls.

'Wer here nw. Come,' he said, jumping out of the car.

I hesitated but followed him because I didn't know where we were, and this location felt ominous. Smerkz was already bopping away from where I stood in the middle of the car park, looking around. No one was about and I couldn't see any signs to indicate where we were either.

'Smerkz? Where we?' I asked, finally catching up to him.

'Farm,' he said, not making any eye contact with me. I'd heard of the Broadwater Farm riot, and me and Shanice had met some boys from Farm at a shubz one time, but I'd never been there. It was like massive imposing blocks that housed concrete mazes. For an estate that big, it was strangely quiet. We walked back in the direction Smerkz had driven in, then he took a sharp left and approached two cars parked between two walls further down. I could hear the rumble of bass, and made out a group of mandem in the cars through the tinted windscreens.

'Wha gwarn u man?' Smerkz said as he approached the cars. I didn't wanna go closer, so I stopped in the middle of the road, hoping no cars would drive in forcing me to move. Smerkz turned around, seeing me standing there. 'Come, Keisha.'

I hesitated. I could feel everyone's eyes on me. I didn't want to look dumb standing so far away, so I walked over. I smiled quickly at the clearest figure I could make out, sat behind the steering wheel in the silver car on my right, then averted my eyes downward, looking at my shoes. I focused on the mud specks on the front of my Air Maxes and I thought about how I would wipe them off when I got home and change into my all-black Converse which I'd bought from Sports World, because I didn't mind them getting muddy. They wiped off easily and they were cheap anyway.

'Oi, Keisha, sit down,' Smerkz said, bringing me out of my thoughts and pointing to the back seat of the silver car. 'I'm gna bill dis den we can duck.' I looked to the driver of the car Smerkz said I should sit inside, for some confirmation that my taking a seat was okay, but he met my gaze with an expressionless stare. Feeling conflicted, I sat down anyway, silently praying he didn't switch and tell me to get out of his car. I sat on the back seat behind the driver's seat with the door open, while Smerkz stood between both cars talking and building his zoot. Smerkz talked and talked, and I sat there partly feeling some ease at the fact he was back to being talkative, but also willing him to hurry the fuck up with the zoot.

'Ur Ricardo's gyal, init?'

I looked up to see the breh in the driver's seat staring at me through the gap in the headrest. He wore a black hoodie which hugged his face tightly, making his big nose and big lips stand out. His eyes were slightly red like he'd been drinking or smoking.

'Yeah,' I said quietly. He didn't say anything else, turning away to refocus on the chatter outside.

Smerkz and his lot started passing the zoot around. They passed it to the breh in the driver's seat and I learned his name was Kubez. It came round to me and I contemplated declining but took it anyway, toking slowly. Kubez turned to me again.

'I've heard abat u still,' he said.

I didn't know what to say so I just said, 'Skeen.'

'Yeah, I've heard abat u still.' He paused for a second, his eyes lingering on me.

'Take off ur trouserz,' he said flippantly.

I nearly choked on the zoot. Clearing my throat, I spluttered, 'W-wot?'

'Take off ur trouserz,' he repeated coolly.

I was completely taken aback. What was he saying? Was he joking? I waited to clock a smile creeping onto his lips. I looked to my right, wondering if Smerkz and the other man in the other car had heard what Kubez was asking me. I met several pairs of eyes gazing at me, expressionless. They could well hear and this wasn't a joke.

'Woz goin on?' I asked quietly, looking back at Kubez.

'Nuffin. Do as ur told. Take off da trouserz.' He said it like he was asking me to pass the lighter.

Kubez turned his back to me and opened the glovebox, his hand coming back out clasping a shank.

'Take dem off or man will slice dem off u,' he said calmly, inspecting the shank in his hand and rubbing a spot on it.

My head felt like it had developed its own heartbeat. WHAT THE FUCK WAS GOING ON?????? I looked towards Smerkz again but he was walking away. I looked back at Kubez. He held my gaze through the gap in the headrest, waiting. I looked over again at the other car, and the three men in there were all looking at me, waiting too. I didn't even know where the zoot was anymore because the next thing I knew I was peeling my trousers off in the back of the car. Smerkz reappeared, having parked his car horizontally in front of the other two, blocking us in and concealing what was about to happen from any possible spying eye.

'Get on all 4z,' Kubez said. My mind was racing but my body moved slowly as I continued to peel off my jeans. They were damp from the rain, making them hard to get down over my thighs. I began untying my shoes. My head was pulsating with thoughts. What was happening to me? What were they going to do to me? Why this and why me?

I'd long kept my distance from the brehs from my block. Since the situation with Michael, I was reluctant to trust anyone. I was paranoid about what I presumed people were thinking and saying, and I was ashamed. Every day for the remainder of my school years, I'd wanted to slip under the radar and move around invisibly. I remember Moses being the first person I resumed saying hello to, and slowly, when I absolutely had to walk past the cage or Dean's house, I'd nod and mumble 'hi', hoping that on this occasion no one was in a silly mood and would conspicuously shout 'sket' as soon as I passed.

'Get on all fuckin 4z, I sed,' Kubez said aggressively. I began to roll onto my hip and position myself on all fours, with my trousers still round my ankles on the back seat.

'Out ere, out ere,' Kubez barked, pointing the shank in the space between the cars.

My head was spinning. I was scared and confused. I felt trapped between the cars and in my damp jeans. I shuffled out of the car, and got down on my hands and knees on the gritty, cold, wet floor. Before I could take a full breath in, someone thrust their manhood in me. I let out a scream from the shock and pain. Whoever it was thrusted mercilessly. I felt like I was being torn in half. Their fingers dug into my skin and I could feel the gritty ground beneath my hands and knees, and the pain of whoever it was thrusting shot through my hips and legs. The shock and discomfort made me want to collapse on the ground. My elbow buckled and whoever was behind me grabbed my shoulder, forcing me to stay up.

'Suck it,' demanded another voice. I raised my head to see a dick dangling in front of me.

I couldn't muster enough strength to raise my head further and look at the face of who was attempting to force themselves in my mouth. It didn't matter anymore, anyway. They took hold of themselves, eagerly forcing their soft, red-toned genitalia into my unwilling mouth. I held him in my dry mouth and moved my head back and forth with the little effort I could manage, attempting to generate some movement that at least mimicked stimulation. He impatiently grabbed my head and thrust himself in and out. I felt the glands in my mouth generating wetness. I wondered if it was saliva or blood. He thrust until he came, forcing himself into the back of my mouth as he steadied himself by clasping the back of my head. I hawked his semen out of my throat, wincing at the burning sting taking over my tonsils. Whoever was pounding away behind me finished as I spluttered, kicking me in my side as he got up. I tumbled over and the sting of the cold wet floor ripped through me. And then another one mounted me. I wasn't wet, I was just scared. His hands clawed at my hips, so when he got off of me, he left stinging, bloody scratches on my skin. I wiped at the blood, trying to focus on something else, and then I blacked out.

The searing scream of a car horn woke me up. As I came to, they got longer and louder in my head until I opened my eyes fully and saw the white concrete ceiling and felt the gritty hard floor underneath me. I could see my bag in the distance. I tried to reach for it, slowly rolling onto my hip and feeling pain erupt in what felt like every point of my body. My throat felt raw, my hips and knees stung, and my hands and ribs felt bruised. I glanced at my legs, struggling not to panic but remembering the last images before I blacked out. My jeans were pulled up, and covered in dark wet stains. The car in front of me blew its horn again. I raised my head just enough to make out a black middle-aged couple peering at me with confusion and concern etched all over their faces through the windshield. The man, who was in the driver's seat, rolled down his window. 'Are you okay?' he called out.

'H-help me. Please take me home,' I cried out. I got up onto my feet. My mind raced as the inquisition in the man's voice reverberated in the echoey car park like a lifeline. I wanted to run to him. I limped to my bag, snatching it up and turning to move as fast as I could towards my saviours.

As the car crept over to me, I felt relief washing over me.

'Please help me,' I whimpered, approaching the couple's car. Standing at their window I noticed the man's grey hair and thick-rimmed glasses and I began to cry. Their expressions softened to worry as I got closer.

'Darlin, what happened to you?' the lady asked from the passenger seat, as her man silently stared at me. She wore a colourful headwrap, and in those five words I decided that I wanted a mum like her.

'I-I-I wanna – I wanna go home,' I squealed, stammering as I tried to breathe.

'Well, where do you live, hun?' the lady asked, the worry on her face deepening.

'Lansdowne Drive,' I told them, giving the name of Ricardo's street. I couldn't go home like this. I knew my mum couldn't do anything for me.

'Curtis, can you drive there?' the lady asked.

'Yes, yes of course.' Curtis nodded with urgency.

'Get in darlin,' she said. I opened the door and got in the back. I started sobbing immediately, perhaps relieved, and Curtis sped out of the car park.

'So, hun, what happened to you? You have a bruise coming up on your face and your clothes . . . why were you on the floor, darlin? Do you want us to take you to the police station, it's just coming up on the left here,' the lady said, peering at me in the back seat, looking me over.

'P-p-p-please. Please j-j-jus tke me h-hme. I wnna s-s-see Ricardo,' I stuttered back, struggling to regulate my breathing.

I burst into tears in shock, relief, pain and frustration that I couldn't get my words out. I couldn't stop crying for the whole journey. When we finally turned onto Ricardo's road, I flew out of the car before it could come to a stop, and shuffled down the road as fast as I could towards his house. I got to the front door and banged with all my strength.

'KEISHA!' Ricardo shouted, grabbing me in his arms and bringing me into the house.

'Hu did dis 2 u, baby girl. Tell me hu did dis 2 u???' Ricardo asked hurriedly. His eyes big like saucers in his panic.

'S-Smerkz a-a-an K-K-Kubez n der boiz,' I managed to spit out.

'SHANICCCCCCCCCCEEEEEEEEEE!' Ricardo shouted up da stairs.

'WOT?' Shanice shouted back, full of attitude, unaware of what was happening downstairs.

He waited for her to appear at the top of the stairs before instructing: 'Bring ma fone n reach unda da bed, u'll feel a gym bag. Go in it and ders a pouch. Bring da pouch.'

Within seconds, Shanice's footsteps came pattering down the stairs. When she saw the state of me there in Ricardo's arms she dropped everything and ran to me. They helped me over to the sofa and Ricardo helped me to lie down. He hurriedly reached into the pouch and took out something wrapped in plastic bags and stuffed it in the waistband of his trousers, then dialled a number on the phone Shanice had brought down.

'Yeah, yeah. Cum 2 ma yard now n bring all da goonz. Yeah, cuz. Ridin,' he said and hung up. He perched on his knees next to me.

'Keisha Keisha Keisha.' He shook his head. 'How?' His eyes looked wet.

He brushed my hair out of my face.

'I dnt kno, Ricardo. Dey jus made me . . .' I tried to explain.

'Made u wot?' he persisted, getting impatient.

'M-m-made me d-do stuff, ly—' I was stammering as I began realising I was scared of what Ricardo might do or say to me. I hadn't wanted what happened, but they'd made me. How was this the second difficult thing I was explaining to him? How would he believe me now? I wanted the sofa to swallow me whole because I couldn't face explaining this one.

'Stuff lyk wot? Wot u tellin me? Wot did dees man do 2 u, Keisha?' Ricardo was raising his voice and tilting his head in confusion. Anger and frustration pierced every word. I was scared.

I started sobbing.

'TELL ME WOT HAPPENED!' he bellowed.

'Rico, calm down, man!' Shanice shouted, rubbing my arm. 'Iz okay, Keish, take ur tym. Did Smerkz hit u?' she asked me gently.

'I-I dnt knw,' I sobbed.

'Okay. So wot did Smerkz do den?' she coaxed.

'H-he made me cum Farm wiv him a-an made me fuk Kubez an sum nxt brehs coz Ricardo boied Smerkz's yungas and cousin at da shubz yes2day,' I managed to get out between sobs. I gazed searchingly at Ricardo, trying to discern what he was thinking and predict what he might say.

His face shifted between anger and confusion and disbelief.

'How did man MAKE u fuk Keisha?' he blazed, jumping up. I felt Shanice flinch next to me. 'Dem man RAPED YOU KEISHA. DEM MAN FUCKIN RAPED MA GYAL!!!' he screamed.

Ricardo started booting the dining chairs in a rage. Shanice leapt up. 'Ricardo man, stop! Y u doin dat?' she shouted, trying to stop him, but her attempt to pacify him couldn't match his rage in the moment. She tried to contain him, reaching and sympathetically holding his arm but he snatched it from her. He kicked and kicked the chairs, the sound of wood cracking and his rage-filled kicks filling the silence. I just lay on the sofa sobbing, terrified of what he was thinking and what he might do next, but too weak to do or say anything.

Ricardo gave the glass dining table one firm boot into the wall, denting it, then a car horn started blaring outside. Ricardo snapped out of his rage immediately and charged towards the front door without a word.

When the sound of the door slamming shut and engines roaring outside invaded the silence, new panic started whirring round in my head. What was he going to do? What was going to happen? Would he be okay? When would I know whether or not he still loved me?

8

Hours later, Ricardo's key turned in the lock in the front door. He strolled into the living room, pulling off his gloves and dashing them to one side. I lay in my spot on the sofa, my eyes fixed on him. I was aware that I had no strength to jump up and ask him a hundred questions, check to make sure he was okay and embrace him. He came to me and held me close and tight. I felt numb. I'd lain there possessed by my thoughts all evening, and my brain had stopped.

I finally pulled away to look at him. He didn't have war in his eyes anymore. I couldn't see or read anything in his face.

'Wot did u do, Ricardo?' I quietly asked.

'Da truth?' he breathed.

'Please, da truth.'

'I can't tell you,' he said flatly.

I relaxed back in his arms, resigned. I stared at the TV blankly. Thoughts popped into my mind through the fog of numbness. Reprisal. Police. Prison. I wondered what he had actually done, but I had no strength to imagine the possibilities.

'Don't worry abat it,' he said out of the blue. It woz like he could hear my thoughts. 'Do you trust me?' he asked next.

'Yeah,' I blurted out straight away. I didn't care to think about my answer and I was just glad he was here, holding me.

We sat staring at the TV, lost in private thought.

It was two months since the rape. I had been at Ricardo's house the majority of the time. Though we hadn't had sex in two months, I felt more safe, reassured and connected to him than ever before. Maybe it was because he didn't seem to be phased by the lack of sex. Perhaps I felt accepted as I was, despite what had happened. Perhaps I felt believed and therefore heard for the first time in a very long time.

It was a Saturday afternoon and I had reached Ricardo's yard after shopping in Oxford Street. I let myself in with the key he had given me. I was in awe of how at home I felt. I ran up the stairs to his room to find him sitting on his side of bed counting money. I dropped my JD and Primark bags on the floor as he mumbled the count, expertly flicking each note between his fingers in quick succession.

'I'm comin. Lemme go chek Shan,' I said, turning to walk back out the door.

'Not even a kiss, ya na?' he muttered, opening a drawer to stuff the wad in.

I ran over to him, playfully planting a big wet kiss on him, then ran back out. I hadn't seen Shanice properly in a couple weeks and we were basically *living* together. She was seldom home, and when she was, she seemed to be glued to her phone. Kareem was back on the scene, and the hard and fast rule was Kareem was cool, Shanice could stay at his, but Kareem was not allowed to sleep over here. Ricardo wasn't compromising on that. I, of course, knew that Shanice got around that when and where she could.

I knocked on her bedroom door and didn't wait for an answer. Shanice was lying in bed.

'U ite, Shan?'

'Yeah b,' she replied, softly. 'Keisha? I need 2 tell u sumfin.'

'Wot iz it?' I asked, searching her eyes for what she might be about to tell me.

'I'm eight weeks pregnant,' she said, almost whispering.

I gasped. 'Wot! U an Kareem?'

'Yeah . . .' she said, smiling.

'Dus he kno?' I asked.

'Yeah. He's happy n everyfin. He wants us 2 get a yard n all dat.'

'Awwww das gud u kno. U kno how moss of dese wasteman r dees days, dey jus wanna plant der seed n dukle.'

'U get me, Keish,' Shanice replied, laughing softly.

'I'm happs 4 u doe, Shan. Ur gonna b such a gud mum u know,' I said, reaching to hug her.

'I hope so u know,' she said, sighing.

'U will b,' I said quietly, still holding her tight in a hug.

'Wot do u fink itz gonna be?' I asked as we parted from our embrace.

'A boy u know. Kareem wants a boy.' She gazed down at her belly. 'Rico's first nephew,' she murmured. 'Howz tingz wit u n him?' she asked, looking up at me.

'We're good u know,' I breathed. 'I didn't know how he mite be afta wot happened in Farm.'

'I know,' Shanice said sympathetically. 'U alrite doe, Keish?' she asked after a moment passed.

'Im blessical,' I said, smiling.

'R u sure, Keish? U knw u can chat 2 me,' Shanice said, looking me in my eyes.

'I know. I'm gud, Shan, trus,' I reassured her, feeling like I meant every word.

'Ite. I need 2 gt ma ars up an go c Kareem!' Shanice moved to get up slowly.

'Ite den, ill leve u 2 it. Bt errrmmm, Ricardo doesn't know abat da baby, does he?' I asked cautiously.

'No. I'm gnna tell him soonish when Kareem's ready,' she said, looking slightly worried. She knew Ricardo's initial reaction would likely be to hit the roof – he wanted Shanice to finish college and get a job before any babies.

'Ite den. Make sure doe. ASAP!' I said, leaving her.

I returned to Ricardo's room. He was watching TV. I'd picked up the shopping bags and begun sorting through my purchases when Ricardo teasingly asked, 'Oi, erm excuse me, where's ma hug?' I feigned annoyance, pretending to drag myself over to him to fulfil his request. I perched on the bed in front of him and lazily draped my arm around him. 'An ma kiss, please?!' he said in a childish voice. I held back my laughter at his ridiculousness. Instead, I rolled my eyes and sighed before giving him a kiss on the cheek. 'An my REAL kiss?' he continued, play-acting a sassy child. I couldn't help but laugh as I moved my face to meet his, defiantly looking at his lips instead of going in for a kiss. He didn't wait before lunging for my mouth, passionately savouring my lips and kissing me in a way we'd tacitly refrained from since what happened to me in Farm. He pulled back. We were both perceiving the same thing. He held my gaze for a few moments, then asked: 'An ma sex?'

Suddenly, the smell of his cologne intensified and heat began rising around my ears. My mind began to flood with memories and imagery of our bodies entangled on the bed, and the pulsating between my legs deepened. I *had* to be ready but more importantly, two months was a long time, and he had his needs. He'd been patient and I believed I had a responsibility to look after my man. If I didn't look after him, who would? I rationalised.

I held his gaze, confirming we were having sex. He got up and proceeded to undress me. He peeled off every item of clothing smoothly, gently pushing me back onto the bed to slide me out of my brown velour trousers. He held my hands and kissed the fading marks where I'd been scratched. With every piece of my clothing he removed, I fought the feeling like I wanted to hide. I felt confused. Ricardo was tenderly holding my hands and kissing my scars and telling me he'd missed me, but I couldn't fight the thoughts and feelings churning around my mind and body. I felt nervous and guilty and as though I had to try harder to breathe.

*

He gently took my legs in his hands and spread them. I closed my eyes, focusing on the throbbing that betrayed me. A warm sensation filled my belly as he gently stroked my clit with his tongue. It felt physically amazing. I forced my eyes open to watch him at work. I knew Ricardo had never done this before. Seeing him between my legs amplified the conflict I felt internally. I closed my eyes again and tried to connect with the physical pleasure. I was so aware of how much better I'd feel if we were having penetrative sex or if I were performing oral sex on him instead. I half waited for him to finish.

He came up and kissed me and I reached for his belt instantly.

'We don't hav to do this, u kno,' he said earnestly.

'I want to,' I reassured him.

9

The next day I awoke with a familiar ache between my legs. Ricardo lay beside me fast asleep. I looked over at the old dust-covered alarm clock next to the PlayStation which read 12:03 in big red numbers. Midday and he was still asleep . . . 'so lazy,' I smirked to myself.

I climbed out of the bed feeling the ache more as I stood.

I crept to the other side of his room and noticed a drawer slightly open. I don't know what made me do it on this day of all days, because Ricardo trusted me in his room even when he wasn't home so I had ample time to snoop when he probably wouldn't catch me, but I slid the drawer towards me while he snored away behind me. What met my eyes shocked me. There was so much money rolled up into thick rolls and three different-coloured balloons tied tightly. I knew what they were from my Michael days. I was VEX! I don't know if I assumed that Ricardo had stopped shotting the night he told me about his mum, but I couldn't fathom how he could have such a lucid understanding of how drugs had affected his mum and his entire life. And more, after the raid, why did he have all this shit in the house with me and Shanice here? I was no shotter but I knew that smart ones didn't keep their shit in the house.

I was ready to blast him as soon as he got his big head out of bed. I went to the bathroom to have a shower so I could get ready and duck. I showered quickly, got dressed and did my hair. I pottered around quietly, clearing away some of my things – I didn't expect to sleep there another night until all that shit was shifted. When I finished getting ready, I had to sit and wait for Ricardo to finally wake up so I could confront him. I contemplated waking him up because I was getting more and more annoyed with each snore he let out. I paced up and down, thinking that if I woke him up and he was moving all tired and shit, and couldn't understand what I was chatting about, I'd just get more pissed off. I looked over at the drawers again and decided to look at what was in the second one. More money and a shank. I shook my head and closed the drawer, forgetting to be gentle. Ricardo started stirring and eventually woke up.

'Wha gwarn b . . . y u screwfacin?' he asked, still half asleep.

'Wot da FUCK iz alla dis?' I shouted, yanking open the top drawer and dangling a balloon in front of his face.

'You know wot it iz,' he said, sounding cool and calm but in his eyes I spied the alarm. He climbed out of bed and reached for the balloon.

'Wot da fuck u doin wit all dis kina shit in da house, Ricardo? Ur da sme person dat told me dat story abat ur mum n ur sellin de sme ting dat fucked up ur family! Wots rong wit u?' I shouted.

'Wot da fuckz rong wiv u?' he shot back at me. 'Y u goin thru manz draws n screamin all up in manz face aswell? An dnt chat abt manz family, blud, are you fuckin dumb? Ur screamin up in ma fce in my yard. Dnt ever think u can move lyk dat in my yard. Imma bad man u kno.' He screamed in my face, taking the balloon from me and stuffing it back in the drawer. I was in too much shock to say more! What was WRONG with him? I just looked at him, kissed my teeth, picked up my bag and left. I ran down the stairs and out the front door. Ricardo came running after me.

He ran up to the end of the porch. 'Keisha! KEISHA, cum ere! Ay, I said cum ere? U kno I do my ting, cum here, man . . . got man shoutin on da roads n dat.'

'Yesss I kno, Ricardo. U do ur ting. Wateva yeah,' I replied, and turned to march off down the road.

Ricardo called my name a couple more times and followed me as I marched down his road. I walked so fast, charging through the streets and got to my house in no time. I let myself in with my key and went straight to my bedroom and threw my bags to one side. I changed into a pair of shorts and a t-shirt and climbed in my bed. I slept for so long that when I woke up it was dusk. I got up and unpacked my bags, still thinking about earlier. 'How could he have me sleeping in his yard with all that shit there? How could he chat to me like that as well?' I checked my phone to see Ricardo had left six missed calls, three voicemail messages and two texts. I paced around my room with the voicemail on loudspeaker and ran through the texts he'd sent, all of which basically said the same ting: 'Im sorry bby', 'Keisha pik up ur fone', 'lets talk'. I just kissed my teeth. I put my phone down, fed up of all the messages, and went downstairs to the kitchen, where I found my mum cooking. She looked surprised to see me.

'Hello madam. Lng tym no c? Da las tym I checked u still lived here, or has that changed?'

'Hi Mum,' I breathed. When Mum weren't drinking, she had a short temper, got rude, and we argued bare, and I weren't in the mood. I would have preferred if right now she was in bed vomiting and I had to fry her bread and bacon. Ricardo had pissed me off enough and I didn't have the patience to deal with her.

She was dishing up some brown stew chicken and rice and peas for herself, and took a second plate and dished me up some and sat down across the small stained kitchen table. I started yamming it down. One thing about Mum, she could cook. The old people at the care home loved it when she was on shift.

Mum tried to make conversation while I ate. 'U okay? Hw come I ain't seen u den? U dnt hav time 4 me no more?'

'Yeah I'm bless,' I said. Concentraing on eating my food.

'Fank u 4 lookin afta me da otha day. Dt woz a bad 1,' she said.

I stopped eating. I was surprised because I don't think Mum had ever said thank you to me before. Usually after Mum had a 'bad 1' she would give me the silent treatment for a few days.

'Iz alrite,' I said and we both continued eating. As soon as I finished, I put my plate in the sink and went back to my room. I stood in front of the mirror and stared at myself. What was I gonna do when staying with Mum felt like too much, I wondered to myself. Ricardo's felt like home now but how was I gonna go back there after what I'd found today? I caught myself starting to feel stressed and tempted to call Ricardo to squash it, but I took a DVD off the rack and went downstairs instead. I was halfway through *Honey* when my phone started ringing. 'Rico <3' flashed on the screen. I wanted to pick up so bad. Mum was gonna be drunk soon and I just weren't in the mood today, but I left it to ring out. 'If he calls again, I'll let it ring out and call him back,' I reasoned. Within thirty seconds, he called back and I smiled, relieved that we were probably gonna squash the beef tonight. I called him back.

'Come outside,' he said, picking up on the first ring.

'Erm, okay den,' I said, a bit baffled. I looked through the peephole before opening the door, and spotted Ricardo closing his car door with flowers in his hand.

I opened the front door excitedly but didn't show it as I walked over to Ricardo, standing by his car holding what I now saw were three bunches of flowers in his hand.

'The shop didn't have a big bunch, so I got you three small ones,' he said as I stood there looking him up and down.

'Skeen,' I replied, making sure I didn't smile.

'Gimme my ring back,' he said.

'Why?' I said with bare attitude.

'Blud, give me my ring, man,' he said, holding out his hand. I pulled the sovereign off my thumb and handed it over. He slipped it into the front pocket of his jeans and then reached into his back pocket.

'Take dees,' he said, handing me the flowers and smiling. 'Ur trouble u knw, Keisha. Fuckin 'ell. Man wnted 2 giv u dis.' He handed me a small blue box. I looked at him before reaching for it. The smile was still spread across his face as I hesitantly opened it. Inside was a sparkly ring. It looked like a diamond but I weren't gonna ask, I was too swept up in the moment to care what it was.

'Iz a promise ring. Das y man didn't wnt u goin thru ma drawz n shit,' Ricardo said as I stared at the ring. 'Put it on den, cum,' he said, taking the flowers from me.

I stood there, speechless. After a minute I replied, 'N-no, Ricardo. I cnt wen ur doin fingz lyk dat on ur doorstep!'

'Dnt worry abt all dat shit, Keisha. I want me n u 2 b 2geva and I'm promising u dat 1 day wer gonna do dis ting properly. I won't hav 2 do nun of dat shit, jus gimme tym. I promise u.'

I looked up at him, I believed him. He was just trying to be a man.

'U believe me, yeah? U gna put on da ring?'

'Yes Ricardo,' I replied, smiling, tears of joy streaming down my face. I put the ring on my wedding ring finger and it fit perfectly.

Ricardo pulled me into a tight hug, squashing the flowers into my chest and kissing my neck till I laughed.

'I luv u,' he whispered.

'I luv u 2,' I whispered back.

10

The sun was still shining, but the holidays were over and I was going into my second year at college. Life looked completely different. I was with Ricardo. He'd given me a ring. Shan was preggers. Rah. I'd ended up spending near enough my whole summer with Ricardo and Shanice, and though summer was officially over, I didn't want to go home and face Mum or her drinking just yet. I walked through the doors into the college foyer and saw some old faces. I went to the common room and was greeted with a couple new faces. They were standing by the door with Mrs Barkley, who was waiting to ask students if we'd take a newbie with us to class if they were on our course. I didn't want her to ask me so I quickly went over to the window seats where I usually sat with Kayla and Alisha. They were already there waiting for me. I'd missed them. We did the same course. They were from South and we had gotten close over time.

'OMG. Iz dat a ring on ur finga?' Kayla was gawping at the ring as I sat down.

'Yup,' I said proudly.

'Hus da lucky cunt den?' asked Alisha, grabbing my hand to examine it.

'Ricardo.'

'Ricardo hu? Shanice's Ricardo?' Alisha asked, dropping my hand in shock.

'Yep.' I nodded.

'Dnt lie!' they said in unision.

'Swear down,' I said.

'Where is Shanice n e way? I thought she was comin dis year?' asked Kayla, looking around.

'She's preggers. She's like two months,' I told them.

'Awwwwwwwwwwwwwwwww!' they both squealed.

'*And* she's gettin her own yard! She's in hostel now,' I gossiped excitedly.

'Oh my gosh, nah, dat is sick!' Kayla began, lifting her hand over her mouth, 'She's gonna get her yard bare quick u kn—'

'ATTENTION EVERYONE,' Mrs Barkley bellowed over the chatter. She was a tiny woman and the power in her voice didn't match her frame. Everyone would buss up in amusment at the mismatch and Mrs Barkley would wait for the room to settle; it had been like this since our first year in college.

When we fell quiet, she continued: 'Now, we have three new students joining this year. We have Rianne and Eliza,' she said, pointing to the two black girls standing awkwardly at the front of the room on her left. 'And here we have Malachi,' she said, pointing to the sexc brown-skinned yute standing on her right. Malachi's face was screwed up and he shuffled from leg to leg. He wore a white Nike t-shirt and his white string vest hung out the bottom. He was bussing low batty with some grey Nike tracksuit bottoms and some grey and white crep, and he had on a black and grey New Era cap. He looked sexxxxc. He woz tall, easily six foot, and had some sexc strong arms. His lips were thick and juicy and he kept licking them. He had a professional shape-up that you could see under his tilted New Era.

I caught him spying me in the back with my girls. Mrs Barkley carried on pairing the new students up with people from last year when our eyes met. He licked his soft, thick lips. I smiled. He smiled back, showing perfect pearly white teeth.

'Keisha man, n e wayz, wenz da weddin?' asked Kayla, totally snapping me out of my trance.

'Huh . . . O, da weddin . . . I duno,' I fumbled, not bothering to inform her it was a promise ring.

As we continued to chatter, I spotted Malachi being paired with Karl and he sat down just by the lockers where Karl and Paulo, the guys that me, Kayla and Alisha usually jammed with, were always cotching.

'Wha gwarn, u kl,' said Karl.

'Kool kool kool,' replied Malachi, his deep sexc voice rumbling. He spudded both Karl and Paulo as he spoke. 'Yo fam, ur Jamal's bredrin, init?' Paulo inquired.

'Yeah cuz,' Malachi replied coolly.

'Ah skeen . . . where is he?' Paulo asked.

'I fink he's comin later u kno.'

'U kno hw dt fool iz, gt 2 much p 2 worry wit bein on time 4 no bludclart EMA at da end of da week,' Karl said.

'Tru say, tru say,' Malachi replied.

'Oh yeah, lemme introduce u 2 our laydees,' Paulo said, turning to face me, Alisha and Kayla over on the other side of the room.

'Oi, fat hedz, cum ere,' Paulo called across to us. He was such an attention seeker and was always getting into it with Kayla. We all thought Paulo liked her, but Kayla swore up and down it could never happen. 'He's so pale and skinny man, neva!' she'd grimace.

'Wot?' Kayla shot back, annoyed.

'Ders sum1 I wnt u 2 meet, abat "wot",' Paulo said, turning back to his boys and screwing up his face. 'Abat she's tryna boy man,' he continued to mumble.

We went over to the table they were cotching on. I ended up with a seat next to Malachi. He was looking at me as I sat down. I felt heat creeping into my cheeks and I had to stop myself from bussing up.

'Dis iz Malachi, u lot. Jamal's bredrin,' said Karl.

Karl and Jamal were a year older than all of us. I'd known Karl since secondary school through Shanice and Ricardo. He was in the year below Ricardo at their all-boys school near Old Street and had become one of Ricardo's youngers. Karl had one foot firmly in the roads and the other, perhaps less so, in his education, his rationale being that he had to look after his Mum and his little brother since his Dad had been deported.

'Hi,' Alisha said.

'Hi,' Kayla said.

'Hey.' I smiled.

'Kool kool kool,' he said back – nodding at each of us.

An awkward silence descended and again I had to stop myself from giggling. Malachi sat back in his chair, slouching, and I could feel him letting his eyes scan over me. I started to doubt how buff I'd decided I looked before leaving the house as he continued silently surveying me. Feeling summery when I woke up to the sun high in the sky, I'd put on my white shorts, black Air Force 1s and a black and white Rocawear top. I had my hair up in a ponytail, and large hoop earrings in. I had on a gold chain with a diamond crucifix, and my favourite rings on, including the one Ricardo got me, of course. When I couldn't resist glancing over at Malachi to try and decipher what he was thinking or what he was observing, our eyes met and the smile on his lips widened and he coolly looked away. He put his arm around the back of my chair and slouched further down in his. He took his other hand and put it down the front of his trousers. 'He's sooo sexxxc,' my mind screamed.

'Na, but where's Jamal? It's the first day u knw,' Kayla laughed, breaking the silence.

'Why u on to Jamal, blud?' Paulo teased.

'Why are *you* on *me* for, P?!' Kayla retorted, rolling her eyes.

'Ahhh! The lovers are at it agen,' Karl taunted, going to tickle Kayla.

'Low it, man. Nah, low dat,' Paulo whined, pretending to be more affronted than he was.

'U lot need 2 fix up man,' Alisha laughed, shaking her head at the silliness.

'U get me,' I said, agreeing with her.

'Yeah, I get u,' Malachi muttered, trying to catch my attention. I let out a laugh and glanced at him, amused by his wit.

'Arrrgh man, I'm slippin today I swear dwn,' Malachi grumbled out of the blue, snapping me out of my thoughts about him. He'd definitely caught my eyes lingering on him as he went on: 'Man couldn't b bovad dis mornin, man.'

'Ay, Jamal! Cum ere fam,' shouted Paulo over the noise of the common room.

Jamal came over, greeting everyone with gender-accordant spuds and hugs as the bell rang. The common room began to empty as people punctually made their way out for their morning classes. We hung back, rummaging in our bags and taking the time to finally study our timetables and work out where we actually needed to be.

'We all got Software Design init,' Karl said.

'Yeah, wot teacher hav u got 4 dat?' I asked.

Everyone studied their new timetables, and after a while we realised that everyone had the same teacher for most of the course except me and Malachi. We had Mrs Jet, and everyone else had Mr White. Mrs Jet's classroom was all the way at the other end of the corridor.

'Ite, cum den, Keisha,' Malachi said as I looked over the rest of my timetable, cross-referencing it with Alisha's.

'Ite. Bless u lot, c u all 18r,' I said.

I felt nervous walking with Malachi. Our trainers sqeaked against the freshly cleaned lino as we walked through the never-ending corridor in silence. 'What if I slip, trip and buss up ma lip?' I kept thinking over and over, being careful to focus on each step I was taking. I was leading the way slightly as Malachi was new and had no clue where he was going, adding to the import-ance of me getting this walk right. Suddenly, he pulled gently at my arm to get my attention. I jumped ever so slightly, so consumed by my concentration.

'Keisha?'

I turned around to face Malachi. 'Ur a peng ting u kno,' he started, cradling one fist in his palm. 'Ur wifey material, man. Definitely. So, man jus wanted 2 kno r u on a linkin ting?'

'Um . . . N . . . I'm engaged,' I stumbled. 'You're not engaged, idiot,' my brain shouted back immediately.

'Ur wot?' he asked in shock, grabbing my hand to confirm what I'd told him. 'Rahhhhh,' he said when he clocked the ring.

'Well, not like officially but lyk . . .' My voice trailed off and I smiled weakly. I felt dumb and embarrassed. I was saying two different things in very quick succession, but also I think I liked this boy a bit. I was confused.

Malachi just stood staring at me.

'Dat rings bare official. R u happy doe?' he asked increduously.

'Yeah yeah, I'm bless,' I said convincingly, remembering myself.

Of course I was happy. I loved Ricardo; he'd done *so* much for me. I'd be lying if I said that I didn't like what I saw with this Malachi breh, and as I contemplated it he weren't really on road if he was in college.

'R u sure doe?' he said, stepping closer to me. He placed his hands round my waist and pulled me closer to him. I moved his hands away.

'Yeah, I'm sure, an low it plz,' I said, shaking my head.

'Y?' he asked, trying to place his hands back where they'd been.

'I've gt a man,' I said quietly as he tried for the third time to hold me close.

'I can sense ur nt fully happy doe,' he sed.

'Get to class now, the pair of you! No hanky-panky in the corridors!' shouted Mr Thorn out of the blue.

We quickly bopped off, Malachi following my lead.

11

As the weeks progressed, Malachi's passes got more frequent and more intense. He knew I had a man, he even had an idea of who Ricardo was via Karl, I was sure. But he didn't seem to care. I threatened him time and time again that I would tell Ricardo about his passes, but he'd grin and say, 'No u won't,' and he was right.

Things with Ricardo were good. Better. We hadn't talked about his plans to stop shotting or the future or anything, but when I tried to bring it up a few weeks back, he'd promised we'd start sorting it when I left college. Sex was better. I felt less like I wanted to hide, and more able to access the pleasure again. But at the same time, I had to admit to niggling thoughts that seemed to invade my mind when Malachi explained databases to me, or boasted about his distinction in the last assignment, and I'd start wondering if Ricardo would ever come off the roads. In the moments that Malachi stepped in to pay for my croissant when Mr White let us leave early on a Thursday morning, I'd wonder could I fall for Malachi and what if I couldn't stay loyal?

I had to admit I enjoyed Malachi's attention as much as I warned him off, and some days the only thing stopping me giving in to his advances was the label that'd followed me around.

The day I lost my virginity, I didn't think I would *crave* sex or want to do it on the regular.

It just happened randomly one day. I'd gone to link one guy called Gabriel from West. We'd met on Face-pic and started chatting on the phone every night. He begged me to come see him in Warwick Avenue. I didn't even know where that was. He gave me in-depth directions that I wrote down on A4 paper and carried with me that day. Shanice and Cleo followed me to the shop to buy a Travelcard. I'd never bought one before. Apart from two trips to the museum in primary school I vaguely remembered, I'd never even been on the tube. I sat on this old, rickety tube train, carefully reading every single Underground station sign emblazoned on the platforms it stopped at until I got to Warwick Avenue.

Gabriel looked just like his pics – curly hair, almond-shaped eyes set below thick dark eyebrows, and thin patches of bum fluff – and took me to the tallest, greyest tower block I'd ever seen. He led me up a dreary staircase that stank on some floors and held the faint tolerable smell of plastic and garbage on others. We settled on what must've been the eighth floor and, after chatting and bussing jokes for hours and hours and hours, I ended up sat on the edge of a block step with his jacket beneath my naked bum, one leg in one leg out of my trousers, losing my virginity. Despite agreeing that we were 'going out' now upon parting ways back at the tube station, I didn't feel like calling Gabriel after that day. And apparently, he didn't feel like calling me either.

A week later, I wanted to do it again. Reece churpsed me. He was cute – not chung or bare buff. He had a nice smile, sharp cheekbones and always had the latest crep and garms without fail. He was just short. Not shorter than me, but too close to my height for my taste. He had been on me for time and kept trying to broach the topic of me and him linking, but I'd always managed to avoid giving him my MSN or number.

As usual I was walking through the ends and a group of boys were cotching by the cage.

'Oi, Keisha. Cum ere 4 a sec,' shouted Reece. Normally I'd keep it short and sweet.

I walked over to him slow. 'Yeah?'

'Manz bin watchin u 4 tymmmm lyk, lemme get ur numba or suttin init,' he pleaded, looking me up and down.

'Yeah, ite den,' I said as I took his phone in my hand. From the look that flashed across his face, he couldn't believe his luck.

'So, wher u goin nw?' he asked after I saved my number and handed him back his 3410.

'Nowher. Got any ideas?' I flirted, cocking my head and licking my lips.

Reece's eyes could've popped out of his head, as he got the message loud and clear.

'My yard?'

'Sounds good,' I replied quietly.

'Follow me,' he said, turning around.

I followed him to his yard. He opened the door with his keys and led me in. He closed the door behind us and stared at my perky breasts as he slipped past me. I followed him across the small flat to his box room. He dashed down his keys on his messy desk in the corner and took off his t-shirt, kicked off his crep and turned to face me. He stepped over to me and held me around my waist and we started kissing. His mouth tasted like the gum in a jawbreaker and his tongue was dry and forceful as he pushed it in and out of my mouth.

He lifted my top over my head, then undid my bra and clawed the straps off my shoulders. He moved his lips from mine and started on my breasts. He simultaneously squeezed and bit my nipples making them harden. I unbuckled his belt and undid the buttons on his jeans. They dropped to the floor and he stepped out of them. He started kissing my lips again and caressing my breasts. He moved his hands down my stomach to my shorts and undid them. They dropped to the floor and he pushed his hand into my knickers and started gliding the palm over my already wet pussy. Ignoring my clit, he then pushed two fingers into me. I started moaning loudly as he moved them in and out faster and faster. He took them out before I started to feel any tingles and he took hold of my hand, leading me two steps to his bed. He lay down and I mounted him confidently even though this was about to be my first time on top. As he entered me I let out a sigh and he grunted, whispering, 'You're so tight.'

I didn't know what to do, so I started bouncing up and down on his dick with all of my strength. His eyes flew open and he spat, 'Oh fuck.' Before I could slow down he groaned, 'I'm gonna buss.' I felt his whole body tense beneath me and before I knew it he was politely rolling over, forcing me to get off of him.

'Hu taught u dat?' he panted.

One Tuesday afternoon at college I made my way to class when Malachi came running up behind me, slapping my bum. I couldn't help but smile – he caught me by serious surprise.

'Double lesson init,' he said, lookin down at me.

'Yup,' I replied.

'Oi. Cum we bunk. Hav u even dun her hwk?'

'Wot hwk?' I gasped. Mrs Jet was one of the strictest, bitchiest IT teachers in the whole college. If you failed to do her homework even once that was you staying behind for as long as it took to complete it.

'Exactly. I only found out 2day so I ain't dun it either.'

'Yeah, we betta jus bunk 4 real. I ain't got tym to stay behind today, man.'

I led us up to a classroom on the third floor that was being redecorated. It was nearly done and we could hide properly because the newspaper was still up over the glass in the door. Malachi closed the door behind him and locked it. I sat on a table. We jammed there chatting about music and listening to tracks on our phones. Eventually, Malachi got onto the subject of 'me an him'.

'U kno I propa lyk u init, Keisha.'

'So u say,' I replied, rolling my eyes. I liked the playful attention, but I was tired of the serious conversations Malachi tried to have with me about his feelings, because how many times was I going to repeat myself?

'Na, I'm bein ova serious. Y dnt u jus giv man a chance lyk?'

'Coz I'm in love n I'm engaged 4 d 100th tym,' I said sternly, looking him directly in the eye.

'Mans got deep feelins for u doe. Ona level, Keisha, I'm slippin rite now, bare spillin out ma feelinz n shit rite abat now, n man lyk me dnt usually do dem 1z, u gt me. But das how much I'm feelin u n das how much I want u to giv man a chance.'

I could hear in his voice and see in his eyes that he was being genuine. I felt guilt wash over me.

'I can't,' I whispered.

'U can,' he shot straight back. 'U can do n e ting if u put ur mind 2 it, Keisha.'

'No, not dis, Malachi.'

We sat in silence for a bit.

Malachi broke the silence again. 'I kno u gt ur man n everyfin, Keisha.' He sounded resolved. 'Man has to tell u how I feel doe. Ur perfect man, u don't undastand. Ur blessed, Keisha, man. I propa want u 2 giv me a chance but I get why ur not tryna hear man.'

Guilt was consuming me. No one had ever told me I was perfect, or described me as blessed. I couldn't help but want him to tell me more. To tell me in what ways I was blessed, and what about me he thought was perfect. How persistent and confident he was in wanting me to give him a chance made me wonder in that moment how much more Malachi might have to offer me. Confusion and guilt whirred around my chest and head.

'Malachi I-I-I . . .' I stammered.

'Shhhh. No wrdz needed,' he whispered, reaching over and placing a finger on my lips. He moved closer and closer and I knew what was coming. I could have stopped it if I wanted. But I didn't want to. So I allowed his lips to touch mine.

I let his tongue in.

I allowed him.

Just this once . . . ?

12

'Oii! Keisha!' Malachi shouted down the corridor as I emerged from my last lesson.

'Oh shit,' I mumbled under my breath. I had been trying to avoid him all day but he'd caught me. I hadn't seen him since yesterday. I felt awkward and didn't know what I'd say after that kiss.

I'd made an excuse to leave the classroom we were hiding out in after the kiss, and faked period pain at Reception and got permission to go home.

'Wha gwarn sexc?' he said, wrapping his arms around me.

'Yeah, hi, u alrite,' I said with a fake smile as I unhooked his arms from around me.

'Woz rong wit u?' he asked, looking puzzled.

'Everyfin. Look wot happened yesterday,' I whispered, getting frustrated.

'Wot? Givin me a chance is da right choice, trus b. R u scared to lock ur man or sumfin?' Malachi asked, clearly in another world.

'WOT?' I almost shouted. 'Lock who? I ain't lockin my man. U got it all wrong.'

'Ur mine after dat kiss yesterday. I swear das wot it meant.'

'Noooooo!' I shouted in frustration. He looked surprised; he'd never seen me frustrated like

I felt in that moment. I calmed down slightly and explained, 'No, Malachi, I'm not urz. Me n Ricardo r stil 2geva n da kiss woz a big mistake an I want us to forget abat it.'

Malachi stared at me like he was trying to understand what I had just said. I waited for confirmation that he'd understood but it didn't come.

'Lyk, hw cn I b ur wifey ova 1 kiss, man?' I continued, trying to reason with him and lighten the growing awkwardness.

His face began to contort into rage, disappointment and confusion all at once. I wanted to run in the opposite direction.

'W-wot?' he sed quietly.

'Look, I'll speak 2 u l8a,' I said, and power-walked off towards the toilets. I dived inside and let out a deep sigh as I leaned against the sink. 'Big fuckin' mistake!' I chided myself under my breath.

Suddenly, the door burst open, crashing into the wall as Malachi came storming in.

'So u mean 2 fuckin tell me dat kiss didnt mean shit 2 u? Iz dat wot ur tryna say?' he screamed.

'Malachi, keep ur voice dwn,' I tried to say as firmly as possible.

'Wot da fuck u mean abat keep my bludclart voice down?' he shouted, lifting his fist to hit. As he did, a group of girls innocently came in.

Malachi quickly dropped his fist and rushed out of the toilet.

'R u alrite yeah?' one of the girls asked me.

'Yeah, yeah, I'm bless,' I said forcing a smile.

I waited a whole ten minutes before I left the toilets, and rushed to the front office looking over my shoulder. I signed out and practically ran out of the building. I was relieved when I spotted the bus approaching the stop as I arrived, dreading having to wait in case I bumped into Malachi again. I rode the bus back to Dalston and gazed out of the window ruminating on the madness. How was I going to avoid Malachi now? What if he turned my bredrins against me? What if he tried to call me a *sket* now because I'd kissed him? I couldn't risk Malachi hating me, and I didn't want him to. This was fucked. I got off at my stop.

'Shanice?' Ricardo called out from the sitting room as I let myself in with his spare key.

'No. Iz me,' I said, walking in and sitting down next to his body sprawled out on the sofa.

'Wot u doin bck home, b?' he asked, looking concerned.

'I wernt bovad wit college 2day,' I said, getting comfortable on the sofa, resting my head on Ricardo's chest.

We gazed at the TV silently.

'Whers my kiss?' Ricardo said abruptly, after some time. I lifted my head and he moved his lips to mine.

'I luv u,' he whispered.

'I luv u too,' I whispered back, feeling sick with shame and guilt.

'U kno ur 18th iz cummin up, init?'

'Yeah,' I breathed.

'Wot do u want for it?'

'Errrr . . . a car,' I joked.

'Skeen,' he said, staring at the random show on the TV.

He fell silent. Perhaps he didn't get the joke, but I had bigger things on my mind. What had happened during the day kept playing over and over in my head. I didn't wanna go back. I had no idea what I was going to do and, worse still, I couldn't tell anyone.

Later that evening as I prepared to shower, my phone rang. 'Withheld caller' flashed on the screen.

'Hello?' I answered.

'Keisha? Listen, don't lock off. Iz Malachi. Mans so so sorry about today, plz forgive me.' I wanted to drop the call immediately. 'U hav 2 undastand man's actions today buh wen we kissed I fort dat ment it woz me n u init, buh den wen u jus boied it, I woz shocked. I woz propa lookin forward 2 cummin college today. I'm bare sorry doe, Keisha.'

'Iz cool,' I responded bluntly.

'Are u sure?'

'Yeah,' I breathed. I just needed all of this to be forgotten.

'We bless now, yeah?' he asked.

Relief surged through me and I audibly released a sigh.

'We're cool, b!' I chirped.

13

'Babez, wake up,' Ricardo said, shaking me. 'Iz 8:45, ur gonna b late.'

'I aint goin in,' I groaned.

'Y not?'

'Coz . . . I'm spending da day wit Shan,' I said, opening one eye to look at him. I was definitely fibbing about any prearranged plans with Shanice, but I didn't feel like facing college *just* yet. Shanice had moved into a temporary hostel a few weeks before, so my story was believable. Though I was relieved me and Malachi were cool after speaking last night, I still felt apprehensive about facing him again. Who should say hi first? Should we still walk to classes together? Was I still going to sit next to him every lesson? And what about asking him for help with databases? There was too much to contemplate and decide, and I couldn't be bothered today.

'Ah, skeen,' said Ricardo.

I got up and rushed to the toilet to pee and brush my teeth, returning to the bedroom to kiss Ricardo good morning with my now acceptable mouth. He knowingly pulled me into an embrace, sitting me on his lap in his desk chair. He nestled his face in my neck, and I felt silly for lying to him and getting myself into a difficult situation in the first place, all over again.

'So, ur goin out an leavin me here on ma jz,' he whispered playfully.

'Yup!' I beamed cheekily, and he bit my neck, making me squirm and giggle.

'Gellof, u animal!' I shrieked.

We laughed and kissed tenderly before I scooped up my towel and phone for the shower. I ran the shower and sat on the loo ready to send Shanice a text to let her know I was coming to see her. She wasn't allowed visitors so she'd have to be ready to meet me outside.

I switched on my phone, and as I waited for it to boot up, message after message streamed in. Who'd been trying to contact me? I wondered. Mild panic started to set in as I started to tell myself it was Mum and something had happened to her. As the screen continued flashing with text after text, I haphazardly opened them at random. Malachi had texted and called over and over and over while my phone had been off through the night. I felt heat rising around my neck as I flicked between messages that were becoming a blur. The first few I'd been able to comprehend read 'SKET' or pleaded with me to contact him, but soon the letters and numbers began to jumble and my mind pulsated with alarm.

What had changed? I didn't understand.

Through the loudness of my racing thoughts, the sound of the shower running was able to break through and I scrambled to get in and under the water before the flood of tears burst through the banks of my shock. This wasn't resolved. This was going to be a repeat of what happened after Michael, but worse. How was Ricardo going to hear me out with this one when I'd lipsed another breh? He'd doubt me on everything that had happened so far. I stood under the water as my chest heaved up and down. I had to stay in here, Ricardo couldn't see me like this. But I had to get out and see Shanice because I needed to know what to do.

'Oi, u kno dat London iz runnin outta water, init?' Ricardo called through the door, making me jump.

'I'm cumin.' I managed to scramble and soap my important bits.

I climbed out, examining my face in the mirror. My eyes looked mad. I'd gotten soap in my eyes I decided on the spot, and then phoned Shanice.

'Im cummin 2 pick u up 2 go shoppin, rite,' I said.

'Okay den. I need sum fingz for wen i go into hospital n e wayz,' she replied.

'Okay, I'll be der in lyk half an hour,' I said and hung up.

'Safe.'

Even though I had my excuse, I still tried to avoid Ricardo before leaving the house. I got dressed in the bathroom and stuffed my phone in my pocket. I was ready to go.

'BABES, I'M GNE, YEAH?' I shouted to Ricardo from the bottom step.

'Wait!' he called back. I rolled my eyes. I really wanted to avoid him, and avoid lying about the state of my eyes.

He came down the stairs with money in hand.

'Rah, wot happened 2 ur eyes? U bin crying?' he asked as he got closer to me.

'N-nah. I got soap in my eyes like a eediat. They were bare stingin,' I lied, avoiding his eyes.

'Ah, skeen. Listen, fuckin, hold dis init. Shanice needs shit. Buy ur self suttin too,' he said, pressing rolled-up notes into the palm of my hand and kissing me. I hugged him round his waist, resting my head on his chest for a lingering moment. 'Sort this out, Keisha,' was all I could think.

I bopped to Shanice's hostel over in Wells Street. I needed the time to think and also decide how much I was going to tell Shanice. Was I gonna tell her about the kiss? Was I gonna admit that I enjoyed Malachi's attention? That we were friends and he helped me and I allowed him to do nice things for me . . .

I one-ringed her when I was downstairs. As I waited, a couple shuffled out of the building. I zoned in on the girl. She wore dingy track-suit bottoms and the laces on her very creased trainers were missing. 'Yeah, we're cumin, darlin . . . Darryl! He's at the fuckin top there . . . at the Tesco yeah, darlin?' She moved between shouting into a tiny phone and at the breh she was with, who'd started marching off in the opposite direction she was apparently intending on going in. As she croaked into the phone and at Darryl, I noticed she had teeth missing and a dark scab in the middle of her lip. She'd slicked the front of her dark hair and it came down just above her eyebrow and swept back into a perfectly neat ponytail which she'd secured with several hairbands and clear bobbles. Her green eyes stood out in the daylight when she peered up at

Darryl as he approached her, mumbling under his breath. I watched the hood of her stained, pink McKenzie jacket bob up and down as it hung off of her shoulders, and they shuffled off at speed. I was wondering what had happened to green-eyed girl when Shanice came out.

'Look at ur belly!' I exclaimed, rubbing her bump. I was always surprised all over again whenever I saw Shanice's swollen belly. She was nearly five months gone now and she'd started waddling and getting out of breath when she had to climb the stairs. I gave her the money Ricardo had sent.

'Awww. He alwayz lookin afta us, init!' She grinned.

'Yeah,' I sang back, a sick feeling washing over me once more. I took a deep breath, reassuring myself that I'd chat to Shanice about it and we'd find a solution together.

We set off for the West End. It was the only place we'd find the biggest and best high street stores to make sure baby got only the best. It was quieter than usual, with most people at work, school or college. The shops on Oxford Street were bursting with the latest in fashion. Every window-display mannequin rocked smart shirts, puffa jackets, chunky gold jewellery, waist belts, neon tights and big-frame geek glasses.

Shanice and I shuffled in and out of shops, picking out cute gender-neutral babygrows and bibs. Shanice got her maternity bag and the most buttaz nightie I'd ever seen from Marks & Spencer. We tested prams, and agreed that Shanice looked buffest with the Mamas & Papas one.

'Kareem sed he's gonna buy da pram in January. Maybe it will go on sale, alie?' she told me as we left Debenhams. We'd had so much fun that I'd forgotten my problems, and almost forgotten about the serious conversation I needed to have with her. We'd bought large milkshakes from McDonald's and strolled our way to Soho as we chatted and drank. Shanice said she needed to make sure she could keep it down before getting on the Underground and vomiting everywhere.

'Iz better if I vomit on da street, alie?'

'True say,' I reasoned, hoping she didn't vomit at all because I definitely didn't have time for that.

We walked the narrow streets, bemused by the sex shops and gay-club promoters parading around in skimpy clubwear in broad daylight.

'Let me jus breav for a min, Keish. Fuck man, I get tired so quick u know,' Shanice said, leaning up against a bollard. This was my opportunity to broach the subject. I stood, slurping my milkshake, mustering up the courage to begin the difficult conversation that'd let my best friend know that I was a top dickhead, when I noticed a tattoo shop across the street.

'Do u dare me 2 get a tattoo?' I said before I realised it.

'Yeah! . . . Double dare,' she said, grinning.

'Ite den.'

We wandered into the tiny parlour. The walls were black, filled with Polaroid pictures of tattoos and piercings. The woman behind the counter had bright pink hair and a massive rose tattoo in the middle of her chest.

'Can I get a tattoo done today?' I asked, realising I wasn't sure *what* I should be asking.

'Yeah, course,' she chirped cheerily, and smiled to expose her perfect teeth, both of which I hadn't expected. 'Do you know what you want?' she asked gently.

'Yeah,' I lied. She held my gaze, waiting for me to tell her. 'A heart an da name "Ricardo",' I said on the spot.

'Okay. Do you know how you'd like it to be designed?' she asked, tilting her head.

'Umm . . . yeah. Like . . .' As I attempted to conjure up a quick image in my head, my eyes wandered, landing on a Polaroid image of a heart tattoo with the name 'Ramona' written in cursive font along the top. 'Like that, there,' I said, pointing at it.

'Oh-kay.' She nodded slowly, very aware that I'd made up my mind on the spot. 'Follow me then . . . is your friend coming?' she said, gesturing towards a heavy velvet curtain that hung behind her.

Two and a half hours later, we emerged back onto the streets of Soho.

'I hope ur gonna b holdin up ma hand lyk dat wen dis baby's ready 2 pass thru,' Shanice laughed as we made our way towards the station.

'Of course I will. Nah, dat *hurt* doe u know. Buh alie iz sexc!' I didn't have a solution for my problems and I still had to face Malachi on Monday, but I was in better spirits, feeling like I'd done something to prove my love for Ricardo.

Shanice and I rode the bus back to the bits from Seven Sisters, parting ways in Dalston where she waddled off, bags in tow, to catch a second bus to her hostel.

I walked towards Ricardo's, wondering if I should've still had the conversation with Shanice, but sure that the tattoo was a good choice all the same. I let myself in with the spare key and found Ricardo in the living room finishing off a call.

'Safe, broski. Man owe you, nah, love.' He dropped the phone, grinning excitedly.

'Wot woz all dat abat?' I inquired.

'I might have a job lined up at a car show-room! Dat woz Fareed, from Bow side. His bruva works der, said he's sortin out a interview for me for next week b!' Ricardo relayed excitedly. I hugged him, beaming. He hugged me tight.

'I'm so proud of u,' I told him as we embraced.

'I wanted it to be a surprise at first, but fuck it. I might have a job!' He was so excited. I was genuinely over the moon but a part of me couldn't help but feel even more stupid. I'd attempted to compare Malachi and Ricardo at one point, telling myself that Malachi being legit was part of the allure. Look at this. Ricardo might have a whole big-boy job.

'I've got a surprise too.'

'Wot?' Ricardo smirked, unsure whether to take me seriously.

'Yeah . . . close ur eyez,' I said, getting up to stand in front of him.

'Wot, woz dis girl on?' he said, reluctantly placing his hands over his eyes.

'Don't peek you know, Ricardo,' I said, unzip-ping my jeans to prematurely remove the dressing over my new body art. 'Okay, you can open ur eyez.'

Ricardo's eyes opened wide like saucers and his jaw dropped. 'Oiii!' he shouted, getting up from the sofa and pulling me into a tight hug.

'Oi, my gyal got ma name tatted on 'er,' he said, over and over. I gushed with pride. He was so happy. I was so happy I'd made him happy.

I hoped it'd be enough for him if shit hit the fan.

14

It was Monday morning and time to face college. I left Ricardo in the bed asleep, showered and found something to wear. I put on my black and white Adidas Respect M.E. tracksuit, all-black crep, and accessorised with my black Just Do It bag. I gave myself a side part and slicked my hair back into a low ponytail, decorating my hairline with shapes I created with the rattail comb and Eco Styler gel.

I arrived at college early and met Kayla and Alisha in the common room. They were sitting by the window opposite the door – our spot for when we needed to convene away from the boys. Though I was relieved they were in early with me, I knew they were sitting by the window to talk about Malachi, and my heart skipped.

'KEISHAAAA!' they both shouted in unison as I bopped in. I was comforted by their cheeriness – perhaps whatever they might have to report back wasn't that bad, I thought to myself as I walked across the common room.

'Where hav u bin, man?' Kayla asked as I approached.

'At home, init. I wernt bovad 2 cum college, man . . .' I said, smiling, willing them to hurry up and broach the Malachi conversation.

'Mmmmm,' grinned Alisha. 'Is that so?' she said, raising her eyebrows. What did she mean by that? I tried to smile.

'So, how iz Shanice?' asked Kayla.

'She's kool. I woz wit 'er on Friday we went up West. I gt a tattoo you know. U lot wnna see?' I said. Why was I changing the conversation, my mind asked me.

'Yeah man, let's see,' enthused Kayla.

I stood up and adjusted my tracksuit bottoms to show them.

They both cooed.

I smiled, covering back up, and sat down.

'So, ur ova serious den, Keisha?' Alisha asked me.

'Yeah man. Ova serious lyk . . . I propa luv him you know, you lot,' I said earnestly, making sure to make eye contact with the both of them. I needed them to believe me.

'Nah, nah, I can tell. Ur in luv propa, but wot u gonna do about Malachi doe?' Kayla said.

'Wot do you mean?' I quizzed, assessing what conversation we were about to have.

'We heard sumfin abat him from Jamal, Keisha. An he's bin movin abit . . .' She contorted her jaw and made her eyes bulge.

'Yeah, you got him SPRUNG,' Alisha jumped in.

'Wot did you hear?' I asked, my heart pounding gently, unsure if I even wanted to know.

'Jamal sed Malachi went away, lyk, to hospital,' she said, leaning in, speaking in a hushed tone.

'Yeah, you know he's one year olda. He missed a year coz he woz in da hospital,' Alisha chimed in.

I couldn't believe what I was hearing. The only people unwell enough for hospital admission talked to themselves. And they certainly weren't one of the mandem. Malachi was young and buff and had nice garms. He got distinctions. This didn't make sense.

'Iz mad, init?' Alisha said, watching me closely.

'Nah, but . . . wot woz he in hospital for?' I stumbled over my words, still registering.

'Jamal wouldn't tell us. He sed bussin dat would be too snakey,' Kayla said matter of factly. My scepticism and confusion only grew with that omission.

'Anywayz, he needs to forget abat me lyk . . . alie doe?' I said, trying to convince myself and them that it was going to be that simple. Before I could be affirmed, the common room door opened and Malachi walked in. He looked like he hadn't ironed his t-shirt and his hat was pulled down low, not how he usually had it tipped to show off a fresh shape-up. As soon as he came in, our eyes met. I looked away quickly and it felt as though tension filled the entire room. I was sure Malachi's eyes were still on me, but I dared not look over at the door again. Though I was staring at them, I couldn't process what Kayla or Alisha were doing or saying.

'Cum bruv,' I heard Karl say, bringing me back into the room. He'd come in behind Malachi.

'Wha gwarn, you lot,' he called to us and made his way over to the corner, knowing not to disturb our very important conversation. Malachi followed.

A few moments later, Mrs Barkley burst into the common room and shouting at us to get moving for lessons and not to wait for the bell, then hurried out, all flustered. We got ourselves together and rose from our chairs slowly. I felt at ease because my first lesson was with Kayla and Alisha, so I had them to walk with. As we approached the common room door, Karl jogged over.

'Lemme chat to u, Keish.' I sensed the gravity in his tone and he didn't bother addressing Kayla and Alisha.

'I'll meet you lot,' I told them, and followed Karl back over to my, Kayla and Alisha's conference space to sit down. The common room emptied and I spied Malachi leaving with Paulo. This was Karl all over – the big, responsible brother. I felt a combination of ease and relief that Karl was apparently stepping in to sort this situation, and fit to bust with enquiries about what Kayla and Alisha had just disclosed.

'Karl, wotz dis about Malachi? Wotz rong wiv him? I mean—' I babbled, shutting up abruptly so Karl could actually answer my many questions.

'Wot? Did Kayla an Alisha tell u?'

'Yeah lyk, wot woz he in for?' I asked quietly

'Man don't know. Jamal won't tell man. But Keisha, ur sendin out da rong signalz. I know abat da kiss, but dese tyms you've got a hubby. U need to set Malachi straight, if u had dun dat from da beginning, u wudnt b in dis shit right now.' My heart sank slightly with guilt and disappointment that Karl didn't know any more than the girls.

'I kno, Karl, but I lyked him I'm nt gnna lie, but I fort it woz jus abit of fun. I didn't know all dis would happen,' I said, feeling desperate. The bell sounded.

'Everyfins gonna be bless, don't worry. Jus don't send wrong signals no more. You better go to ur lesson doe, Keish,' he said as we stood. He reached and enveloped me in a warm, reassuring hug.

'Fank you, Karl,' I said appreciatively. I felt reassured by Karl's last words. 'Can I ask you sumfin, Karl?'

'Go on,' he said, picking up his bag. The common room was empty now.

'Do u fink I'm a sket?' I believed Karl would tell me the truth, he didn't know the ins and outs of my history but he was probably the safest person to ask as he knew about the kiss and the 'friendship' I'd developed with Malachi.

'Nah, Keish, I don't,' he said earnestly. I felt like I could breathe again ever so slightly.

'Fank you, Karl. I luv u man.' He gave me another hug and we made our way to class.

Lunch was welcome after a long morning of back-to-back lessons. I met Kayla and Alisha in the common room and we headed to the chicken and chip shop on the high street for lunch like we did every Monday. I got my number 3 meal – chicken wrap, chips and a Sprite, like always. Slurping our still-full tins of fizzy, we walked back to college and signed back in at reception. Looking slightly out of place, Malachi loitered in the lobby. I avoided his eyes and walked past him, pretending I hadn't seen him. I signed in, chattering away with Alisha and Kayla, who

I heard greet him as I bent down to sign my name. Anxiety crept in as I wondered why he was standing there. And where was Karl?

I had one more lesson before I was done for the day. As soon as the bell went, I headed to the main entrance and signed out. Today had been okay, I admitted. I strolled to the bus stop, reasoning with myself – the last thing I needed to overcome was a lesson with just myself and Malachi, where we sat next to one another, but today had left me feeling some-what confident that I'd overcome that hurdle when it came.

I turned onto the street and jumped. Malachi was standing right there as though waiting. Our eyes locked. 'Oh shit, oh shit,' ran through my head. Pretending I hadn't seen him was out. Before I could contemplate another option, my feet continued moving, carrying me past him.

He grabbed hold of my arm.

'Wot? You can't say hello, nah?' he spat.

'You alrite?' I uttered, unable to move.

'Why you tryna air man? Why did you turn off ur phone?' he questioned me, clearly offended.

'Please let go of me,' I managed. I had no idea how it sounded, but shock and fear was surging through me.

'Fuck off den,' he spat, throwing my arm back to me.

I practically ran off, bolting straight past my bus stop and heading to the next one to get as far away from him as possible.

When I got to Ricardo's, the house was empty. To remedy my surprisingly decent day that had turned sour, I sprawled on the sofa and turned on the TV. Some hours later, Ricardo came in, Chinese food in tow. I smiled when I saw him, feeling like relief and safety had arrived.

'Wot u smilin at? Me or da food?' he said, feigning suspicion.

'You,' I laughed, sitting up. He kissed me before settling on the sofa next to me, handing me my Chinese – a bag of 'ur narsty' mini spring rolls, prawn chow mein, and sweet and sour chicken Hong Kong style.

'Cum. We gotta discuss wha gwarn for ur 18th u kno,' he said, cracking open one of his containers. Ricardo's excessive Chinese order consisted of sweet and sour chicken balls, special fried rice, spare ribs, and salt and pepper wings.

'Okay.' I bit into a spring roll, not in much of a birthday-planning mood.

'So . . . do u want a shubz or wot?'

I shrugged.

'I swear u sed dis. You an Shan . . . for ur 18th. You both sed . . .' he insisted between chunks of deep fried chicken ball.

'Yeah, nah, I do . . .' I couldn't tell him I wasn't in much of a celebratory mood because I'd flirted and lipsed my way into a very sticky situation with another guy.

'Rite. So, das DJ, food, drink . . . das it rly. I'm gonna get you invitations printed tomorrow.' He reached for the remote and switched the channel.

I tried to enjoy my food and focus on the *My Wife and Kids* episode on the TV, but my thoughts whirred round. I didn't deserve a party planned by Ricardo. Today didn't go well, and the Malachi stuff wasn't 'bless' yet.

My birthday was in three weeks. By then, I had to bless things with Malachi, I told myself.

On Wednesday, I stood in the common room at college with Kayla and Alisha, selectively handing out invites. Every invitation decision was made via three-way consultation, with me having the last word.

'Shud I invite Malachi?' I asked them. In my bid to finally bless things, I wondered if an olive branch was the smarter option.

'NO! Dat crazy-ass fool,' Alisha shot back.

'But he's gnna find out abat it anyway, den he myt get even more vex coz u didnt invite him,' Kayla reasoned.

'Yeah, das tru,' Alisha agreed.

'Okay, so I'm invitin him den. He mite not even come, alie?' I said, trying to convince myself, knowing full well he'd be there.

Malachi walked in moments later as if he knew he was being discussed. I gave an invitation to Kayla and she went over and gave it to him. I watched him as he opened the envelope, read it and smiled. He looked over, meeting my eyes and nodded. I smiled back politely. I wanted to feel relief but apprehension and uncertainty filled me. I just hoped I'd made the right decision.

15

It was November 17th. The day of my eighteenth birthday shubz had come round quick and I was excited. I'd gone to visit Mum the day before. Since I'd started staying at Ricardo's seven days a week most weeks, I hardly saw Mum anymore and even though I worried about her, I felt free of stress for the first time in as far back as I could remember.

Most of my positive memories growing up were of birthdays. Mum always tried to do what she could to make them special, and my eighteenth was no exception. When I crept in the house,

Mum was carefully lifting a cake out of the oven with her tatterd red oven mits.

'Keisha!', she squealed. She set it down and shuffled over to me excitedly, drawing me into a hug. Her hair was scraped back in a neat bun and she was wearing a green blouse. She'd made an effort for me. She ushered me over to the kitchen table impatiently and handed me a small gift wrapped in silver paper. I opened the package as she beamed down at me curiously lifting a black velvet jewlerry box lid. Inside was a thick solid gold heart shaped pendant with a 'K' engraved on it.

'Look on the back!' Mum insisted. I lifted it out of the box and read the tiny engraving. *'Mum loves you'* was etched on the back.

'I'll get you a chain to put it on soon', Mum babbled but I was more taken aback by the tears stinging the back of my eyeballs. I reached for her and burrowed my head in her slightly boney chest, grateful for her today and wishing she was like this everyday.

We ate cake and watched DVDs, and she didn't pour herself a drink for my birthday.

But tonight, the party was set to start at 8:30. I'd spent all day resting and being pandered to by Ricardo.

'U lookin forward to tonite?' he asked from his desk chair as I lay on the bed.

'Yeah.' I smiled.

'Got tym for a quickie?' he quipped, a mischevious smile on his face.

'No, der ain't no tym for no quickie, you horny child,' I laughed.

I play-fought my way out of the bedroom to get in the bath Ricardo had run for me. I undressed in the humid bathroom, hearing the faint clank and scrape of pots from downstairs where Shanice and Mighty's cousin organised food prepared by Mighty's granny.

I slipped into the bath and lay back. I envisioned how the night was going to go. I anticipated all of the compliments from my friends. I looked forward to clamouring into the middle to skin out in time for a heavy bass drop. I couldn't wait to grind my behind into Ricardo's crotch, and for his friends to scream their affirmative 'braps'.

I cleared the steamed mirror to begin loosening my doo-doo plaits and meticulously detangle my birthday twist-out. I heard Ricardo climbing the stairs.

'An stop eatin da fuckin jerk chicken, Shanice blud,' he called. I grinned knowingly.

In that moment, I felt at home. I felt part of a whole.

I emerged from the bathroom with my best twist-out to date framing my minimally made-up face – eyeliner, mascara, and lip gloss was the whole 9. I'd found a strappy black Morgan dress in TK Maxx last week. The shiny ruched material hugged me, feeling fitting for my inauguration into womanhood. I'd had my feet and hands worked on by Dalston's best and, despite the hour wait, the diamantés 'Katie' had insisted sticking on my nails for free had made it worthwhile.

'Ohhhh shit! Ma wifeys tryna get pregnant 2day!' Ricardo squealed as I came into the bedroom.

'Shuut up! No babies yet,' I laughed.

'We have to have a quickie, man?' he said, standing behind me and pressing himself against my bum.

'No, man. Ur gonna mash up ma hair.' I turned around and touched the button on his Stone Island shirt.

'U kno u look beautiful' he told me, kissing my forehead.

'Fank u.' I blushed. 'Ur lookin very nice urself.' I smiled, stepping back. Ricardo playfully checked himself out in the mirror, and we laughed.

Downstairs, friends milled around with paper plates balancing portions of curry goat and rice and peas and coleslaw. Ricardo's boys shuffled in and out, clutching bottles of E&J and Alize, answering calls on brick phones that they had to slip out to take. Girlfriends from school and college and endz donned a collection of skimpy skirts and dresses, accessorised with thick metallic waistbelts giving every shape an hour-glass illusion, or strappy belly tops paired with jeans jazzed up with stitchwork and diamanté. They huddled together and self conciously lifted unsatisfactory portions of rice and peas into their mouths on plastic forks. The mandem swaggered through, self-assured, clothed in variations of Goggle Jackets and Boxfresh Varsities, overwhelming the senses with chatter and laughter and Versace Blue Jeans and pungent high-grade and shiny Pradas and bright stitchwork on their dark True Religion jeans.

By 10 p.m., the house, the porch and the pavement outside were buzzing.

Kayla and Alisha sauntered in, feeling slightly out of place as they anticipated being the only South Londoners in attendance.

'Keishaaa! Awww, look at youuu,' they cooed when they spotted me, rushing over to hug me, plastic bags sagging with Lambrini and heels lodged between us as we nestled in a warm group embrace.

The night progressed. Better than I'd imagined in the bath earlier, I was high on compliments and hugs, being hailed up and my cup being generously refilled. The DJ had the mandem screaming the lyrics to Lethal Bizzle's 'Pow! (Forward)' and the gyaldem, warm and relaxed with alcohol, bubbling to Anthony B's 'Tease Her'.

I'd spied Malachi.

In the weeks after giving him an invite to the party, things had calmed. We'd been in Mrs Jet's lessons and shared the odd free period. We'd cultivated a friendly distance, and though I remained mindful of his capacity to switch, my anxieties were being pacified day by day. When Jamal reared his head at college after nine days absent, I'd forgotten about quizzing him about Malachi's time away.

'Keisha,' I heard behind me.

'Oh, hi. Fanks 4 cummin.' I turned around to see Malachi. I leaned in, offering him a short, friendly hug.

'U look . . . beautiful,' he said, stepping back from the embrace, looking me up and down. I felt mildly uncomfortable by the compliment.

'Fanks.' I smiled, turning to give my attention elsewhere. Malachi grabbed my arm, his tight grip causing my focus to snap back to him. He sensed my alarm and released my arm, holding his hands up in surrender.

Through the night I forgot about Malachi. I danced, and laughed, and drank, replacing the space I'd otherwise have to ruminate on his earlier behaviour.

Ricardo found me dancing among my girls and tapped me on my shoulder, motioning to me to follow him. We maneuvered through the crowd to where the DJ had set up. Ricardo signalled to him and the DJ cut off the music and handed Ricardo the mic.

'WHA GWARN EVERYBODY? Oi, come we sing 'appy birfday to da birfday girl.' The room broke out in tone-deaf, well-intentioned song. I beamed at the enthusiasm as people swayed along and held up drinks and lighters, illustrating the genuineness of their wishes.

'Ite, ite, now everyone come outside,' Ricardo announced over the mic when the singing of 'Happy Birthday' came to a close. He ushered me out of the room and through the front door. He held my hand, leading me into the middle of the road. Everyone milled around on the pavement, wondering why they'd been brought out into the cold night.

'Ite. Look dat way,' Ricardo instructed, pointing over my shoulder. I turned around expectantly, unsure of what I was looking at or for. The dull sound of a car door clicking open sounded over and over. I turned to look at Ricardo to find him repeatedly pressing a car key.

'A car?!' I shrieked and gasped.

'Ha haaa.' Ricardo jogged past me, gassed. My feet were glued in place as he pulled open the door on a little silver VW Golf, neatly parked.

Partycomers cheered and 'brapped'. My feet finally carried me over to the car to take a look. I beamed with gratitude as I repeatedly thanked and reconfirmed 'you got me a whip?' to an excited Ricardo, who simply wanted to show me and his boys the car's features.

We made our way back into the party. I was on a new high. Surrounded by friends, I danced and laughed to warm-up tunes as the DJ restarted a bashment set.

Malachi politely nudged his way into the middle of the circle that had formed round me, to hand me a card and a small gift box. I took it from him and we shared a genuine smile. I felt too happy and on a high to contemplate the past in that moment.

'Can I hav a dance?' he asked

'Ummm . . . y-yeah,' I responded, slighty caught off guard. I slipped out of the circle and Malachi led me to a corner where a table stood, placing my gift from him on it. He then turned and slipped behind me, attempting to grind up against me.

I laughed, immediately stepping away. 'Ha ha, very funny. I kno u don't fink ur gonna be grindin' up on me lyk *dat*!'

He started laughing. 'Iz dis how ur boyin man?'

I laughed, confident we were sharing a joke. 'Fanks for da gift by da way,' I called over my shoulder as I moved back into the thick of the party.

*

The bass to Beenie Man's 'One Girl' dropped, and Alisha grabbed me before I could even turn around to look for her to bruk out properly to our tune. I was lost in the whinin when Karl grabbed my shoulder.

'Cum, we affi blaze something fi yuh eart'strong!' he insisted, motioning for me to follow him. I followed, leaving my girls shocking out, unaware I'd slipped away.

Outside, Malachi sat on the neighbour's wall by himself.

'Cum we blaze something with Keisha on her birthday, cuzzy,' Karl called to Malachi out the side of his mouth, his attention focused on rolling the zoot. Malachi hopped off and bopped over.

Karl sparked up, handing me the zoot proudly. I giggled.

'Happy eart' strong, bestie,' he said, cheesing.

I took a deep pull on my birthday zoot, eager to heighten the euphoria I already felt.

'Rahhh, you can smoke like *dat*?' Malachi said, and we all bussed up laughing.

We stood in the bitter November night air, laughing and chatting and passing the zoot.

'Oi, come we take your whip for a spin. You got da key?' Karl quipped, handing Malachi the last bit of the zoot. Before thinking, I skipped over to the car, repeatedly pressing the car key excitedly.

We piled in, Malachi getting in the back, me in the passenger and Karl in the driver's seat. He started the engine and turned the radio up before pulling away into the night.

We drove through the empty Hackney streets. Streams of lights zoomed by. I gazed out of the window at the traffic lights, noticing dark figures huddled together on the corner, standing in the night air, sharing a drink or a smoke. I felt safe in the car amidst jokes and the warm air blowing from the heater.

We'd made it up to Upper Clapton.

'Cum we pull up in Stamford Hill estate and bill it,' Karl suggested.

'Yeeeeah and den roll back to my shubz,' I enthused.

We turned into the estate. Karl stopped in a deserted spot. Malachi rolled the zoot in the back when Karl's phone started ringing.

'Oi, 1 sec you lot,' he said, getting out the car.

'I bet its a gyal,' I said to Malachi, watching Karl smile as he talked into the phone.

I gazed out at the shadowy blocks. The windows set uniformly in white frames standing out in the dark.

He joined us back in the car minutes later, not mentioning the call. We got through half the zoot before Karl said, 'Keisha, you drive back to Rico's.'

'What?' I said, laughing. He had to be joking.

'Come man. Don't get too lean. I'll do da gears.' He put the spliff in the ashtray and opened his door. He was serious.

'This is gonna be jokes,' Malachi said, bussing up in da back.

'Nah, you lot, on a level, I can't fuck up.' Laughter from the high and concern from the remenants of sense in my voice.

'Your gonna be alrite,' Karl said, catching the giggles. I opened my door and jogged round to the driver's side. Karl climbed over to the passenger seat and I started the engine.

'Don't let me crash you know, Karl! I swear on my life.'

'You won't, man!'

The high slowed me and I repeatedly asked Karl which pedal I should be pressing, causing both he and Malachi to laugh uncontrollably.

I made it to Dalston when Karl said, 'Oi, let me out here quickly.'

'W-what?!' I spluttered, alarmed. We were so close to Ricardo's, where was he *going*?

'Cum, Malachi, help her init. I need to go do something round here quickly. I'll come back to Rico's in like an hour,' and he was climbing out before the car had fully slowed to a stop.

Malachi climbed into the front. 'Don't worry, it's cool.'

What could I do? I had to trust him and get the car back to Ricardo's.

Malachi changed the gears, calling out which pedal I should be pressing before I asked, making the journey from Dalston toward Ricardo's easier than when Karl was helping. I relaxed.

'Turn here, Keisha,' Malachi suddenly said.

'Dis ain't da way doe,' I said, confused.

'I'm gonna piss myself. I beg you quickly pull up here,' he said, pointing to a park entrance.

'1 sec yeah,' he said, and hopped out as the car came to a stop.

I watched him jog in and disappear into the darkness.

I sat back and waited, grateful that despite a rocky few weeks, he was helping me get my eighteenth birthday present back in one piece. For the most part, he was cool, I admitted to myself.

I remembered the zoot in the ashtray and found the lighter. I got out the car and sparked it.

After a few seconds, Malachi jogged out of the park.

'U cool?'

'Yeah, cum we smoke quickly.' My high was wearing off slightly and I wanted to top it up before returning to my shubz.

'Nah, manz bless,' he declined.

I smoked and chatted with Malachi as we leaned on the bonnet.

'Keisha da smoker u know!' Malachi teased, laughing.

'Shut up, man!' I laughed. 'Can I ask you something, Malachi?'

'Go on.' He nodded.

'How cum ur so up and down? Like . . . one minute ur calm, next minute ur vex?'

'Am I?'

'Yeah man, u are! And why did u think you could whine on me at my party in my manz yard please, Malachi?' I asked, full of attitude.

Malachi laughed.

'Nah, Malachi, it's not even funny like . . .' I said, getting serious. He put his hands up in surrender.

'Ur right. Its ur birthday. I should be on my best behaviour.'

'U better! Or I'll get you rushed,' I laughed. 'Just joking.'

'Rah, isit?'

'I'm jokin, Malachi man. Low it.'

The intensity of the high was creeping up on me. My eyes felt heavy and I felt happiness wash over me.

'Can I ask you one more fing?' I drawled, leaning into the relaxed feeling that invaded my entire being. I didn't wait for Malachi to answer as I continued. 'I heard something, you know. I heard you went hospital. Wot did u go der for?'

Malachi laughed. 'Who told u dat?'

'Nah, answer my question first,' I protested, giggling.

'Whoever sed dat is chatting shit,' I heard him say. I couldn't decipher his tone but in response to his words I felt the uncontrollable urge to laugh. I laughed and laughed, indifferent to the silence. I started walking back round to the driver's side ready to get back.

'Cum we get back to my shubz. I'm going straight to da DJ and telling him to play "Goodas" so I can whine Rico. Alie my shubz is live?' I said, my eyes finally finding Malachi.

'Swear?' he said dryly. He'd not moved from the bonnet.

'Nah, come on man, he got me a car like!' I held my hands out towards the car.

'Let me piss one more time quickly.'

'Rah, again? U must have been drinking bare.'

As he made his way back into the park, I plucked my phone from my bra to see a text from Karl.

I presumed the rustling behind me was Malachi walking through the last of the autumn leaves, emerging from the park. I called out, 'Rico – I mean Malachi. Guess what Karl texted me say—'

I turned, connecting with a solid fist, and my whole world went black.

16

I awakened to black. In the deep darkness, I could hear the faint rumble of voices. I let out a faint whimper of 'help' hoping someone would hear me and help me. I ran my hands over my body as I couldn't see. I felt the fabric of my dress. I felt the wetness of my nose running. My jaw and head were pounding. I ran my hand over my face gently, feeling a stickiness on a particularly painful spot. I realised it was congealed blood. I let out another whimper: 'Help!'

Suddenly, a click filled the room and then light. I looked around, trying to identify my surroundings. The space was vast. The floor was dusty, and light couldn't pass through the windows because they'd been painted over. I spotted Malachi in the doorway and let out a gasp as my last memories of the night before flooded back.

I willed myself to roll onto my side. I got up on my bum, ears and head pounding with exhaustion.

'Wot did you do to me? Where am I?' I sniffled, wanting to sound commanding.

'Do you know wot u did last night?' he spat, brimming with anger and charging towards me. 'You boied man, Keisha. Bare times. Askin man about hospital and shit, tellin me ur gonna get me rushed and dat.'

The bravado I'd attempted crumbled.

'I'm sorry, Malachi, I woz jokin—' I was snivelling and convulsing. How trapped and powerless I felt was eerily familiar. 'I'll never run jokes on you again,' I pleaded.

I used the last of my resolve in an attempt to escape what I feared was coming, and looked in his eyes. He looked chilling and unreasonable.

The urge to plead consumed me and I whimpered 'please' over and over again.

He unbuckled his jeans.

I laid myself down gently on my side in the dust, whispering 'please'.

The pounding in my head intensified, my mouth began to ooze salty saliva and the plug socket on the wall I had focused my eyes on went fuzzy.

*

Ricardo was fuming. Keisha hadn't answered her phone for the past hour. He shuffled through the party growing more and more ignorant, asking everyone he passed if they'd seen her. His anger grew as the response continued to come back the same: 'Nah, I ain't seen 'er in tym.'

'Where da fucks dis girl?' he mumbled as he paced up and down the corridor. The hot and happy atmosphere was beginning to grate on him and he found himself fighting the urge to start throwing people out.

Shanice wandered out of the kitchen.

'Is it still going voicemail?' she asked gently. Ricardo aired her and decided to go outside, not wanting to lash out at his pregnant and genuinely concerned sister. It was 1 a.m. now. Ricardo had last seen Keisha well over an hour ago with her bredrins.

Pacing along the pavement, grateful for the night air cooling him down, he realised Keisha's birthday gift was missing. Thoughts began racing through Ricardo's head: 'Did her whip get robbed? This girl can't drive, so she couldn't have taken it nowhere.'

Ricardo tried to call Karl. No answer.

Ricardo headed back to the house to begin looking for Karl to suggest they roll out to look for Keisha and/or her car, when Kayla and Alisha emerged from the house, clearly making a move for home.

'U alrite, Ricardo? Where's Keisha? We're going now.'

'We wanted to say bye,' they said politely.

'I'm lookin for 'er. When did you last see 'er?' Ricardo barked impatiently.

'Umm, like an hour ago, maybe . . .'

'I saw 'er follow Karl,' Alisha remembered. Slight relief washed over Ricardo following the new information.

'Yeah? When doe?' he inquired.

'I fink lyk a hour ago . . . after you gave 'er da car.'

'Ah, ite. Fank you. Safe for comin. Get home safe an dat,' Ricardo called behind him, busy making his way back indoors to look for Karl.

Ricardo peered into the kitchen. Mighty's cousin was washing pots at the sink.

'Oi, Jodie, you seen Karl?'

'Mi see 'im an Keisha gan outside. Mi nuh see 'im since,' she informed Ricardo. Ricardo tried

Karl again to no avail, heading back out to swing by Keisha's mum's and Karl's.

Driving impatiently through the silent streets, Ricardo turned onto Keisha's mum's road.

'Da car ain't here, blud!' he mumbled. He contemplated knocking at Keisha's mum's but decided against it.

Next stop was Karl's in Hoxton. Ricardo parked his car on Pitfield Street, walking the long way round the block to Karl's, looking out for any sign of Keisha, Karl or the whip. He spotted Karl's Punto parked up and jogged over to feel the bonnet. The car was stone-cold.

More frustrated and confused, Ricardo buzzed Karl's flat. Karl's younger brother, Demitrius, answered the intercom.

'Oi little man, iz Rico. Where's your bruva?' Ricardo growled into the speaker.

'I don't know,' Demetrius replied innocently.

'Tell him to call me,' Ricardo instructed him before marching back to his car, fresh out of ideas. Before starting the engine again, he called both Karl and Keisha. Still no answer.

'FUCK MAN!' he screamed, punching the steering wheel. 'Where da fucks dis gyal blud?' his mind was screaming.

He'd started the engine when his phone started vibrating. 'Karl' flashed on the screen.

'Karl blud, where you? Where's Keisha?' Ricardo babbled.

'Yo Rico, wha gwarn?' Karl sounded sleepy.

'Blud, where you? Where's Keisha?' Frustration was cutting through his words.

'Fuckinnn . . .' sleepy and distracted, Karl drew out the word, trying to refocus. 'Ain't she come back to her party, nah?'

'Blud, where da fucks Keisha? Dat Alisha gyal whatever da fuck her name is and fuckin yardie Jodie said you and Keisha left da shubz time ago and no one's seen 'er since. Where's her car, blud?' Spittle flew from Ricardo's mouth. He sucked air into his chest, feeling drained.

'Jam cuz, she should be coming, blud. She's probably blazing a quick zoot with Malachi.'

Ricardo took a few breaths in and out before responding.

'Blud. Who da fuck is Malachi and when did you leave Keisha, blud? You know she can't drive. Blud, what's really going on?'

Ricardo heard Karl ask someone in the background, 'What time did I reach here?' and a girl responded: 'At 11:45.'

'Fuck. Rico, blud, it's nearly 2. Where's Keisha?' Alarm in Karl's tone.

'Blud, dis is what mans saying!' Ricardo shouted into the phone, more relieved than frustrated now that he was being understood.

'Come link me now. I'm near Argos in Dalston,' Karl instructed.

'Ite, bless.'

Ricardo sped through the streets, hopeful Karl could tell him more and ready to quiz him on who this Malachi brudda was.

Ricardo swung onto Sandringham Road, looking out for Karl impatiently.

As Ricardo went to blaze his horn, Karl came jogging over and jumped in.

'Where did u last see her?' Ricardo asked straight away.

'Right here basically, blud.' Karl looked in the rear-view mirror, noticing a car behind impatiently flashing its lights at Ricardo's stationary vehicle. 'I know where we should go. Cum we get my car first,' he suggested.

Ricardo accelerated through Kingsland High Street, ignoring red lights. He screeched to a stop back on Pitfield Street and Karl hopped out. As he climbed into his own car, Ricardo rolled down his window: 'Oi, where we goin and who da fucks Malachi, blud?'

'Fuck! Yo, follow me,' Karl said, starting his engine.

I was startled by something cold being poured over my head.

'Get up,' Malachi snarled. The sound of his voice unsettled me more than the wetness dribbling over me. The pounding in my head had calmed down.

'We're going now. You can clean up.' He took hold of my arm, forcing me upright.

'Where?' I uttered. He ignored me.

I got to my feet, trying my best to keep up with him. We went out into the cold, the breeze whipping around my body, making goosebumps erupt all over. My car was waiting. Malachi opened the back door, ushering me in. He got into the driver's seat and started the engine. I slumped in the back seat, too exhausted to hold myself up and conscious of the state of myself.

We drove through ends I couldn't make out in the darkness, before hopping on the motorway. I closed my eyes. The stamina to look out for a road sign or work out how I could escape the car at a red light had left me. I appreciated the relative comfort of the car's fabric seat beneath me and the warmth of the enclosed space. I must have drifted off because the next thing I knew, the harsh, cold air was blowing on the backs of my legs.

Malachi had opened the back door on me. Getting my bearings, I looked around the car before seeing him over my shoulder glancing at my exposed skin where my dress had ridden up. I yanked it down, ashamed.

We were in a car park on a block that I couldn't quite make out. There were a couple of cars scattered here and there and I willed myself to place where I was.

We got out. I kept looking around in the middle of the night's silence, searching for a sign as I shuffled behind Malachi over to the block. Malachi opened the block door for me and I took a deep breath as I walked in, no idea how close to home or Ricardo I was.

17

I awoke to the sound of Malachi's voice.

'. . . I went home, blud . . . Blud, I don't know, she was in her car cuz. Man was bare lean so I just went yard after you left . . . Where did I leave her? Like Homerton or something. Man don't remember 100% doe . . . Nah, mans been sleeping, I don't even know where she is . . . Yeah, phone man if you hear anything. Bless.'

He locked the phone off. I knew it was Ricardo and Karl looking for me. We had come to this flat that looked more like a home. I couldn't make out much in the darkness when we came in, but as I opened my eyes in the early morning light, we were in a carpetless room. Thin grey curtains hung over a large window. Paint was peeling around the window frame and I was laid on a mattress on the floor. I wondered what was over on the other side of the room but dared not turn over and let Malachi know I had heard his phone conversation.

'Keisha? Keisha? You up?' Malachi spoke gently. I kept my eyes shut. Malachi settled back down on the mattress and didn't ask again.

Ricardo followed Karl, weaving through the streets of Hackney.

'Karl's a fuckin driver,' Ricardo mumbled to himself, watching as he swerved by a Tesco lorry at speed.

They pulled up at a traffic light near Mare Street finally, and Ricardo took the opportunity to pull up next to Karl.

Rolling down his window, he shouted across: 'Blud, who da fuck is Malachi?'

'Wat cuzzy?' Karl shouted back, rolling down his window and turning his music down.

'Blud, whos dis Malachi yout?'

The light turned green and Karl got ready to put his whip in gear.

'Blud, answer me blud!' Ricardo insisted, defiantly remaining stationary.

'Cuz. Its just a dumb situation but da Malachi breddas head nuh good.' Karl attempted to reassure Ricardo, willing him to move before traffic began forming behind them.

'What da fuck does dat mean, cuz?' Ricardo shouted back belligerently.

A car approached and started blaring its horn.

'TESCO!' Ricardo shouted and zoomed ahead.

Ricardo knew Karl wouldn't have him rolling round on a dickhead ting, but he was confused and started wondering if he'd been a bad judge of character when it came to Keisha. Throughout the short relationship, he'd found out the specifics of what people had said about Keisha, and believed her side of things. Before it felt more personal to him, he'd heard or discerned the odd suggestion that Keisha was 'on tings', but he'd doubted it for the most part, feeling like he *knew* Keisha from when she was young. Being slightly older, Ricardo didn't personally feel like what the younger lot described as 'on tings' could compare to what he'd seen and heard, especially from associating with his dad's old friends. Keisha had also proven herself with saving him at the start of the summer. She was trustworthy. He was sure he'd seen the truth.

Screeching into the car park, ignoring the bays, Ricardo hopped out as Karl came to a stop.

'So, who's Malachi? What's dis brudda got to do with Keisha? Chat to me.' Ricardo approached Karl as he opened his door.

'I told myself I'd keep dis a secret u know . . . Fuck Keisha, man!' Karl started. 'Da Malachi bredda frm college liked her bare, bt on a weird ting cuz. Den dey kissed b—'

'Wait. So you've got man rollin round looking 4 gyal das been cheating, blud?' Ricardo cut Karl off.

'Nah, bredda. Man woz on a madman ting, blud. Keisha was in trouble. Man heard he was in hospital an dat. I try chat 2 da yute but it was all long, cuz.'

Ricardo was pissed off. 'What type of madman ting was this Malachi breh on?' he wondered, finding it hard to believe but finding it equally as hard to believe that Karl was making up an elaborate tale in favour of Keisha.

'I'm gna fone him cah I dnt memba exactly where dis guy lives. I know it's E9.'

Ricardo started pacing around the car park. He just wanted to find Keisha, and give this Malachi brudda a well-deserved spark in the face.

'Yo brudda, call me wen you get dis?' Karl asked into the phone. Ricardo zoned out, resisting the urge to allow his anger to consume him and grab the phone. Frustrated that Karl had obviously failed to reach Malachi, he walked out further into the empty car park and left Karl to handle the madman on the phone.

Moments later, Karl jogged over to Ricardo.

'Voicemail, bro. We're gonna have to find where da yout lives doe. I jus know iz a block in E9.'

Ricardo lifted his arms up and sighed heavily.

'FUCK!' he screamed, and charged towards his car.

'We gotta crawl every block,' Karl said, hopping in his car. 'Come, we go Banister first.'

Karl and Ricardo aggressively ripped through Morning Lane, up Ponsford Street, and broke the lights to turn onto Homerton High Street. Crawling slowly through each block, and winding onto back streets by Homerton Hospital, they stopped and wound down their windows to question anyone they spotted.

Ricardo confrontationally creeped past brehs on their block, rolling down his window to bark, 'Ay, come ere. Who's Malachi?' his aggressive brazenness commanding compliance.

'Man, don't know no Malachi, cuz.'

Ricardo and Karl had crawled their way around Banister, Ballance and Nisbet. No one had heard of Malachi, and no one had seen a silver Golf.

The sun had risen in the sky, and extra-early churchgoers started emerging from their homes.

Karl signalled to Ricardo. He wound down his window.

'What, blud?' he grumbled, unable to hide his frustration.

'I'm phoning da Malachi yout, pull up,' Karl instructed, undeterred by Ricardo's shortness.

Ricardo wound up his window knowingly. He sat back in his seat deflated. A minute or so passed by and he sat up to check what Karl was doing, and spied him talking animatedly with his hands. The Malachi brudda must have picked up, he contemplated, fixated on Karl, wondering what was being said but knowing better than to piss himself off.

Karl finally wound down his window again.

'Suttin sus is goin on still. I don't trust da brudda. He said he last seen Keisha near E9. Cum we keep lookin.'

'Oi, do u fink we shud fone da Malachi yout and tell him to cum help us look 4 her den,' Ricardo asked Karl, trying to contain the anger rising in him.

'Iz 6:30. Iz too early. Let's keep lookin. When it gets to 8 I'll fone him again and ask.' Ricardo nodded at Karl, appreciating his reasoning.

They crawled through residential roads, making their way towards Kingsmead.

They turned in, weaving in and out of the red-brick blocks at a snail's pace, peering through their front windows, ignoring innocent families looking back suspiciously.

Ricardo spotted it first. Keisha's car neatly parked in front of a block.

'Blud! Keisha's car, blud. How can she be parked all bate like dis?' he shouted out loud.

He flashed his lights at Karl and gave his horn a little tap to alert him, before pulling into a space. Karl followed suit.

Ricardo hopped out, jogging over to Karl. 'What do u want to do?' Karl asked.

'I don't know, blud. What, should man start pressing buzzers?' Ricardo asked, at a loss.

Karl looked around. 'Look, I fink we shud chill and wait, u kno. Cum we sit in my whip and see what happens. When it gets to 8 I'll fone Malachi an see wot he says abat helpin us look.'

'Not gonna lie, Karl blud, I want to fone da brudda now,' Ricardo panted, getting in the car.

'Nah, he could say iz too early to come out or sum shit. U get it?'

'True say, true say,' Ricardo acknowledged.

They waited. Ricardo restlessly waited for the minutes to tick by. He put on some grime, trying to zone out. After less than half an hour, he turned to Karl: 'Blud, fone da pussy.'

Karl tried calling three times. Voicemail each time.

'Blud, I'm getting vex. Bun dis,' Ricardo screamed, getting out of the car and walking over to Keisha's birthday present.

'KEISHAAAAAA,' he started shouting.

'OI, KEISHAAAAA.' A horn started blowing. He looked over, slightly taken aback, clocking Karl blaring his horn.

A woman on the second floor opened her window at that moment and screamed, 'FUCKING SHUT UP WILL YOU!' slamming it closed.

Ricardo walked back over to Karl. 'What floor do u fink he's on?'

Karl shook his head. 'Cuzzy, I dnt hav a clue.'

Ricardo marched over to the block door and began pressing down on as many buzzers as he could at one time, shouting, 'KEISHAAA!!!!'

An old man opened his window on the ground floor and called, 'What are you doing? I've got a good mind to call the police!'

He glared at the old man and spat, 'Why don't u shut da fuck up, u prick!'

Karl jogged over, grabbing him by the arm and leading him back to the car.

'Blud, what the fuck? Wha gwarn? Why she not coming out?' Ricardo stressed, pacing, peering up at the tall block.

'Cool down. Don't mek the police come here,' Karl warned.

Ricardo stared at Keisha's car. 'Blud, the car has an alarm on it. Let me try set it off.'

He began touching and tapping the car in different places, trying to set off the alarm.

Nothing happened. Karl came over to help but the car didn't make a sound.

'Iz not working. Wot else can we do?' Karl asked.

'I've got an idea. You're not gonna like it doe.' Ricardo smiled mischievously, jogging over to a far wall with loose bricks. He picked one up and jogged back over to the car.

'Blud, wot you tryna do?' Karl asked, bewildered.

'Its my property, alie. Man bought dis,' he replied, hurling the brick into the passenger-side window. The car alarm started screeching.

He dropped the brick, dusting off his hands, smiling. 'She's got to come out now,' he said, looking over at Karl.

'What the fuck? Listen, you better follow me downstairs to tell them to fuck off and stop the car alarm!' Malachi panicked, getting in my face. The alarm on my car had been screaming for the last ten minutes at least.

I'd been lying on the mattress wide awake, staying as still as I could manage. In the close, muted silence of the flat I'd faintly heard my name being screamed from a distance. Over and over. Accompanied by a car horn blaring. Malachi jumped up, catching me awake as my eyes shot open when I realised it was Ricardo shouting my name.

Malachi stood by the window, peering out like a hostage-taker hiding from the police.

'I can't tell Ricardo and Karl to fuck off,' I told Malachi as he pulled me towards the front door and opened it.

We travelled down in the lift, my teeth starting to chatter. I tried to smooth down my hair before Ricardo and Karl saw me. Malachi looked afraid.

We stepped off the lift and Malachi pushed the block door open with force, getting the attention of Karl, Ricardo and the two nosy people standing around my blaring car. Ricardo had a brick in his hand, arguing with an old man. He looked at me and I saw the shock flash on his face. The rage in his face and demeanour drained away, and confusion and sorrow washed over him. I ran to him, my bare feet slapping against the pavement. He scooped me into an embrace and I sobbed into his shoulder, my whole body convulsing.

Suddenly, I heard sirens ringing out above the noise of the car alarm. I didn't think Ricardo could hear them. He pushed me off of him. Karl pulled me into an embrace and I could hear him saying my name. I struggled to disentangle myself from his arms to see where Ricardo had gone. I turned in time to see him repeatedly hurl the brick in his hands into Malachi, blow after blow landing. I felt myself scream as the old man attempted to stop Ricardo, just as three police cars swooped in. Bumbling officers rushed to grab Ricardo, their jaws clenched and red faces seething with hate. The first officer to reach him snatched his arm brandishing the brick, and pulled it back, causing him to scream and drop it. The pain made him tumble to the floor as officer after officer surrounded him, concealing the reasons for the screams that continued to reverberate amidst the screaming alarm.

Everything felt like it was moving in slow motion from that point. I wanted to run over to the officers and explain it was Malachi they should be grabbing, not Ricardo, but my feet felt heavy. I felt arms round me and I froze moment-arily, feeling afraid and unprotected again.

'It's okay, Keish.' It was Karl holding me, stop-ping me from running into the chaos.

Malachi was crumpled on the floor by the block door, nosy neighbours milling around him, nursing his injuries sympathetically.

'What you doing, blud? What the fuck, man?' Ricardo began shouting. 'Take these off me, blud, I've come to get my girl. This is my car!' Two burly officers were lifting Ricardo from the floor.

He was cuffed. Shirt torn. Mouth bloodied. A bruise coming up on his eye.

'We are arresting you on suspicion of ABH, criminal damage, possession of a weapon with intent to harm, and breach of the peace. You do not have to say anything. But it may harm your defence if you do not mention when questioned something which you later rely on in court. Anything you do say may be given in evidence. Do you understand, sir?'

'FUCK OFF,' Ricardo screams.

18

I walked the long, quiet way home from the bus stop so the news could soak in. The sun was bright in the sky, and it beamed down on me through the trees' naked branches. It had been a long time since I'd walked this way home to contemplate something positive.

I had first walked this way when I was making my way home from Michael's house, the day I had to make the decision all alone to get an abortion because I was too scared to tell my mum or try to reason with Michael again. The dark warehouses along the quiet pavement featuring graffiti and mural paintings, that Mum told me used to hold the wickedest dances back in the day, loomed over me. This way was quiet, and aside from people coming round this way to get up to no good, spying me with their shifty eyes that wondered what my deal was, it was uneventful and allowed me to be with my thoughts. I started taking this way to avoid the mandem cotching on the high road in the years after Michael. I took this long way lots after college or after work at the part-time job I'd got at Claire's to think about Ricardo. I wondered how he was, what he was thinking, how much he might hate me, and if he believed that I had loved him.

It was nearly a year and a half since he had gone away.

The last time I'd seen him was when they'd dragged him away in cuffs outside of Malachi's block. Everyone had had their breath held in limbo while he was on remand. I naively believed he'd be out once he got to the police station and the officers had heard the whole story. I thought they'd march over to Malachi's immediately, realising their error. But Ricardo never came out. First it was remand, then he had a court date, then the next thing I heard was he'd gotten eleven years. I'd asked Shanice as much as I could, between her having her baby boy and trying not to let it be known that I'd not heard from Ricardo even once since the day he was arrested.

I was too embarrassed to tell anyone that the person I loved so much and thought loved me hadn't responded to any of my letters, hadn't thanked me for the money I'd sent him, hadn't sent me a VO or called me. I'd been lucky to even get his prisoner number, but in the madness of him getting arrested, Shanice sent it to everyone in a text. I just pretended to people that I'd hear from him from time to time and that he hadn't said much, that he didn't have much credit.

All that time, I'd actually been waiting by the phone, going to the post office to ask them if my post was blocked or something, phoned the prison, *everything*. I'd taken the long way home to cry and wonder if I had to wait five and a half years to get an answer from him. For him to tell me himself just how much he hated me and how I'd ruined his life. As I continued down the road lost in my thoughts, I spotted my mum in the distance. I completely forgot what I had been thinking about as I approached her, wondering what she was doing here.

'What you doing here, Mum? Ain't your meeting at 3?' I asked, going into my pocket and pulling out my phone. I was sure it was 3 p.m.

'Yeah, I was waiting for you! I didn't want to leave before you came back . . . so, what happened?' Mum asked excitedly, practically jumping up and down. I paused for a second to leave her in suspense. She blinked at me impatiently.

'Well . . . they offered me a place, Mum!' I finally exclaimed.

'Oh my Lord!!!' Mum squealed 'Keisha! They offered you a place at university! My daughter is going to university!!!' Mum cried, holding my face while tears streamed down hers.

'Okay, okay, Mum. Your meeting, come on, get your skates on,' I said hurriedly. Mum had been in AA for forty-two weeks and attending meetings every few days. I'd been counting and, I had to admit, she was beginning to remind me of the mum I knew before the drink.

I needed that mum; she'd helped me on my bad days through the Ricardo situation.

After walking the quiet, deserted street and coming in with my eyes puffy, I'd collapse into her arms and sob. In those moments we'd developed a mother-daughter intimacy I felt more and more sure would've helped me navigate my teenage troubles. I'd told her about the abortion, and she'd shared her many scars too.

'Fuck the meeting, my daughters going uni!' Mum exclaimed.

'No, seriously Mum! Come on, you've got to go to your meeting,' I said, feeling worry creeping into my thoughts.

'Okay, okay,' she said. 'I'll see you when I get back.' I'd turned to make my way towards home when Mum called out to me.

'Keisha? I'm so, so proud of you,' she said.

'I'm proud of you too, Mum. I'll see you later.'

I turned and walked towards the house feeling warm inside.

I opened our front door, and Mum had put a letter in the middle of the kitchen table which meant it was for me. The small square brown envelope, the black stamp over the postage and the letters and numbers scrawled on the back let me know who it was from immediately. My hands trembled and I had to take three deep breaths to stop my heart from beating so fast. I had been waiting for this for over a year. I pulled the tape from the envelope flap and carefully pulled out one thin sheet of paper. My heart dropped a little – I wanted to open an envelope to pages and pages of his writing that would dry every tear I'd cried since November 2007.

Dear Keisha,
How are you? Mans alright in here, you know how it goes. Sorry I've took so long to write you back and sorry I ain't sent you a VO. I've just had bare tings on my mind init. Still do. Thank you for sending man ps. You know you don't have to do any of that.
    Shanice said you was applying for uni. Hearing that made my day. You're a smart girl Keisha, don't let no one tell you different. I know its all fucked because of the situation

but trust me, I don't hate you. I know you're thinking that. They arrested me for having the brick, making bare noise and damaging my own car that day, but that ain't the reason they're trying to keep man here. Trust me, Keisha. I don't blame you for nothing because a man will always reap what he sows. I just want you to do what's best for you.

I don't think you should wait for man. Not because I hate you or because anything was fake either so don't start thinking that! Just trust me, you're a good girl Keisha. Man remember everything, trust me. You're gonna be alrite.

I'm always rooting for you. You and Shan look after my nephew.

RICO X

Heat rose in my neck and ears, and my heart continued to pound in my chest. I burst into tears.

I was relieved.

I'd often left relationships and loves feeling like something about me had to change. When I'd wanted to be loved and thought I was loving, something always went so wrong and someone got hurt. Michael had gone wrong. Malachi had gone wrong. And for the last 18 months I'd believed Ricardo had gone so disastrously wrong.

I sobbed and reread Ricardo's letter, needing his words to heal the parts of me that felt wrong and bad and unacceptable and ruinous.

I rested my head on the dingy kitchen table when I'd sobbed so much that it felt too heavy to continue to hold up. I closed my eyes.

I was proud of myself. I'd stayed loyal to Ricardo, even with him not here. I'd established something to work towards in his absence and I'd achieved it. I was going to university.

The brevity and closure in his letter stung parts of me. I wanted him to come back and love me and save me like he had done before. I breathed a deep sigh into the table and felt the warmth of my breath out heat my face momentarily. I sat back up and looked around the kitchen. Nothing appeared to have changed – the Wanis calendar still hung lopsided and old grease buildup was still thick on the walls, but the cupboards no longer held bottles of Whisky. I didn't need to be saved from my home or my mum anymore, or from boys.

I sat back in the chair playing with the corner of Ricardo's letter between my fingers. The sadness started to subside as I began to realise that his letter was the reassurance I'd been waiting on. In his short letter he affirmed that the parts of me that had long felt corrupted and defiled weren't so broken, and that I was strong enough to see what life had in store, even if I was going at it alone.

THE
ESSAYS*

Sexc

Candice Carty-Williams

I looked in da mirror. I admired ma sexc full body an smiled. I thought bck 2 wen i woz a yute wen i fort i woz so fat an buttaz an used 2 h8 da way i looked. But now, i woz in luv wit ma figure! Blessed wit a big bum an chest, a firm flat stomach an sexc thickish thighs.
— *Keisha the Sket: The OG*

There is so much I could say about *Keisha the Sket*. I could write about how reading something written in slang and Ebonics for the first time made me feel seen, and how it made me feel understood; it pushed the limits of what I believed writing could be. I could write paragraph after paragraph of how the spelling of 'sexy' as 'sexc' or 'sexxxxi' or 'sexxxxxxxxx-cccccccc' was, and still is, nothing short of revolutionary. Through a mix of alternative spellings, the fact that it's written in dialect, and with numbers and symbols in place of letters ('4rm' as 'from', and

'@' in the place of 'at', for example), *Keisha the Sket*'s author, Jade LB, refused to follow the rules of literature, and what's better than that? As I started to read more as I got older, only Irvine Welsh's *Trainspotting*, written in Scottish dialect, came close to what Jade LB did in *Keisha the Sket*.

In this essay, it feels important to talk about *Keisha the Sket* in the context of Black female sexuality. As an adult, *Keisha the Sket* – a story I first read as a teenager – has been a surprisingly large part of my life. Before its author was revealed, around once a month I would catch myself thinking about Keisha: What would Keisha be up to now? How old would she be? Would she have settled down and had kids? What was her job? But most importantly, and more realistically, I wondered who the author was, what they were doing, and if they'd written anything since. I wondered because I wanted the author to know the impact they'd had on the culture, and to understand how this piece of fiction is still very much part of the memories of Black women today. In my WhatsApp group chat – a set of five Black women working in the creative fields – we'd discuss it constantly. But, as we were adults now, we wouldn't just talk about the story of Keisha. We'd talk about the cultural implications. We'd talk about what it had meant to us when we were growing up. We'd talk about the extremely graphic sex this fictional teenager had, and wonder how that had come about in the mind of the young woman who'd written it, and why.

One early afternoon in November 2019 (I'm a night owl), before I'd woken up enough to reply to any messages, I ignored all of my WhatsApp notifications and went onto Twitter. I scrolled and scrolled, one sleepy eye open, and sat up with a start when I saw a tweet from the *Black Ballad* account. *Black Ballad*, a cultural platform developed by Tobi Oredein with Black women in mind, had found the author of *Keisha the Sket*. I couldn't believe my eyes. I sent the tweet to the group chat, and saw that one of us had already said, 'omg guys. Have you seen *Black Ballad* has found the girl who wrote *Keisha the Sket*? Just came out of a workshop and six people have already texted me about it lol. It's like Christmas, I'm so excited.' None of us could believe it. I checked the rest of my messages and three other friends had already sent the article to me too. Before having a brand was a thing, *Keisha the Sket* was already unknowingly a brand of its own – one that so many of us had been subscribed to, either actively or subconsciously, for over half of our lives.

I can't put a precise age on when I first read it, but it feels to me that Keisha was very present in my teenage years. I went to Haberdashers' Aske's Hatcham College (yes, it was a mouthful to say back then, and now) in New Cross, a school that

I understood would have been a private school if it hadn't been funded by a set of old white men, the Haberdashers, who we never saw but heard *so* much about. My South London school was split by gender, with the boys at another site up the hill, and was overwhelmingly white, with a handful of Black kids in each class. The handful of Black kids tried our best to hold form in this space, and held on to every single bit of Black culture we could sneak into that school. Our hairstyles were policed, as was the way we wore our uniforms, and by Year 11, when most of us were sixteen, we were having to hide playing Snake on our Nokia phones – which gives you a sense of the kind of technology we were working with.

What we did have, though, just about, was the internet. And, like most people of my generation, I spent my evenings tapping away on MSN Messenger or downloading music that would give the family computer various viruses. Then I overheard a girl in my science class talking about *Keisha the Sket*, and thought, 'Who is Keisha? There's no Keisha at this school?' Until I understood that Keisha was a fictional character – and not in a book, but in a story going around on this internet thing.

Back then, Google wasn't as helpful a resource as it is now. I think Ask Jeeves was the reigning search engine, and when I asked Jeeves, he didn't show me *Keisha the Sket*. You had to be *sent* Keisha in order to access her story, or you needed to be friends with someone who had the story on their phone. Either way, if you were able to read the story, you'd truly be *in the know*. And that was the kind of cultural currency that money cannot buy when you're at school.

When I first read *Keisha the Sket* in all of its instalments, I had absolutely not had sex. One of my friends had had sex, and I remember being pretty frightened of it, but through reading I was pulled into this world where sex, or the excitement of sex, coursed through every single page.

Ma legz den bcame rly weak an shaky an i came on his dick, which was now gettin biga an biga insyd of me. He came in me soon afta me an slowed dwn 2 nufin.

I couldn't read it fast enough. Of course, in my school years, talk of sex was all around. The boys at the other site would come down the hill, and while they lined up for their Design Technology class, they'd effectively catcall us. When we'd exchange numbers with them, we'd talk about sex, sure – their main line of questioning was 'Are you a virgin?' 'What bra size are you?' and 'What have you done?' – but we wouldn't *have* sex with them. *Keisha the Sket*, for me, was my entry point to understanding what sex was. It was also where I understood the perceived value of the Black female body.

'Oi. Erm excuse me miss, but ehh, whers ma hug?' i went
ova 2 him n gve him a hug. 'N ma kiss?' i gve him a
kiss on da cheek. 'N ma REAL kiss?' i moved ma mouf
directly facin his n he bought his lipz 2 mine n opened
his mouf. I sat on his lap passionatley lickin n tastin his
full lips n warm mouf. Wen we finished (afta a gd 5minz)
he looked @ me n sed 'An ma sex?' He asked seductively.

Keisha, in essence, is completely and utterly driven by sex. More specifically, she is driven by the sex that men want from her, and the desire they have for her (terrifyingly young) body. Her young body is described as adult in every way conceivable: 'Blessed wit a big bum an chest, a firm flat stomach an sexc thickish thighs.' And before Keisha even tells us about her body, the way she dresses herself is highly sexualised: 'i opened my wardrobe, it woz a sunny day so I took out some shorrrrrrrrt white rah rah skirt an a pink vest top.' That skirt was certainly short for there to be nine 'r's in its description.

On every other page, Keisha is either operating on her own sexual desire, the promise of sex or how she's going to fulfil a boy's sexual fantasy, either through what she plans to do or what she plans to wear:

An hour n a half later i woz slippin in2 da small black
dress i had picked out 4rm a store up west. It hugged ma
body, bringin out ma curvez, big pert titties n apple ass.

I slipped ma well pedicured feet in2 sum blck 'killa' heels.
I looked in da mirror n lyked-no-loved wot i sw. Ma hair
woz out n curly an abit wet so i jus put sum moisturizer
in it n put it up inna clip. I neva wore no makeup except
4 lip gloss but i made da effort by putin on sum eyeline
n mascara. Picture perfect.

'Ohhhh shit! Ma wifeys tryna gt pregnant 2day!' ricardo
sed as he walked thru da bedroom door.

The men who desire Keisha's seventeen-year-old body, and the men who have sex with her, are all obsessed with this body above all else. They either want to have sex with her, or protect her body, or abuse her body, or all of the above. Later on in the story, after various trials and tribulations with the men in her life (and with very little look-in from any adults, caregivers or even Keisha's friends), Keisha is kidnapped at her eighteenth birthday party by Malachi, a spurned admirer. She is then repeatedly sexually assaulted by Malachi as a punishment for not wanting to be with him.

I understood, on reading *Keisha the Sket* as an adult, that how Keisha is treated by men is a product of how we as Black women understood our capital and our worth when we ourselves were teenagers. Sex was all around – not just in the conversations at school, but in the music videos we'd watch every day *after* school and in the other media we consumed. Of course, back then, our representation in books was, as it is today, lacking, so we were hardly going to find any Black female role models in literature.

This representation – or lack of – plays into three or so key tropes that Black women have long felt the need to fulfil in the presentations of us that society has given us, and that popular culture has reinforced. The first is the mammy – the big-breasted, strong, house slave woman. Her role is to look after everyone, while seldom looking after her own children or even herself. The needs of others come before her own.

The second trope is the magical negro, a Black character who exists simply to help a white person. Key examples of this are Oda Mae Brown, Whoopi Goldberg's character in the film *Ghost* (1990), who allows the spirit of white man Sam Wheat to jump inside her body, in order for him to avenge his own murder and also say goodbye to his grieving girlfriend; and Jennifer Hudson in the *Sex and the City* movie (2008), playing Carrie Bradshaw's one-dimensional and plucky assistant who is employed to help Carrie with *admin alone* but ends up having to cross way too many employee boundaries in order to help her boss, a white woman, get over her heartbreak.

The third trope, and the one we see play out in *Keisha the Sket*, is that of the highly sexualised Black woman. She can be found in pretty much any hip-hop music video, and she's usually sassy and confident – but more than anything, this Black woman exists mainly as a desirable body that comprises big breasts, a small waist and a big bum. She says little to nothing apart from when she's being sassy and confident, and is usually there to be looked at and to have sex with. It makes total sense, considering the representation that Black women have had in the aforementioned music videos, and before the days of social media, that Keisha would perform the actions of the trope closest to her age range. Quite the cocktail.

Keisha's narrative makes total sense, given how the Black female body has always been positioned in society. We understand, from anecdotal research, that Black female children are seen as adult from a young age, in stark contrast to how society sees their white female counterparts. In the *New York Times* article 'Why Won't Society Let Black Girls Be Children?' written by A. Rochaun Meadows-Fernandez – a Black content writer specialising in sociology, health and parenting – the author recounts her childhood experiences, saying that 'I was experiencing what academics call "adultification", in which teachers, law enforcement officials and even parents view black girls as less innocent and more adult-like than their white peers.'[*] The 2017 report *Girlhood Interrupted: The Erasure of Black Girls' Childhood*, written by Rebecca

---

[*] A. Rochaun Meadows-Fernandez, 'Why Won't Society Let Black Girls Be Children?', *New York Times*, 17 April 2020, https://www.nytimes.com/2020/04/17/parenting/adultification-black-girls.html.

Epstein and Jamilia Blake, found that 'adults believe black girls ages 5–19 need less nurturing, protection, support and comfort than white girls of the same age, and that black girls are more independent, know more about adult topics, and know more about sex than white girls.'* So, of course, when these children grow into teenagers, it's almost impossible for them to see themselves as children. We're thrust into the world of sex before most of us are ready to be.

When we first meet Ricardo, the brother of Keisha's best friend Shanice, who becomes Keisha's boyfriend and supposed protector, after he's said a few words to her he smacks her on the bum:

> 'Rarrrr . . . u sure ur lookin 4 shanice an nt me!' he sed lookin me up an dwn.
>
> I laughed an jus moved him outa da way an walked in 2 da corridor. He turned round an slaped ma bum. I didn't do nufin bcoz her brova woz ova buff.

A few minutes later, she's on top of him and they're having sex in his room while Shanice is downstairs.

---

* Georgetown Law, 'Research Confirms that Black Girls Feel the Sting of Adultification Bias Identified in Earlier Georgetown Law Study', 15 May 2019, https://www.law.georgetown.edu/news/research-confirms-that-black-girls-feel-the-sting-of-adultification-bias-identified-in-earlier-georgetown-law-study/.

A couple of hours later, Keisha and Shanice go to the house of Ramel, whom Keisha arranged to meet in the story's opening. Keisha has sex with Ramel while Shanice has sex with his friend Sean downstairs:

> *Ramel led me upstairs an i left shanice dwn stairs in da passage wit sean kissin. Wen gt 2 da floor dat his room woz on he opened his bedroom door an looked bck at me wit a sexc look in his eyes. I folowed him in2 da bedroom an closed it bhind me. As soon as da door shut he span round an started lipsin me rly hard an ruff. He woz feelin up al ma body an takin ma top off. He woz alredy topless wit jus jeanz an boxerz on. He gt me dwn on his bed an gt on top of me an put his face in ma chest an started lickin an suckin ma chest.*

But again, this makes total sense coming from the teenage mind of the writer of *Keisha the Sket*. When sex is presented as your only way of connecting with men on a meaningful level, what else is the story of a seventeen-year-old Black girl written by a thirteen-year-old Black girl going to be? The imagination effectively comes up with variations of what's around it. The environment that we as Black female teenagers were existing in was an ecosystem of sexual capital. And this isn't harmless – far from it. This under-standing of what the Black female body can give is pervasive, and it's damaging.

When I was writing *Queenie*, of course, Keisha was wandering around the chambers of my mind. Like Keisha, Queenie (even though she is twenty-five and not seventeen) understands – through the ways that men speak to her, and her bodily attributes that they can't help but refer to – that sex is something she *should* do. It is a way that she can connect with men, and a way for men to give her the attention she needs in place of the love that she *actually* needs. In the article that broke the Black girls' internet in November 2019, *Keisha the Sket*'s author, Jade LB, wrote that *KTS* is 'a story about a girl who, despite the ways in which she was deemed socially undesirable, found love'. Neither Keisha nor Queenie completely understand that they have much more to offer than their bodies. Which isn't to say that they don't have strong personalities. Keisha is confident, playful and bright, and Queenie is emotionally driven and funny. And they both know what it's like to *want* to love, despite how society sees them.

I have so much love for *Keisha the Sket*. And that enduring love is more than fifteen years strong. Keisha was, to me, one of the first Black female characters that I understood as part of my world. So much so that she's stayed in my world for over half of my life. Even though teenage me couldn't relate to her shenanigans, adult me understands her and loves her even more than I did back then. Putting the politics aside, she reminds me what it meant to be young, to flirt with abandon, to be unworldly, and above all else, what it meant to get wrapped up in the adolescent flurry of sex, desire and excitement. And bringing the politics into focus, Keisha is the product of an upbringing we all understand – one of hypersexualisation coming at us from all sides – and of the narrative that sex is the mission.

Either way, Keisha the Sket is one of the most important literary characters of all time. And for that, she'll go down in Black girl history as one of *our* first literary heroines.

Sex and Masculinity in the Endz

Caleb Femi

Reading *Keisha the Sket* as an adult makes me swoon at the richness of its nostalgia; it takes me back to a time when every endz in London was buzzing with the excitement of being visible in literature, of feeling like part of something bigger. I think about how the technology at the time was quintessential to the form of writing, how communication and the sharing of stories was shaped by it. I think about the clothes we wore, the teenage dreams we had, and about the overwhelming possibilities of the future. I think about what it was like being a hormonally charged-up teenager during the holidays looking to do nothing but spend your days with your friends. While the weather was still bitterly cold, you and the mandem would chill on the block, anticipating your summer antics and how effortlessly the gyaldem would give you their numbers because your outfit that gleamed in the sun and your general swagger of being *that* guy would have done the heavy lifting. Fast-forward to summer and it was now your time to shine; you had your white t-shirt, grey jogger shorts and brand-new white Air Forces, and you were ready to scorch the streets and announce yourself as *that* guy on the endz. You and your friends would go on group links (where an all-boys group of friends meet up and hang out with an all-girl group of friends) as a way of helping each other navigate the new and exciting landscape that was romance.

My first encounter with *Keisha the Sket* (*KTS*) was at one of these group links with girls from North West London. The six of us, three boys and three girls, hung out in the upstairs seating area of a McDonald's that was fragranced with faint toilet odour. We boys tried to run game as best we could, but all the girls wanted to talk about was *KTS*. It didn't take us long to cave and ask for a brief synopsis of the plot, and in moments we found ourselves leaning forward and paying attention as one of the girls began to read us an extract that she had printed out.

'Duno boi, dat sexc bwoi ramel iz invitin me 2 his yard
4 a lash init but i duno if i gna reach it or not'
'go man!!!! 4rm wot ive seen dat bwoi iz 22 buff!'
'I knooooooo! Oh my dayz! da boi! Wot u on 2day doe?'
'Nuttin rly u kno, u wnna jam an den ill escort u 2
ramelz yrd?'

'Ye, ite den. Arrrr i jus gt 1 gully idea, ramel sed hell
fne me, wen he dus ill ask him if he wil bring his bredrin
4 u'
'Wot bredrin??'
'Sean, hes nufffff peng aswel!'
'Wot dus he look lyk?'
'Lite skin, peng green eyes, cain row, nuff tall'

What we heard captured the mechanisms behind
making a group link happen from the perspective of
a girl. A perspective we, the boys, had only ever
imagined and fabricated out of our own teenage egos.
As she read on, our (my) fascination fattened, because
for most of us on the endz, the stories of relationships
(if we can even call them that) and romantic/sexual
links that were heard through gossipy grapevines or
the bragging lyrics of our favourite rappers/MCs were
almost exclusively male-centred. But in this confes-
sional, we were presented with the perspective of the
usually silenced voice. A voice that spoke exactly like
me, my boys and all the girls we knew. A voice that
spoke her truth, devoid of shame or fear of criticism.
Admittedly, at the time, the crux of my interest in
KTS was to gain a romantic understanding of what
girls thought about boys: what their desires and expectations were ('dat sexc bwoi ramel iz invitin me 2 his
yard 4 a lash'), what they found attractive in boys
('Lite skin, peng green eyes, cain row, nuff tall'), and
so many other curiosities. I saw it as a guide to the

intricate labyrinth of a girl's mind – one that, beyond the superficial benefits, would give me a better understanding of my own perspective on romantic interactions.

It was years later, in my early twenties, after having nostalgia-soaked conversations about *KTS* with my peers, that I revisited the bits of the text I could find online and saw that it held up a mirror to society, exposing the harsh consequences of our patriarchal framework and this brand of masculinity that dictated how teenagers like us, uninformed and naive, went about exploring the complex landscape of romance. But what were the sources in and around the endz that informed this harmful brand of masculinity?

When I turned thirteen, I remember becoming very aware of my sexuality, my body and masculinity. I was attempting to make sense of the urges and emotions awakened in my pubescent body. A new version of myself was hatching out of the shell of an obsolete version. The problem was that there was no manual on how to navigate the world as this new version of myself, and there were limited spaces to freely and safely discuss topics such as sex and intimacy. So I looked to my peers, who were also in various stages of the process of puberty. Our discussions became less about football and TV, and more about sex and status.

In hindsight, none of us had the experience or knowledge to give sound advice or provide credible insight. A lot of fact-checks were done by referring to the songs that underpinned many of our discussions: Boya Dee's 'Gash by the Hour' and Dizzee Rascal's 'I Luv U' and 'Jezebel'. These songs endorsed the commodification of women, the absence of intimacy and the glamorisation of social status, and we took such songs as a reflection of the psyche of the older male figures we aspired to be like.

These songs stressed that a good social status was paramount to 'sexual conquest'; none of us wanted to be the 'prick' in 'I Luv U' or 'Ricky' in 'Jezebel'. In the endz, having a good social status went beyond enjoying the celebrity of being cool; for many of us, it was a survival tool. Being seen as *that* guy on the endz meant that you could move between spaces knowing you were protected from everyday dangers like getting bullied, robbed, beaten up or even killed. It meant that you were accepted and seen as a valued (in all its many meanings) member of the community, and, of course, one who was romantically desired. We see this patriarchal sign post reflected throughout *KTS*, particularly in Keisha's initial reasons for choosing Ricardo as a partner: 'n e tym i felt dwn or had n e truble wit n e dickhed boiz den i knew i culd turn 2 him 2 shank n e prick inna dem eye!'

It should be noted that, in many cases, a good status came with its own dire consequences, as it increased your visibility around the endz and often made you a target for others who were aiming to ascend the social pecking order. One of the many paradoxes of the endz, proving that ultimately no one is entirely safe.

The male figures we watched at home, in our place of worship, at school, cruising through our estates or flexing on Channel U also informed our masculinity and our approach to romance. They showed us how to look the part – the clothes, the trainers, the kempt look – and more importantly how to perform the part, by copying the machismo they exhibited. We followed a prescribed set of rigid behaviours – a dos and don'ts, if you will – when approaching sex, romance and intimacy, and those who did not adhere to these behaviours often found themselves vulnerable to ostracisation. We see this demonstrated in Chapter 5, when the boys harass Keisha for her sexual autonomy and Ricardo for publicly claiming romantic involvement with her. What fuels the boys' behaviour in that scene is their understanding that (heterosexual) sexual relations, for men, are about dominance and the affirmation of manhood and the shaming of intimacy. And for women, they're about submission and bartering and the shaming of sexual autonomy. In the endz, shame is a powerful tool used to police gender roles, and *KTS* serves as a monument that challenges that shame. In its title alone, there is a disarming of the power of shame by owning the very verbal weapon – 'sket' – that would otherwise be used against a girl (like Keisha) for engaging in and enjoying sexual encounters.

Furthermore, rereading *KTS* as adult, I question the nature of the supposed enjoyment of Keisha's sexual encounters. Throughout *KTS*, there is no extensive demonstration of Keisha's own sexual pleasure being prioritised by any of her consensual partners. In fact, the bandwidth of her sexual pleasure is limited to the satisfaction of her partner, absolving him of any responsibility and leaving it solely up to her to orchestrate her own moments of sexual pleasure. Another example of our warped perception of sex and intimacy.

It is impossible to speak about sex and this brand of masculinity without talking about the violence that fortifies it. There are various forms of violence that plague the endz. Some violence makes the news (youth violence or state-sanctioned violence); while other acts such as the sexual violence committed against girls and women, like the harrowing events of Chapter 7 in *KTS*, slip under the radar and often go unreported and unaddressed.

As a teenager, I was able to point to and deplore the act of rape, but my understanding of rape culture and how much we as a society perpetuate it was very limited. I often think about how the culture of sexual violence permeates aspects of our everyday lives. Hiding in plain sight in the most common of places – like our language, for instance. There are violent overtones in the words we use in reference to sex. Let's consider the slang terms used for the word 'sex' (as teenagers, and perhaps even today): beat, smash, tear, cut, slam, fuck (I'm sure you have examples of your own); these are clearly words loaded with violent energy, and they shape an impressionable teenager's perception of how they are expected to perform during the act. This is reinforced in the general depiction of heterosexual sex in porn, film and social media: we often see rough and hard ramming with no sense of intimacy, where the man remains silent unless he's talking 'dirty' (but actually disrespectfully) to the woman, and the woman screams loudly, leaving us wondering if she is in pain or feeling pleasure. As teenage boys, we often took these violent performances as an indication of 'good sex', or at least sex done right. And so the violent language we use around sex, along with the violence of the generally prescribed performance of heterosexual sex, results in the dehumanisation of the bodies involved – particularly that of the woman – and ultimately contributes to the culture of rape and sexual violence against women.

It took me a decade to understand how the internalisation of this brand of masculinity damaged my psyche. This was only due to the access I had to the literature and educational spaces that addressed the matter. But not everyone in the endz has access to such spaces, hence why it's important for the men who do have such access to have conversations with men and teenage boys from the endz on the topics of sex and masculinity. I have been in conversation with men who have experienced, to different degrees, a pressure to adhere to this brand of masculinity. Men who have felt the negative impact it has had on their lives and the lives of those they've come in contact with. Some of us have been able to see the link between our mental health issues and the internalisation of these unhealthy ideals of masculinity. But the truth is, these conversations are not happening as frequently or widely as they should. Perhaps this is due to a lack of safe spaces in which we can talk honestly and freely about our physical and mental development as men, in order to prevent another generation of men from normalising and perpetuating the ideologies that uphold rape culture and inflict abuse, violence, suicide, depression and anxiety.

There is much to be said about the mentality many boys from the endz have in regard to masculinity and sex: the performance of machismo; their warped expectations of sex; and at times their dangerous interactions with girls. I believe that literature like *KTS* can serve as a gateway to having these necessary conversations that enable a collective push to unlearn these ideologies and to re-educate boys (and men) on better forms of masculinity. For example, masculinity that sees strength in vulnerability, that prioritises consent and an equally collaborative approach to sexual activity, that makes space for gender and sex fluidity. It is important that this push is led by men since historically it is women who take on this responsibility.

A Million Footsteps

Aniefiok Ekpoudom

I heard So Solid Crew before I saw them. Among the South London sprawl, their local anthems beat out of battered car speakers and rattled from home-built sound systems. In some of my misty memories from when I was a boy, huddled on the curbsides off Lee High Road, I heard songs carved on PCs bleeding through pirate radio dials. I heard MCs in bold tones, UKG becoming something else. I heard rhythm. I heard resistance. I heard a resilient people pushing through glass ceilings, wading through hostile territory like all the artists gifted and Black and British who came before. Every generation of ours on this island has forged diamonds from scraps.

In the first years of the new millennium, So Solid wavered over the country like a long British summer. After early outings on pirate stations like Supreme FM and dances held in venues like the Stratford Rex, the crew of thirty-plus from estates around Battersea found themselves at the Brit Awards in 2002, packed into the exhibition centre at Earls Court and nominated for Best Breakthrough Act and Best Video for '21 Seconds'. The latter was a crowded category. They were a jewel among a sea of mainstream British artists, nominated alongside Coldplay and Elton John, Robbie Williams and Kylie Minogue, in a contest decided by the popular vote.

American actor Michael Madsen presented the award that evening, and stood on stage alongside hosts Frank Skinner and Zoe Ball, waving a white card in his fingers as he read, 'The winner is,' before a pause, '21 Seconds, So Solid Crew.' Shrieks rose in the arena, and gun fingers raised from palms to toast the evening air. The crew filed from their seats onto the stage, flashing past broadcast cameras in a catwalk procession of thick fur coats and cocoa-butter cream blazers, mesh vests and New Era caps, denim skirts and blue bandanas saddled on glistening foreheads. They scattered across the stage like toddlers in a school playground, and applauded the screaming supporters in the audience. At moments, they extended their arms in a salute, as if reaching through the TV screen to their people watching back home. This win was bigger than them.

Black musicians paint murals on the eardrums of their people. Songs are more than melodies – they are cave paintings of our existence, oral recordings of how a people has lived and endured and flourished and sustained themselves here in Britain. Decades before So Solid won the Brit Award, sound selectors

Count Suckle and Duke Vin built Britain's first sound systems from spare parts in Ladbroke Grove during the 1950s, and played reggae in basement parties at a time when their people were still barred from the freeing weekend release of London's nightclubs. Generations later, grime kids in East London risked their lives on council flat rooftops and hung aerials from tower block windows to transmit their music across the city. A spirit of enterprise and resistance has hovered over working-class Black art for as long as communities have called these regions home.

Both the sound selectors and the grime kids were greeted with hostility from state and from country – as were So Solid. The early basement parties in the 1950s were firebombed by white gangs in Notting Hill, till houses burned and attendees fled to the roof-tops. The UK's culture minister described So Solid as a 'cultural problem' in 2003, and the grime kids who came after had their music banned from club raves and were smothered by Form 696. Resistance is encoded into the DNA of our sounds. Black music emerges in spite of censorship, leaving faint tracks in the earth for the generations who follow.

Music echoes through the original *Keisha the Sket* manuscript. Among the high dramas and deep-seated traumas of Keisha's life, sound and rhythm thread through the quiet moments of the story, linking the lives of a young, working-class London. Bashment plays at house parties, with 'a whole leepa blck ppl dancin an whinin up'; grime MCs spill out of speakers when teenage friends retreat to their bedrooms from the heat of a North London summer.

In one scene, Jade writes about 'sum bashy music playin full blast'. It's a fleeting ode to Bashy, an MC-cum-rapper out of North West London, a local giant of his time who moonlighted as a bus driver and a postman while chasing down his music dreams. He recorded early mixtapes in a bedroom studio where he fashioned recording booths from open ward-robe doors and a set of towels draped over the top. To market his project *The Chupa Chups Mixtape*, he ordered boxes of lollipops from eBay and then sat in his parents' home in Kensal Rise, taping Chupa Chup after Chupa Chup to over a thousand CD covers.

Bashy's fleeting presence within *Keisha the Sket* is a signpost of this wider enterprise at work, a symbol of how these sounds of resistance hung over the text and its young readers, a sense of daring passed down among unseen community lines. *Keisha the Sket* is a product of the same essence that forged grime on East London rooftops and cleaved So Solid Crew from Battersea council estates, is of the same spirit that saw Duke Vin forming sound systems from rubble, and new immigrant communities pulling in close for house parties in West London basements.

Like the innovators who came before, the text is a mural and a tribute to the sums of its parts, pulling from the threads of historic working-class Black art in this country and watering the soil for the generations who will come after. These endeavours are a communal pooling, a village reaping and sowing. Black art in Britain survives by these means.

In 2015, I sat in the stalls at an arena on the Essex Road in North London. Across the floor, a scattering of musicians and managers and producers and DJs and A&Rs were clad in sharp suits and fedora hats and tracksuits and bomber jackets and elegant dresses and pristine white trainers. We had gathered under the lights for the first edition of the Rated Awards, an award show founded by the YouTube platform GRM Daily. Among those in attendance that evening were community figures young and old from cities north and south, huddled together in tight stalls to welcome in the first award show to exclusively celebrate the genres of UK rap and grime.

A solo violinist opened the event, pulling and arching his bow over tense strings as 'Ghetto Kyote' flowed through the room, his fingers and his instrument mimicking the celestial rhythms of the cult grime instrumental that pulsed from Nokia brick phones and Walkman headsets across the country in the new millennium. A mood of celebration and pride moved through the room, and as the performances unfolded and awards were placed in palms, I remember a sense of reverence among those in attendance.

Harvey and Megaman of So Solid were present at the show. They presented Stormzy with Best Video. The crowd cheered as they strolled onto the stage. 'You can imagine how proud we are watching this,' Harvey said, leaning over the microphone and staring out into the crowd, 'because when we came out in '98, '99, we had no Black people to share it with. To see this barrier being broken and seeing us united together, just make sure you lot behave, man, and make the night go well.'

In recent years, Black music and Black art have come to dominate mainstream culture and conversation in Britain. In 2019, we watched Stormzy grace a Glastonbury stage with Black ballet dancers and Black BMX riders and Black choirs. In 2017 I was among an audience at the Roundhouse in Camden to see the rapper Little Simz throw her own festival in the same halls she first freestyled in as a fifteen-year-old. At home with my mother one evening in 2016, we watched Skepta collect the Mercury Prize for his fourth album, *Konnichiwa*, and we smiled as he stared at the trophy in near disbelief, his mother and his father at his side in traditional Nigerian dress on a family-crowded stage. The community has entrenched itself on the industry's front lines.

But among the accolades of this time, in Stormzy and Skepta, in rappers like Little Simz and writers like Michaela Coel, are the forefathers and fore-mothers who laid the gravel for their passing. I see echoes of legendary radio station Choice FM in new online station No Signal Radio, So Solid infused in grime, and grime flowering in the flow patterns of UK drill and UK rap. And *Keisha the Sket* too is etched into our storytelling, has crumbled the borders around literature and moved others to pull the nuances of local and personal experiences into words, its pieces lingering in the songs and the new authors of today. They are staggered generations meeting in quiet communion, waves lapping at a stubborn shore, eroding the coastline and gradually moulding the texture of a land that has long resisted us.

Skepta won Artist of the Year that evening in 2015, and Kano won the first GRM Legacy Award, saying: 'It means so much for me to collect this . . . but it wouldn't be right for me to stand here and not big up some of the people that I think I'm a part of *their* legacy. I'm talking about Wiley, I'm talking about So Solid, I'm talking about the Heartless Crew.'

A year after the Rated Awards, a friend gifted me some spare tickets to his show at Brixton Academy. It was the homecoming leg of his Made in the Manor Tour. There were spotlights roving the stage Kano stalked, and a live band dressed in uniform black garments. The number '86' was emblazoned on his jacket, an ode to his old family home in East London. We were up in the bleachers, where the sounds of the instruments wafted in a thickening crescendo, and a balcony hovered over the thousands in the pits, swaying in the current.

We danced to songs that made us young. Arms wrapped around strangers. Punters became backing vocalists. A few rows ahead of me, a man had lost his friends and was alone with his arms aloft, hollering every lyric, fingers conducting every harmony. He was a stranger who, by his association with these songs and albums, had become a close relative of the rest of the audience. By the close of the evening, when Kano was playing his final few songs, the man stood alone in the gangway, stilled now by the rhythms, shaking his head slowly, overwhelmed by the moment. There is release in celebration.

Black music and Black art hold space for community and carve out room for kinfolk to see themselves. Those of us reflected in these murals find shelter in the melodic embrace. Whenever I look back on those scenes at Brixton Academy, I think of the early innovators who fought and endured to pull out space for their people. 'We come over to England and we didn't have no halls of our own,' said Duke Vin in an interview before he passed. His friend Count Suckle echoed his sentiments: 'There was no place for Black people to go. They wouldn't let us in clubs, they say you got to be a member but there was no membership for Black people.'

A collective rising that never melted in the face of suppression is perhaps why we celebrate how we celebrate; why community award shows are founded and become holy grounds; why anthems blare out of car stereo systems in South London; why a man at a Kano gig wanders by himself into the aisles of Brixton Academy and sheds years in the gangway. It's a subtle realisation of a gnawing truth: that for the institutional forces who conspired at large to demonise music and ban shows and firebomb house parties, it was never meant to be like this.

In its own sense, *Keisha the Sket* is a piece of this collective rising; it made space for those who came out of London searching for themselves in the years after the new millennium. Bashy plays in teenage bedrooms. Bashment binds the house parties. Young boys dress in New Era caps and Nike t-shirts with string vests concealed underneath. Young girls are in hoop earrings with black Just Do It bags and rock diamond crucifixes. Together, they feel their way through adolescence. The fragments of Black life for a generation are etched into stone on these passages and pages – and, by doing so, are preserved for the next.

The Blacker the Berry, The Penger the Juice

ENNY

During my time at school, specifically years seven, eight and nine, the most important thing in my life was catching the 401 bus after school. I could have made the 3.40 one if I hadn't been hanging out with my friends in the shopping centre – but I wasn't interested in that bus. I also could have caught the 3.20 one, the one my mum expected me to get on, but I wasn't interested in that bus either. It *had* to be the bus at four o'clock; you see, that 401 bus was unlike any other. It was as if, from that very moment, we could blissfully leave the mildly racist suburbs of Bexleyheath and head back to our respective area codes where we were just black naive adolescents trying to express ourselves as much as we could.

For some, that journey on the 401 bus wasn't taking them home – they were catching the bus to take them to their next escapade. School was the pre-drinks; the afterwards was the party and where the real learning started. For others, including myself, catching the bus home was like social nectar – I immersed myself and lived in their world for a few hours. It was the thrill of watching students from the nearby boys' school scuffle outside McDonald's because they were in opposing gangs, or watching the girl three years above me lock lips with her boyfriend in front of the school gates.

I'm talking about a period of time when the top deck of the bus was like walking through Notting Hill Carnival, and putting your phone in the corner pocket of the windows was the original Bluetooth speaker. I'm talking coloured shoelaces tied into braids, side fringes slicked down with Jam hair gel, gems stuck on teeth, and ears decorated with huge fake diamond studs from the Asian-owned black hair shop. What a time to be alive. A time when social media was still taking its first baby steps with MSN and Piczo, and the pressures of beauty standards were not as intense as they are now. Being able to just exist in the moment, because that's all we had.

It was during this formative time period that I first read *Keisha the Sket*. I didn't fully realise it at the time, but *Keisha the Sket* was a cultural moment. Never before had we seen our vernacular and lives written and reflected like that in literature.

There was nothing like the thrill of getting your hands on a new chapter. I remember the feeling as if it were yesterday, the constant questions about 'who's got part three?' ringing through the playground, and transferring the content from USB to USB like it was contraband. Sneakily trying to read it on the low in a year eight IT lesson, or erasing the evidence from the family computer because you knew the ass-whooping you would get if your mum saw what you were reading. *Keisha the Sket* was a whole experience.

But it was also more than that experience – it was raw and it was real. It was the first time we realised it was possible to use literature as a form of expression. We saw that you could write a story in slang, you could use swear words, and you could express yourself on the page in the same way that we expressed ourselves in real life. All those thoughts were running round my adolescent brain when, two years later, I began writing short stories and sharing them in the playground amongst my peers, even embarking on a short-lived Wattpad career.

Rereading *Keisha the Sket* as an adult gave me an insight into the thought processes of our teenage selves. How we used to think, the things we thought were important, how we thought we knew it all, and even some very uneducated attitudes towards sex. Reading *Keisha the Sket* as a twelve or thirteen-year-old was similar to that journey on the 401 bus – some of us related to the themes and events, whereas others were being enlightened. This was particularly true of the all-girls school that I attended.

Being at a single-gender Catholic school meant that interactions with the opposite sex happened only when they could, after school – or maybe never, depending on the person. We read *Keisha the Sket,* discussing the events of the story, trying to learn from them – but in reality we were all as clueless as each other. I attribute a lot of who I am today as a woman to the five years I spent at secondary school. That time shaped a lot of the ideals and values I carry till this day, and I don't mean that in regards to my faith or my education, but more so in terms of my relationships with other women, how I see myself and even how I express myself. I sometimes wonder, if we'd had more teachers that looked like us, would we have been a bit more ready for the world outside those school gates?

Though not a predominantly black school, I was lucky enough to be surrounded by a community of girls who looked like me and with whom I shared the same heritage (*waves Nigerian flag*). There's a safeness when there are more of you in the room, and it's not something you really understand till you get a bit older and begin to realise the system we live in. I remember being in year nine, when the deputy head tried to implement a rule that black girls would no longer be allowed to wear hair braid extensions to school. Can you imagine – the one protective hairstyle black girls are known to wear, and they wanted to take that away? It was such a laughable idea that it didn't get taken any further. We would discuss in the girls' toilets how our mothers would react, imitating their responses: 'Eh heh, the teacher should come to our house every morning to be doing your hair, what nonsense mtchew.'

Hair was such an important piece of our identity at school. When everyone was dressed in the same uniform, there were only a few ways we were able to express our individuality – and those were through hair or accessories. Remember the feeling after a half-term break when you'd return to school that Monday with a fresh new hairstyle, and walk to the pre-school hangout spot to meet your batch who were ready to gas up your hairdo? Or how you'd walk into your first lesson a little bit late just so you could make that grand entrance and stunt on your class, like 'new hair who this'?

Your hair would sometimes even represent where you stood in the social hierarchy at school. I always felt I was treated a bit differently depending on how my hair looked. Growing up, my mum was so very hands-on when it came to my hair, it was very rare she would let me have mine out of a protective hair-style, which is probably why I don't have the greatest relationship with my natural now (we don't really kick it like that). When first entering secondary school, she finally stopped plaiting my natural hair and allowed me to do more hairstyles with extensions. That was my big-girl look, but it wasn't till I walked through the gates that my eyes were opened to a whole world of hairstyles. Hairstyles she wouldn't let me do. What I would've given to wear my relaxed hair in a slicked-up ponytail, with my baby hairs gelled down and four zigzag cornrows on the left side of my head. I mean, that's what all the other girls were doing, but my mum had her own preconceptions of girls that wore their hair like that. They were the 'hoodlums', the 'gangster girls', and she didn't want her daughter to be associated with the likes of them. Gel was like contraband; she would throw away any container of gel she saw in my room. That didn't stop me, though.

I remember there was one occasion when I wore my hair out to school, and one of my classmates spent twenty minutes slicking down all my baby hairs and my side fringe. You couldn't tell me nothing! I was now South East London's finest; it was as if everything had changed. I walked out of the school gates a new girl, blazer collar popped, school shoes swapped for a pair of Vans and ready for the 401 bus. It's funny how hair has the ability to change your confidence or how people perceive you. For that hour and thirty minutes I felt like a different person – like I had unlocked a new level of 'cool'. But all that ceased when I finally got off the bus and saw my mum's convertible in the car park.

She'd gotten home before me.

Through no fault of our own, I think we rarely praise the style and creativity that is birthed from young black girls. Some of the bespoke fashion trends that may have been seen as rebellious and silly by our educational institutions were truly just forms of expression – and they most certainly should've been nurtured more appropriately. We can't pretend that we don't now see the things we were once scrutinised for being celebrated in popular culture. Slicked edges are gentrified, batty riders are universal, subculture has become popular, but we're still not the beneficiaries of it. I'm sure if they could bottle up the young black girl experience and sell it in a department store, they would. I always describe it as a feeling, an energy – or like when you catch a whiff of a familiar fragrance and you can't exactly remember how you know it, but the scent alone sends a warm feeling through your body.

We are only now seeing it portrayed in TV and film. No gimmicks, no side stories, but the main event. When making the 'Peng Black Girls' video, all I wanted was to capture who I was and how I grew up using fashion and visuals, and Otis Dominique, the video director, executed it to a T. So much so that I was shocked at the response from both black and white people alike. Many black women and men spoke on how it was nice to finally see their sisters, nieces and daughters shown in a light that truly represented them. People of other races spoke on how they had allegedly never seen black women in this space, and it dawned on me that seeing black women being portrayed without being fetishised or carrying plight is not something we see often. And that's what's important to me: to show the duality of being a black girl and to show there's not only one way to be one. To break down preconceptions perpetuated by media, and outdated stereotypes that have never served us.

I always say the culture – from Channel U and fashion, to literature such as *Keisha the Sket* or films like *Kidulthood* – had a hand in raising us. These things felt like ours, even if we didn't know what that meant back then.

Acknowledgements

God foremost.

Alexis. Not going to go into it too tough, but put simply, irrespective of the external reverence for *KTS*, this categorically would not be as it is today without you. Fact.

Thank you for loving me from a pure and true place. It was direction-shifting.

Thank you to Suli Breaks. You woke me up and nurtured me into gear. I'm infinitely grateful.

The team who believed. Rachel Mann, first and foremost – thank you for bringing your unwavering belief on this journey, and holding my hand too. You've carried me and reminded me that I can walk so perfectly. I felt throughout and continue to feel very, very blessed to have been looked after by you.

Lemara Lindsay-Prince. Thank you for everything, my real G. It's been a hell of a ride and I'm eternally grateful for your steadfast support and belief in both the project and in Keisha. As much as this is glorious,

I recognise we've both learned formative lessons in this time that we'll certainly never forget. I hope so many more writers experience your infectious energy.

Thank you Donna (JULA) and Tallulah (#Merky Books) for all of your support too. Both myself and this project needed your co-sign and various forms of support throughout. Thank you for your adaptability and the peace you offered to the process.

Thank you Helen Conford (#Merky Books). You stepped in just before the frenzy of the announcement and gracefully grabbed the bull by the horns. Thank you for giving both myself and the project your time and attention. I'm extremely grateful for how you prioritised *KTS* and committed to the project's success straight away.

To the wider #Merky Books team – I couldn't have asked for more in terms of your creativity. Everything has **slapped**. Thank you for hearing me and staying in alignment with what the project needed aesthetically.

The contributors. Thank you endlessly for being a part of this and making it what my vision needed it to be. Not only in the midst of a pandemic, but also juggling hectic schedules that were already mad when we came along with this, you came through like the Dream Team for real. Thank you thank you thank you!

Research was central to this project. I couldn't have completed the rewrite without the support of the guys that played cultural historians and experts in historical linguistics. This lot helped to draw out the finer details by prodding my memory or offering their own, and answering questions as basic as 'Did we used to call it a "spliff" or a "zoot" in secondary school?'

Thank you Jimmy Trill, Imahni J New and Deji 'Deej' Ade for helping me birth the rewrite and answering my hundreds of crazy questions at all times of the day/night.

The inner circle – you lot know yourselves. Short and sweet: I love you all. Thank you for loving me in all the ways you know how. You've simultaneously let me lean on you while supporting me to lean into myself.

I've got to shout up my therapist. You've supported me in making changes that have truly transformed my life. I don't think I'll ever tire of writing or talking about the chapters of my life that you helped me with, and how much I have learned about myself through your love-filled practice.

Last but not least, thank you to every last person who has kept Keisha the Sket relevant over the years. I wouldn't have had the confidence to knock on doors or sit and project my voice at tables without being reaffirmed at every turn that this was backed by you lot.

In re-producing this, some self-work, deep reflection and growing up has occurred. I've been forced to look back at teenage me and acknowledge all of her 'stuff'. I feel extremely lucky to have done it feeling, in some ways, like I was being cheered on by you all. This has been a full-circle period that most people don't get the opportunity to experience in their lifetimes.

I'm eternally grateful.

Contributor Biographies

Candice Carty-Williams

Candice Carty-Williams is a writer and the author of the *Sunday Times* bestseller and British Book of the Year Award–winning *Queenie*, as well as the upcoming *People Person* and the young adult novella *Empress & Aniya*. Candice has contributed to essay collections such as *New Daughters of Africa*, edited by Margaret Busby, *Girl: Essays on Black Womanhood*, edited by Kenya Hunt, and more. In 2016, Candice created and launched the *Guardian* and 4th Estate Short Story Prize for underrepresented writers – the first inclusive initiative of its kind in book publishing. Candice was formerly the *Guardian Review* books columnist and has written for the *Guardian*, *i-D*, *Vogue*, every iteration of the *Sunday Times*, *BEAT Magazine*, *Black Ballad*, and many other publications. She will probably always live in South London.

Aniefiok Ekpoudom

Aniefiok 'Neef' Ekpoudom is a writer from South London who documents and explores culture in Britain. In his work, Aniefiok tells stories about the people, sounds and communities shaping the country as it exists today. He has written for and worked with the *Guardian*, the *Observer*, *GQ*, *Vogue*, GRM Daily, Netflix and more. He has contributed essays to *Safe: 20 Ways to be a Black Man in Britain Today* and the forthcoming #Merky Books title *A New Formation: How Black Footballers Made the Modern Game*. His first book, *Where We Come From*, will be released via Faber & Faber in 2023.

Caleb Femi

Raised on the North Peckham estate in South London, Caleb Femi is a poet and director. His debut collection, *Poor*, was published in 2020 by Penguin Press. He has written and directed short films for the BBC, Channel 4, Bottega Veneta and Louis Vuitton. A former Young People's Laureate, Caleb has been short-listed for the Forward Prize (2021) and the Rathbones Folio Prize (2021), and longlisted for the Jhalak Prize (2021). He has been featured in the Dazed 100 list of the next generation shaping youth culture.

ENNY

ENNY dropped an anthem at the end of 2020. A celebration of, and for, Black women, 'Peng Black Girls' quickly gained traction when it was released in November, but when Jorja Smith jumped on a remix it blew up. Smith consequently signed ENNY to her label, certifying the twenty-five-year-old as a rising star and a vital, unique and important young voice. South London born and raised, ENNY – born Enitan Adepitan – found early musical inspiration in what the family would play at home: gospel, hip-hop, jazz and indie records. This smorgasbord of early influences is reflected in ENNY's style: mellow freestyles sit atop rich, contemporary instrumentals. She has been featured in the Dazed 100 list, graced the covers of *Crack Magazine*, *POP*, *Wonderland* and the *Guardian Guide*, and has been playlisted across BBC Radio 1, 1Xtra and Rinse FM, making her TV debut on *Later . . . with Jools Holland*.